THE FEY'S FORTUNE

THE FEY'S FORTUNE

HALEY KNAPP

Haley Knapp

ISBN 979-8-9876359-0-2
EISBN 979-8-9876359-1-9

Published by the Author, Haley Knapp

Cover Design through Canva

First Printing, 2023

To all of my players, my love is etched in continents and seas.

I

Remington Darkwalker looked out over the bow of his ship lost in the thoughts of his past. He used to be handsome, a young man with the whole world to conquer. He closed his eyes attempting to remember that last night of feeling, that last night of satisfaction. He held in his emotions, needing to be strong, but he was angry at the world for the curse that now lay upon him. No, not the world, the River King. The creature that took everything from him.

"Captain, ship's been spotted ahead, what's the course?"

Remington quickly snapped out of his daydream. Not many people can surprise him, but he could never hear the approach of his first mate T'kocht. Many of the crew believed T'kocht's feet did not touch the ground, though none have been able to get close enough to prove it. Remington took in the appearance of his best friend. T'kocht's pale green skin courtesy of his bastard father covered in tattoos in a poor attempt to hide the coloring, was starting to show tinges of red from the never-ending sun. His face, gnarled from years on the sea and combat against his enemies, slowly succumbing to the curse. Remington could see the lengthening tentacles growing from his chin, drawing attention away from the small tusks that stuck out over his top lip. His crew did not deserve this, did the punishment really fit the crime?

"Capt'n?"

"What? Oh, yes. Lower the sails and get into position. Let's see what chaos we can cause this time."

His voice spoke clearly, but without joy. There was once a time nothing would make him happier than causing chaos on the seas. He was a pirate after all, isn't that what pirates do? But how he felt did not matter. He had a job to do, a deal to keep.

He looked across the boat, watching as his crew went to their stations. Some hiding amongst the crates of food and barrels of rum. Why did they even have this on board, he wondered, their hunger and thirst are never satiated. The food tasted of nothing, of pure salt. Others began slipping into their stolen skins, the magic held within transforming the crew to appear as seals lounging on the deck. Remington looked at his own seal skin, draped across his wide shoulders. He remembered its previous owner. He thought about her every day, and what he lost when he chose to leave that island. Without meaning to he whispered his thoughts, "Focus, the other ship will be here soon. They always come."

Though Remington was young, not yet 32, he understood the seas, and he understood people. An abandoned ship floating on the water seemingly inhabited by seals always brought them in for a closer look. Some came hoping to loot what they could from what was abandoned, others looking to help any survivors aboard. Remington was always disappointed when it was the second group, but the world was cruel and it was their fault for not learning it sooner. Or at least that's what he told himself. He had a reputation to keep. With a deep sigh, he slipped into his seal form, and without hope attempted to feel the warmth of the sun on his skin. He felt nothing.

As the crew lounged upon the deck, the ship in the distance pulled up alongside, the opposing crew placed a plank to cross over to investigate. The cruel looks upon their faces quickly told

Remington that these were fellow pirates. Did they follow under the Pirate King, the horrible man that dared to call himself a King, or were they part of the rebels, those that call themselves the Nautilus? The answer did not matter to him, no one was safe upon the seas.

They watched as the newcomers began to investigate the boat, signs of confusion slowly spreading across their faces. The confusion always happened right about now when the invaders truly took in their surroundings. Standing on the deck of The Fey's Fortune, one could imagine the magnificence this ship once held. Three 30-foot-tall masts lined the center of the ship, cannons lined both sides on the lower decks, and a beautifully carved wooden wheel stood at the helm, the spokes appearing as crashing waves. Hanging off the bow was a beautiful maiden clad only in seaweed, her delicate hand pointing her crew toward their destiny. But that age of glory was no more. Now the ship seemed abandoned, the carefully painted name on the side barely readable. Green moss grew from the cracks in the boards, corals and various mollusks growing from all areas. Seaweed draped across the maiden on the bow, the full scene giving the impression that this ship was raised from the depths of the ocean after a long rest on the bottom.

Remington quickly lost his patience. In the beginning he found some entertainment in this confusion, watching as his victims attempted to pet his crew in their seal forms. But it did not take long for the charm to wear off. Remington slipped from his seal skin as he has done a thousand times before, effortlessly slipping the skin over his shoulders where it always remained.

The gasping sounds of his victims echoed across the hull. Some were gasp of recognition, others of fear at the sight they beheld. Before them stood Remington in his full glory. Standing tall at 6'3", his square jawline framed a rugged face. He wore a fine dark blue cloak that reached almost to his feet, carefully embroidered with golden threads. Upon his head sat a matching tricorne hat, whose shadow hid his delicate eyes that were as blue as the sea itself. However, these fine wares were not what drew the eyes on onlookers. For fish scales grew over parts of his skin. Along the right side of his face, a starfish seemed to have fused to where his ear should be. Peaking from his coat, coral grew from near his collar bone. All around, he was dripping wet, as if he was pulled from the sea like the ship he commands.

"Hello gentlemen," his low smooth voice breaking the silence that had followed. "It seems that some of you recognize me. Tell me, what do they say of me these days?"

At this, the rest of his crew came out of their forms and hiding places surrounding those on deck. Drawing their swords and without hesitation the crew slaughtered their visitors leaving only one alive as the captain always requested. This poor soul was dragged before the captain. His voice shook with his body.

"You's the Drowned Captain ain't you? I-I've heard stories about you. They says your soul is so cruel, that when your boat went down, the ocean spat you back out."

Remington let out a hearty laugh, amplified by the rest of his crew. "Oh really, that is fascinating. Did you hear that boys, the ocean itself spat me out!" Remington knelt down to the man, and grabbed his face with large, strong hands forcing the terrified man to look into his eyes.

"You learn a lot by looking into a man's eyes. What do you see in mine?"

"I, uh, see yous's power, and, and strength to take over the Pirate King"

"Oh? So you are one of those that think I should rule the seas?" Remington leaned in uncomfortably close, his hands crushing the man's cheeks, his breath cold against the man's ear. "Let me let you in on a secret. The ocean did not spit me out. It was the River that spat on me and doomed me to this life on the seas. I do not desire the power so many of you want to give to me. I want my freedom, I want to feel something, anything again. I want to turn back the clocks."

With a slow motion, Remington drew his scimitar across the man's throat, watching as the blood soaked into his ship. He stood up to look at the rest of his crew who were awaiting his orders. Remington flicked his hand in indifference as he headed towards the captain's quarters, "Loot and burn the ship, then make for land." T'kocht bellowed out, "Alright, you heard the captain! Clean up this mess and set course for Tortuga." He watched Remington with pity as he walked away, wanting to help, to share the weight that his captain always carried on his shoulders.

2

As Remington stormed into his cabin, the door slamming shut behind him, he grabbed his bottle of rum and took a swig. He questioned the purpose of it. To him and his crew, the rum tasted the same as water: salty nothingness. At this point it was more of a habitual ritual, a memory of the times when the alcohol actually made things better.

Remington curled up into his hammock. Every day he tried so hard to appear strong in front of his crew. To use his stoic face as a beacon to them to continue their mission, to continue "life" though that word was used loosely. He found sanctuary in his cabin, the crew knew not to bother him there, he was safe.

Drinking the last drops of the bottle, he threw it across the cabin, the glass shattering against the opposite wall. He stared at the familiar walls that he called his for the past 6 years. Remington listened to the drip of water from the ceiling in the back right corner, the creaking of the hull of the boat as it rocked back and forth in the waves. He looked around at the room, the walls finely decorated with fine paintings, fancy swords won in various exploits, and bejeweled decorations reminiscent of anchors and wheels.

His eyes finally landed and focused on a portrait of himself in his younger years. Bright-eyed and ready to take on the world. A knife stuck from the painting, right about where his heart would be and various rips strung across the painting, where the knife had been stuck before.

As he stared into the eyes of his past self, he found himself thinking back to before his misfortunes started, to before that last fateful night on the beach.

Remington grew up in the Saxe Empire, in the city of Rivenport. Rivenport was known as Paradise City, the place that rich folk went to relax, sunbathe, and party to forget their woes. Remington was not rich. His mother and father were soldiers in the Saxe Empire's army. They were killed during a skirmish with the local thieves guild when Remington was only 5.

From then on, he learned how to survive on the streets. Some of the older kids taught him how to beg, steal, and find odd jobs to keep himself fed. As he grew, he quickly proved himself to be cunning and swift. He came up with elaborate plans and soon found himself with a comfortable living. But Remington had no love for this city that had no love for him. When he was old enough at the age of 15, Remington found commission as a crewmate on a small trading vessel. For a year, he worked hard, hauling heavy barrels of supplies on and off the boat, learning the trade of a sailor.

On a dark night in the month of Tredichar, a massive storm hit the ship, ripping it apart board by board. Remington did not remember much from that night after the storm, but he could still hear the roars of the winds and waves battering the side of the hull, each hit cracking the wood of the small boat. The sound and sight of the crew rushing around the deck, fighting for every step against the merciless rain. They had done everything right, tying themselves to the main mast to make sure they were not flung off the side

Remington had been desperately retightening ropes keeping the sails stowed away, trying to salvage what he could from the ship. A flash of lighting burst just to the right of him, the blast of thunder deafening as shrapnel flew towards him, severing his safety net to the ship. He reached forward for the other half of his ties, trying to reconnect them, but the storm did not wait. Another flash of lighting slammed into the mast, not 15 feet from where Remington was standing. He did not have time to register what happened before the force of the bolt sent him flying off the side of the ship, chunks of wood slicing into him, following him into the water.

Remington knew how to swim, but it was dark, and he soon became disoriented, not knowing which way was up, his lungs screaming for air. His eyes caught sight of flames over taking the ship. Swimming towards the light, Remington felt hopeful, but it did not last long. As his head broke the surface of the water, the ship exploded, the black powder it was carrying igniting, sending pieces of the ship bulleting in every direction. Remington felt the sharp pain of one of the larger pieces cracking against his head and then slipped into darkness.

Remington woke up cold and soaking wet on an unfamiliar ship. His hands tied behind his back, his clothing ripped and tattered. He could feel the warmth of his own blood on his head dripping into his eye causing it to sting and his vision to be blurry.

He heard a voice from off to his right, "Check it out gentlemen, the runt lives. Ha! Maybe he is stronger than he looks!". At 16, Remington was nothing like a runt. Already standing at his full height, strong muscles formed from his time at sea, he knew this man was trying to provoke him. He felt a foot impact his side, "Get up pip squeak," the man demanded, "The captain will want to see you."

Remington shifted himself the best he could to see his surroundings. Looking around, he immediately recognized his situation. He saw the black sails that hung from the masts, the stench from the crew that couldn't care less about a bath, and the look of the man in front of him; He was on a pirate ship. Remington analyzed the pirate in front of him. The pirate was large, pushing 230 pounds of muscle, his black hair matted and tangled, tied with a sun-bleached ribbon. But even with all this mass, Remington could tell this man was only a brute. He was slow, both physically and mentally. If he wanted to, Remington could escape pretty easily, but he had nowhere to go. They were on the open seas with no land in sight.

The brute grabbed Remington by the shoulder blades, yanking him to his feet rather roughly. As he found his footing, it hit him how sore his body was. He felt his ankle buckle beneath him, it must be sprained. He tried his best to hide the pain, and limped forward, feeling the point of a sword at the small of his back.

Eventually he was forced to the helm of the ship, where a woman in her mid 30's stood at the wheel. Her reddish-blonde hair pulled back out of her soft round face, revealing bright green eyes that held a coldness behind them. Her waist tightened by a black corset that opened up to a long flowy skirt that billowed from the ocean winds. Remington stared, mouth slightly ajar, both in surprise and in admiration of the beauty that stood before him.

Her siren like laughter knocked him out of his stupor. Her voice soft, yet firm spoke toward him, "Not what you were expecting am I? My name is Captain Areliel Atrigul. Welcome aboard the Sickening Rose. And what may we call you?"

Remington hesitated to answer, attempting to figure out her game, what her motivations are, why was he alive. His quick analysis showed she was not a patient woman; she would be expecting an answer. He bowed low, the blood still rushing into his eye, "Remington Darkwalker, at your service ma'am."

"Remington? That's a nice name." she responded. "Tell me Remington," leaning in close, her warm breath upon his ear causing goosebumps to rise upon his skin, "what misfortunes brought you into my domain?"

Before he even had time to think, Remington spilled his short life story to the captain, ending with his near-death disaster. Carefully she listened to his story, taking in every word that he said. When he was finished, she looked down at him, a seductive smile crawling across her face. "Well Remington," she said, "I have good news for you. You get to live another day. I like you, there is something… different about the way you hold yourself. Come, I will take you as a member of my crew, maybe we can make a decent pirate out of you."

Remington blinked at her and did not say anything. Though initially he held an admiration, he did not like the look of the smile on her face, nor the feeling of power she currently held over him. He understood though, that he had no other choice but to accept, if he wanted to find his way back to anywhere. Captain Atrigul took this silence as an acceptance. "Good, you already know when to keep your mouth shut. That is one less thing I will have to teach you." She caressed her hand along his cheek and underneath his chin, before returning to the wheel.

Atrigul without even looking barked orders toward the brute, "Brend, show our new crewmate to his quarters, he must be ever so tired after his ordeal. And find him something to wear, we want to look nice now don't we."

Brend grabbed Remington's shoulder (which Remington thought was probably bruised by now) and led him below decks. As Remington was dragged along, Brend in a gruff voice said, "Now the captain may have taken a liking to you, she tends to enjoy young lads like you, but don't think that will grant you any special privileges from the crew. Make any missteps, say anything wrong to your superiors, and you will be punished just like the rest of these rats. Rest up while you can, for your work starts tomorrow, and we don't take kindly to slackers."

Eventually, they made their way down 3 levels of the ship, to an open room with many hammocks hung about. Just like any ship, there was no privacy to be found here. Remington was led to an empty hammock near the outer edge of the hull, where the warmth did not quite reach. He could see the hammock above his was currently occupied, and the faint sounds of snores could be heard emanating from it. Brend reached up and pulled down on the hammock, causing its occupant to flip out of it with a heavy bang onto the wooden deck and a loud "Oof" coming from the body. Brend let out a cruel chuckle. "Get up!" he yelled as the man began to recover from the fall, "we got a new crew member here, Captain says he needs something to wear. Go find him something, I ain't doing it." With that, Brend stormed out of the barracks, probably to go torment someone else.

Remington now got a clear view of this crewman. Standing before him was a strong lad, Remington guessed him to be around 20 years old though he was not sure. The pale greenish-grey skin, and small tusk like teeth protruding from his bottom lip in a large grin, immediately gave away the man's heritage as a half-orc. His dark reddish, almost black hair was roughly chopped just above his shoulders. His eyes were black in color, but not showing the aggression that Remington expected of his kind. He was wearing a vest that cut off at the shoulders, revealing the start of what would be a long line of tattoos. This one, was a simple mermaid, with her tail wrapped around his bicep, the mermaid herself seemingly dragged down by chains, unable to escape. Remington tried to figure out what this said about the man before his thoughts were interrupted by a coarse voice much deeper than Remington expected, "Welcome aboard, you look like shit. You can ignore that bilge-sucker, he is an ass to everyone. Let's see if we can find you anything drier. Name's T'kocht by the way."

"Remington," he replied offering no further discussion. Though Remington was not in the mood for making friends at the moment, he could not help but like T'kocht. Eventually, they were able to find a spare linen shirt, and cut off pants that would serve better than the scraps he was currently wearing.

Returning to their hammocks, T'kocht turned to Remington and said, "you should try to get some rest, this ship gets pretty busy, especially when we are nearing a jump. Find me if you need anything, you seem like a decent bloke." Remington attempted to ask what T'kocht meant by "the jump", but T'kocht's snores were already echoing through the chamber. Finding himself exhausted, and not seeing any other options at the moment, Remington climbed into his hammock and quickly slipped into a deep sleep.

3

Remington was not sure what time it was when he was awoken by a crewmate. He thought it was sometime after midnight considering the darkness outside. She was quietly shaking him and whispering to wake up. As Remington shifted to get a better look, the crewmate was a younger half elven woman, who Remington thought could have been quite pretty at one point, but her missing eye and scarred right half of her face showed this woman had faced hell at some point in her life. "The Captain wants to see you," she whispered, "move quietly".

Remington slipped out of the hammock and went to follow the woman. He saw now that many of the other living spaces were now occupied, only a small portion of the crew working the night shift. One of those being T'kocht. As they made their way up the various decks of the ship, they eventually made their way across the upper deck. The cold sea air blowing his hair into his face, he saw T'kocht quietly humming a shanty while tying down some rope. Remington gave a slight nod in his direction, but T'kocht made no indication that he saw it, though Remington knew he was looking right at him. Remington wondered why T'kocht acted as if he was not there, but before he had time to truly contemplate, they arrived at a set of doors that led into the Captain's quarters. His escort quietly turned, leaving Remington alone outside. Taking a deep breath, Remington knocked on the door.

"Oh! There you are, I have been waiting. Come on in, don't be shy." Captain Atrigul's voice rang through clearly, with a tone that was both soft yet commanding.

As Remington entered, he saw Captain Atrigul facing a large desk in the back of the room, pouring what appeared to be rum into two glasses. She was wearing nothing but a shear silk robe. Remington immediately began to feel uncomfortable, feeling as though he walked into a scene he should not be in. She slowly turned around, revealing the robe to be very loosely tied in the front. Her hair was now let down, the soft waves of each strand, positioned in just a way to cover her what otherwise would be exposed breasts.

"Do you drink Remington?" she asked, a coy smile on her face. "When I can," he responded curtly. Remington did not want to play games. Taking the glass from her hands he asked point blank, "Why am I here? What do you want from me?"

Captain Atrigul tilted her head to the side, took a sip from the glass and responded, "Isn't it obvious? You are young though, so maybe it's not. I may be captain of this ship but being away from land can be so lonely. I have a need for company, and many of these *ruffians* are so beneath me. And too many of those on shore are broken in, so boring. When my crew saw you floating in the sea, I saw potential. You are young, handsome, and quite strong." She set her glass down on the table, walking over to Remington. She caressed her hand across his face as when they first met, slowly sliding herself behind him. With nimble fingers she began untying the strings of his shirt, revealing his bare chest, just starting to grow chest hair. "And I have much to teach you," she whispered in his ear, slightly nibbling on his lobe.

Remington quickly tried to step away from her, feeling himself trapped like a deer that has been cornered. But she was fast and grabbed onto his arm so that he could not get to far away. He spun around to face her, panic having entered into his eyes. "I don't think this is appropriate," he stated trying to maintain a steadiness in his voice, "if you do not mind, I will be returning to my cabin now." But her grip did not release.

"Oh, my dear Remington, it seems there is a bit of a misunderstanding here. You do not have much of a choice in this matter. For you see, I am the captain of this vessel, and every single man and woman on this ship will follow my orders without question. And if I ordered them to throw you back to the ocean where we found you, they will do it without blinking. We don't want that to happen now do we? So why not be a good lad and follow my orders." She gave him a predatorial smile and half dragging him, led him towards the large bed that sat in the corner of the room.

Remington at this point recognized his situation: accept the part as hers to do with as she will, or death. It was then that Remington learned his first of many lessons from the Captain: power brings obedience and he followed her without saying anything further. He passed his first of many nights as a pirate, in the company of his captain, drinking as much as he could to ease his unrest.

4

Remington awoke in the morning cold and alone. His whole body ached from the previous day's activities. A splitting pain coursed through his head, a result of the rum from the night. He looked down at his shirtless chest, seeing the large purple bruise spreading across his shoulder from where Brend had gripped him. He saw the smaller bruises across his stomach and chest, gifts left by the captain as a firm reminder of the night's events. He shivered.

He slowly got up from the bed, and found his shirt, which had been tossed to the middle of the room and quickly put it on. Remington knew he had a long day ahead of him, so with a deep breath he exited the room onto the top deck of the ship. Immediately, Brend was there to greet him, "Look who has finally awoken from his beauty sleep! Ha, it did not do much to help that face of yours. Time to get to work!" Remington rubbed his hands on his face, feeling where scabs had been forming and bruises were beginning to heal. He looked around the ship, seeing now clearly the crew, which was a wide mix of species and genders, though none of them looked favorable. Many of them were staring at him as he exited the room, some were shaking their heads. He saw off in the corner T'kocht working on cleaning some swords.

"Hello," Remington greeted T'kocht attempting to appear

friendly, "need any help?" T'kocht looked up, a short frown upon his face melting into a smile. "Aye, I could use some help, and you could use a friend. Not many of the crew members are going to like that entrance you made this morning."

Remington involuntarily flinched a bit at that comment, failing in his attempt to hide how he felt. T'kocht noticed. "I'm sorry about that. When the captain wants something, she tends to get it. You don't got to, but if you ever need it, you can talk to me. You are not the first boy she's adopted."

"I'm not a boy, I can take care of myself," Remington responded, a bit more aggressively than he intended. Immediately he felt bad, T'kocht was right he did need someone he could trust on this ship. But Remington was a proud man, never wanting to show weakness, as that allowed people to take advantage of you. He remained silent.

Seeing Remington's discomfort, he quickly attempted to change the subject. "Alright, alright, I meant no offense, but you can't be more than what 17 or 18?"

"16, I will be 17 in less than a few months."

"Yer young to be out on the waters, any family? Where did you come from before washing up on the Sickening Rose? You don't sound like you come from any of the islands of the Northern Keys."

"Saxe Empire. No family, just me."

"Well, with no family, you can take some comfort know'n no one will be missing ya. Saxe Empire eh? I heard they have been making serious contraptions up there. Ileviel told me they even have ships that can fly through the air like a bird. I told her she was talking non-sense, ships can't fly. But she insisted she'd seen it with her own two eyes, I think it was the booze personally. Apparently, the Pirate King is planning on making a trade agreement..."

Before T'kocht could continue his rambling, Remington interrupted, his interest now peaked. "The Pirate King?" he asked. "Who's that?"

T'kocht looked over at Remington in shock. "You mean to tell me you have never heard of the Pirate King before?" Remington shook his head.

"The Pirate King is a title that is passed down to who ever holds leadership over the community. It's a powerful position, though you usually don't stay there very long. There is always someone who wants to take your place. Once someone takes the throne, they lose their name and work to keep some form of order on the seas. The current king beheaded the old one not but 4 years ago. Seems to have a good following too, I think he will stay on the throne a lot longer than most. Rumors say he even has a dragon turtle on his side, a creature so large, some sailors mistake it for an island. I heard he has big plans for unifying the pirates but I personally..."

T'kocht was cut off by the arrival of Brend. "You would do good to respect the king. Get on his bad side and good luck trying to live," Brend harshly added. "T'kocht, yer shifts over, get out of my sight. Remington, Captain wants to talk."

T'kocht put away the sword he was polishing and stood up. He let his hand rest briefly on Remington's shoulder, giving it a short pat. "Don't be so angry Brend, it will ruin your pretty face, oh wait, I think it might be too late for that," T'kocht teased. Brend attempted a wide swing at T'kocht who very nimbly dodged out of the way, laughing as he headed to the lower decks.

Remington could not help but let out a slight chuckle, which caused his rib cage to hurt. One look from Brend told Remington it was probably not a good idea to push him much further. Remington got up with a deep inhale and made his way towards the helm, where Captain Atrigul was checking a strange map and comparing it with a watch and compass. He cleared his throat, announcing his arrival.

"Ah, Remington! I hope you slept well. Looks like you are getting along on my ship, even making a friend. I'm glad. But we do need to find you a role on this ship during the day, the night shift is just a bonus." She said with a wink. "So tell me, what other skills do you have?"

Remington stared at her, attempting to show a dead pan face of no expression. "Not much ma'am. I only worked on a shipping vessel, working sails, moving creates. I can sneak when needed, but that's about it."

The Captain let out a soft chuckle, he could tell she did not fully trust his answer. "You really are fresh meat aren't you. I cannot have you be useless, plus I think you have some *untapped* potential. It is decided then. You will learn the various skills needed to survive on my ship from the crew. We can start with your fighting training. Go find Nicky, if anyone can teach you to use a sword, it's her. Oh, and when you are on duty, call me captain."

After asking around for Nicky for a bit, Remington was eventually directed toward the mess hall where he saw a familiar face. It was the young half elven woman who woke him up the night before. Now that it was light out, he could see her a bit more clearly. She looked a bit older than he originally thought, though still very much in her prime. Her blonde hair cut very short, only slightly combing over her head. Currently, Remington could only see the left side of her face which was fair and had soft curves, though it seemed a little bit burnt from the sun. Her hazel eye starring at him though she did not acknowledge him, her attention focused on the apple she was eating.

Remington put on his most dashing smile and approached. During his walk to the mess hall, he had come up with a plan to survive, and this plan involved making many friends. Luckily, this was something Remington was very good at when he wanted to be. "Hello there," he greeted her, "my name is Remington, I am guessing you are Nicky? Truly a pleasure to meet you. The Captain told me to find you to train with a sword."

Nicky slowly turned toward him, a smile growing across her face. He could now see the right side of her face was not burned, or at least not burned by fire. It seemed to have been a cold burn, leaving the skin cracked and blistered. Her right eye was replaced by glass, and her right ear was completely missing. She did not seem to care.

"Hiya," she responded followed by a slight pause as she took the time to look him up and down. "Oh yup, now I see why the captain wanted ye. If yer looking for Nicky well you found her! The best swordswoman on this ship."

Remington couldn't help but genuinely smile at her confidence, another great ally to gain.

"So, Remington right?" She swallowed the last chunk of apple. "What is your fighting experience like? Any professional training?"

"Got a bit of basic self-defense skill with a knife that I learned on the streets, but that's about it. Got pretty good aim when needed." Remington decided it was best to not lie to Nicky. Lies bring distrust, and that was not something he needed right now.

"Oh goodie," she squealed, "that means I won't have to un-teach you anything. Alright, let's go pick you out a weapon and see what you can do." With that, she swung herself out of her seat and practically dragged Remington to the armory on board. He followed, doing his best to keep up with her swift speed.

After going through quite a few hallways, they eventually reached a small room that was packed with various weapons. There were all sorts of archery equipment, cross bows, daggers, and swords of various shapes and sizes. Some seemed plain while others were finely decorated with runes and gems. Remington saw in the corner a pile of swords he recognized as the swords he and T'kocht were cleaning earlier. He thought to himself these must be the spoils of battle. The rest of the equipment in this room was well organized, sorted by type and size, and everything was well polished.

"I like to keep them clean, some say that a dirty weapon shows the fights it has been in, but I think it just causes them to rust." Nicky explained. "But a man's weapon is his lifeline, it protects its owner and becomes one with him. Take a look around, see what calls to you. The blade you pick says a lot about a person. No pressure or anything." She added a fun wink to the last line.

Remington let out a small chuckle before beginning to look around the room. His eyes washed over a couple of swords that were about as tall as he was and shudder to even think about trying to lift them. He turned his eyes to the one-handed weapons. There were a wide variety to choose from, some were simple short swords, sharp to a point, good for slashing and stabbing. Others were long and narrow, coming to a needle nose point, easy to handle but not very versatile. As he carefully weighed his options a reflection caught his eye.

As he turned to look, Remington found a curved blade carved with intricate elvish writing. It was attached to an ornate handle, where the cross guard was designed to look like faery wings, delicate but sturdy. The wings themselves extended about 6 inches to either side, iron framing the outside of the wings and the veins that ran through them. Another metal, one that looked almost silverish, filled in the wings so thin it was practically see through. Remington cautiously tapped the metal and it felt as though he was tapping on a block of iron. It did not give way or puncture whatsoever. The hilt seemed to be made of a smooth black glass, with various gems inlayed around the bottom, and a blue leather wrapped around for grip. He gripped it in his hand, feeling the balance of the blade. He looked around the room, and quickly picked up a spare dagger to keep in his opposite hand. He looked toward Nicky.

"Interesting choice," she said curiously. "You know, Captain was actually planning on selling that sword next time we are ashore. Been on the ship for years and no one has wanted it. It fits you though, I think it will serve you well. It even has a name if you read the writing. Calls itself the Fortune Teller. Well, it's not very safe to practice indoors. Follow me!" Remington grabbed the matching sheath for the scimitar and followed her onto the deck.

There the sun was out in full force, Remington guessed it was sometime midafternoon. He realized he had not eaten since the explosion, and his stomach let out a tremendous grumble. Nicky turned around laughing, shocked at how loud his stomach's complaint was. "Well we can't have you starving to death on the first day. Go grab some food and then we can get going. I'm not in any rush. Plus, I need to talk to Brend. Meet me back here in 30 minutes!" Nicky ran off to go find Brend.

Remington returned to the mess hall, grabbing himself some stale bread and cheeses. With some digging, he eventually found himself an apple similar to the one Nicky was eating. Remington was impressed by the amount on the ship, most likely he thought, stolen from other ships. This fact did not matter much to him, he quickly finished eating then made his way back up.

There he once again found Nicky, who was using a sharpening stone on her own weapon, a delicate rapier that ended at a point so sharp it glinted in the sun. Remington began to sweat with nervousness at the sharpness of the blade. However, to his relief, she sheathed her sword and picked up a wooden practicing stick. She handed him a similar practice stick, curved like his own sword. "It's a bad idea to start straight away with the sharp stuff! First, we start with technique, then when I say you can, we can switch to your fancy sword".

"Yes ma'am," responded Remington, adding a teasing salute to the end of it. However, before he even realized what had happened, he felt his head smack against the deck of the ship, his legs having been swept out from under him. A chorus of laughter could be heard across the ship. He looked up at Nicky, whose playful demeanor had been replaced with a serious focus.

As she reached down to help him up she said, "Rule number one, always be prepared, for no one will fight fairly." Remington took her hand and as he began to stand up, she dropped him. "Rule number 2. Don't ever expect anyone to help you. If you want to live, you need to help yourself." Remington quickly scrambled up, his pride hurt more than his head.

For the next 4 hours, Remington learned proper techniques, stances, and earned himself a few bruises for not paying attention. By the end, he was sore, exhausted, but proud of the progress he made. Even Nicky, for how much she insulted him during the training, complimented him on being a quick learner.

As Remington headed towards the stairs that lead down to the crews' quarters, he felt a hand land on his shoulder. Turning to look Captain Atrigul was standing behind him. "You did well for your first day, looks like I made a good decision after all. Go ahead and rest for a couple of hours, then meet me in my quarters." She smiled at him, with that wolfish look in her eyes. Remington hated this look, it made him feel like he was her next meal, which in her mind, he was. But Remington had a plan, and if he was to follow through with it, he will have to suffer first. "Of course, Captain. Anything else?" he responded.

"That will be all." With that, Remington headed to his hammock, hoping to catch at least a few hours of sleep.

5

Remington felt like he had just closed his eyes when he felt himself being shaken awake. He lazily opened his eyes to see T'kocht, who promised to wake Remington up when his shift was about to start so that Remington would not miss his appointment with the Captain. T'kocht gave him a slight nod, "You going to be okay?"

"Yeah," responded Remington. Remington quietly slipped out and made his way to the upper deck.

Once again, Remington knocked on the Captain's doors, hearing the sickening voice beckoning him to come in. He squared up his shoulders and walked in. As he entered, he saw Captain Atrigul working to undo her braid. She was struggling as a few strands of hair had knotted together from the strong winds that day. "Do you need help?" asked Remington, putting on his friendliest tone.

She put her hands down, giving up on trying to work blind, "Yes, come over here."

Remington made his way over and with dexterous hands from working ropes on a ship, began untangling the knots, trying not to pull too hard. "So, Captain" Remington started, "I heard a couple of crewmates talking about an upcoming jump, what do they mean?"

She reached her hand back, slightly patting him on the shoulder. "It's a well-kept secret, only a few other captains know. If you continue to prove useful after we stop for provisions, then you can learn more."

"We are making for land? Where?" asked Remington curiously, with a bit more enthusiasm than he intended. He reined it in.

"Halitona" she answered almost absent mindedly, "but don't get too excited, I am not going to let you slip away that easily." He could see her cheeks rise in a smile.

"I would not dream of it," Remington shot back. The last of the knots were finally undone.

He stepped back, waiting for the Captain to make the next move. He needed to gain her trust, but he did not want to move too quickly. That could raise her suspicion. He watched as she stood and moved over to her fine china cabinet, pulling out two glasses and a bottle of rum. She poured a glass for herself and Remington and took a sip. She looked at him and said nothing for a while. Finally, she walked over to him and wrapped her arms around him. He did not resist. "Come, I need to blow off some steam. We can save the questions for later."

For the next week, Remington became more acquainted with the rest of the crew. He continued working 3 hours a day with Nicky on his swordsman skills, still not having graduated in her eyes to the privilege to use his own sword. The rest of the time, he spent rotating between other crewmen, slowly learning the ropes. Every night he visited the Captain, entertaining her and keeping her company as she demanded.

One early morning, only 9 days after his arrival on the Sickening Rose, Remington was working with a dwarven man who called himself Glazzglek on repairing small rips in the sails when a shrill whistle rang out across the ship. Remington stopped his shotty needlework and looked towards Glazzglek, "What was that?"

"That be th' lookout lad, a ship haes bin spotted. Th' eagle mist hae seen something worth taking. Ye better climb doon, th' rammy micht git messy. Ah hawp Nicky taught ye weel, huv a go nae tae die in yer foremaist combat." Glazzglek slid down the mast, leaving Remington sitting on the cross posts. Remington often had difficulty understanding what Glazzglek was trying to say and was taking a minute attempting to translate Glazzglek's explanation. Eventually, Remington unraveled it and looked across the Nandiac Ocean. He saw a sailing vessel on the horizon and felt the ship turning to head in that direction. Remington gathered his basket of mending supplies and made his way down the mast after Glazzglek.

After untying himself from the safety line, he joined the rest of the crew gathering under the helm waiting for Captain Atrigul to speak. Shortly after everyone quieted down, Captain Atrigul spoke. "Alright crew, we got a target up ahead. Remember, the less fighting we start, the easier this will be. We will fire a warning shot to test their reaction. If they show aggression back, then give them hell. Do not forget, just because we are pirates, does not mean we are savages. If they surrender, let them live. Let's take what we need and get out of there. Alright, stop standing around looking useless and get to work!"

Immediately the group dispersed to work the sails to increase their speed and move their way down to the cannons in preparation. Remington moved to join the group working the ropes, though he still did not quite have a place in this battle plan. As they approached, Remington could better see their target. The flag it flew, a red cross passing over a golden background, indicated it was from the Saxe Empire but not military. The military always had extra white stripes underneath the red. Remington was relieved to realize that unless they had hired mercenaries, this should be an easy capture.

BOOM! The warning shot fired as the cannon ball splashed

harmlessly into the ocean near the other ship. There was silence as the Sickening Rose waited to see if there was a response. The other boat seemed to slow as if inviting them to come closer. Taking this as a surrender, Captain Atrigul navigated the Rose closer to the other ship. The two ships were naught but 200 feet from each other when the first volley of arrows peppered the deck. One of the crewmen that Remington had not met yet had been struck in the shoulder, wounded, but alive. The Captain shouted out, "Looks like we got a fighter! Eagle take to the sky and the rest of you prepare to board!"

Remington did not even notice T'kocht in the mass of people, but now saw him very quickly scrambling up the mast to the bird's nest with a heavy cross bow in his hand. T'kocht carefully took aim at the other boat. Remington watched as a bolt flew from the cross-bow and into the neck of one of the awaiting enemies. Not many could make such an accurate shot. Remington made note of that.

The rest of the crew scrambled to avoid the incoming volley of arrows while also preparing to board the other ship. Eventually the two ships were close enough that members of the Sickening Rose could swing over to the other side, landing into the middle of the fight. Remington could see there were about 12 or so very well-trained fighters on the other side. These men were much more skilled than the normal guards or army. There must be something very valuable on board. Remington felt a pull on his arm, "Come on boy!" yelled Brend. "You got arms and legs get fighting!"

Remington drew his sword, feeling the weight of it in his hands before rushing to the stern of the boat where a plank was being laid to cross over. Eventually the two boats were close enough to allow the gap to be bridged and Remington along with 5 others ran across. Remington felt sick as he watched the blood spraying from the various combatants. One of the mercenaries saw Remington in his confusion and began to charge. Almost too late, Remington noticed the man and as he attempted to ready himself, he watched the man drop to the ground at his feet, a heavy crossbow bolt in the back of his head. T'kocht.

This near-death moment snapped Remington out of his stupor, and he joined in the fray. Attempting to use the techniques Nicky had taught him, Remington entered a dueling contest with one of the guards. Time seemed to slow for Remington as he watched his opponents blade swing towards his right shoulder. He ducked out of the way, nimbly taking a step back as he was taught. He swung his scimitar to the left, before pulling it back just as his opponent went to parry. Seeing now the opening they had left on their left side, Remington seized the opportunity. With one fluid motion he sliced his blade across the neck, one of the few openings in their armor, causing the head to almost become detached. At this point Remington did become sick.

As he finished his retching onto the deck of the ship, he looked up to see that the battle was won. 4 of the 12 original mercenaries were still alive, but gravely wounded and surrendering. Many of his crewmates were wounded as well, and he could see one amongst the dead. He looked down at his opponent that now lay dead on the deck, the warm blood still flowing from their neck. He could see now that she was an older woman, maybe in her late 30's, Human. He began to wonder if she had a family, what was she protecting that was worth dying for, and most importantly did he have to take her life.

"It happens to all of us eventually," the familiar voice of Nicky appearing behind him. "It's best not to think about it too much. A man's first kill is always the hardest. It was either you or her. You did good." She put her hand on his back, which gave him some comfort.

The crowd parted as Captain Atrigul finally made her way across. She paced in front of the 4 survivors, looking each one in the eye.

"You fine folk really put up a good fight didn't you? You were smart to surrender when you did, but you must be guarding something quite valuable. Now let's just make this whole thing easier and tell me where we can find it so we do not have to turn this ship upside down hmm?"

The mercenaries looked at each other, a silent agreement passing between them. They looked back toward the captain and remained silent.

"So that is how we are going to play huh? Rinva, Errich, go start searching the decks, grab anything that seems useful. Brend, follow them and bring up the first person you can find, for I am sure there are others on board." A human woman with platinum blonde hair and a small halfling man began to make their way to the lower decks, followed by Brend. A few minutes later, Brend returned dragging a man by his collar, choking him in the process. Brend dumped the body at Captain Atrigul's feet.

She looked down at the poor man who was coughing trying to regain his breath, shaking with fear. She smiled. "Now I am going to ask again, where is the item you are protecting. We are going to find it eventually, but if you help us, maybe we will show a little bit of mercy. If not, I am sure your friend here doesn't need all of his fingers, right?"

Her blade was drawn, long yet slender as the heel of her boot crushed the wrist of the man before her. The mercenaries once again had their silent debate. It seems they were attempting to call her bluff. Unfortunately for their fellow crewmember, Captain Atrigul never bluffed. With a slow and purposefully painful movement she removed all five fingers from his hand. He screamed in pain, those viewing wincing in sympathy.

Captain Atrigul reached down and picked up one of the fingers. She playfully bit the severed finger, and caressed the man's face with it, wiping away his tears. "Now again, where is the item you are guarding? Hmm, his nose seems a bit long don't you think? Maybe I can fix that for him." As she reached down toward his face, the sound of his tears was broken by Rinva returning. "I think we found it Capt'n, you are going to like it too." The captain chuckled releasing the man and made her way over to Rinva, who was holding a small wooden box.

Remington attempted to get a view of the box, but Captain Atrigul had positioned herself in a way as to block the view from her crew. "Magical I assume?" he heard her ask Rinva. "Yes, Capt'n. Allows you to spy on people far away when you want, even talk to them if you wish. Very rare object, and very expensive too." The Captain nodded her head and turned back toward the mercenaries.

"This is quite the cargo. Something I would expect to find on a military vessel. Unless you did not want to be connected to the Lords of Lebdi? I am curious who was this for?" At this point one of the mercenaries spoke up, a tall bulky man with a terrible wound in his shoulder. "We are not connected with the Lords, though this is a gift for your King. I suggest you return it and allow it to reach its destination, he is expecting it." Remington could tell the man was lying, or at least partly. They were working for the Lords. He could tell the captain knew this as well. The man was not a good liar.

Captain Atrigul raised an eye at this. "For the Pirate King you say? Hmm, well from where I am standing, he is not here is he and I want this oh so very much. What ever shall I do?" She turned around and looked toward Brend, "Kill them, restock the Rose, then send this ship to the depths. Leave no witnesses." As she finished this sentence, she plunged her sword behind her into the gut of the mercenary who spoke. Brend smiled back, "With pleasure," he responded. It did not take long to dispatch the other three, who were now weaponless.

Remington stood on the ship in shock, but soon realized this was the life of pirates. They do not keep their words, and opinions can change on a copper if opportunity was upon them. He tried to ignore the danger this new life brought him and helped move cargo from one ship to the other. As the final boxes of food were brought on board they pushed off, and set the other boat ablaze, now a ghost ship with only corpses to carry.

Remington watched the blaze as they sailed away from the carnage, remembering the life he was responsible for ending. Remington wished he could say it never got easier, but it did. As he was contemplating, T'kocht quietly approached making Remington jump at his appearance. Remington quickly put on a fake smile.

"That was some nice shooting, where did you learn to be such a sharpshooter?" Remington asked.

"Started my training young, shooting birds in the streets. It's harder than you think. How are you doing?" T'kocht responded, ignoring Remington's attempt to steer the conversation away from himself.

For most of Remington's life, he never trusted anyone. Most of the people he met were greedy and selfish and would not hesitate to throw some random kid under the cart. This caused Remington to keep to himself and to never tell anyone anything. But seeing T'kocht now, he could see the sincerity in his eyes. This man actually cared about how Remington was feeling, and real empathy was rare. Remington knew if he wanted to make it out of this with any sanity, he would need someone he could trust. So he decided for once in his life to be honest.

"Not the best to be honest. I have never taken a life before and I am not sure how I feel. Is this line of work always like this? Why did you join this crew?"

T'kocht smiled and slid along the walls of the ship until he was sitting on the deck with his long legs stretched out. "It's not always like this. Usually raids actually go peacefully and don't happen very often. Typically it's just weeks at sea, enjoying the open air and if we are lucky, we get to do some explorations of islands."

"As for why I joined," he continued, "Well look at me. I know most people in society see me as a monster. They get one look at my tusks and green skin and immediately think I am going to eat their children. You have spent enough time with me to know I don't even eat meat. Growing up the bastard son of a whore, I did not have many options to survive. I could always have chosen to go into my mother's line of work but I wanted more freedom. So, I ran into the captain recruiting some new crew at a bar in Halitona and signed up. Quickly proved myself as a sharpshooter, earned me the nickname Eagle. At this point I am not even sure the captain knows my real name, but it does not bother me. Pirating is not for everyone; many don't make it their first 3 months at sea. But for many of us outcasts, it allows us to find success, and to turn our backs on the society that turned its back on us. The crew have become a family out here, and I can see you have the strength to survive in this family. I want you to survive."

Remington joined him sitting on the deck of the ship and pondered for a bit what he said. He wondered, even if he did ever get off this ship, what waited for him back in Rivenport. He did not have a family; he did not have friends. He could find another job on a merchant vessel, but he found no life in that. It was just another way to stay alive. He thought about the past week and a half on the Sickening Rose. He saw what T'kocht talked about, the crew acted as a family and they quickly accepted him as one of their own. However, he did not see the freedom. From the moment he was dragged aboard, he was an object of possession of the Captain, a tool to be used for her own pleasure. He remembered the threats made, and the obedience of her first mate Brend to carry out any violence she requested.

Remington looked over at T'kocht who was watching him closely. "I see what you mean, the crew does act like a family and I am a survivor. Maybe I can find what I am looking for out here, on the water. You're a good friend T'kocht. Thank you for being here." With that, Remington stood up and began to head towards the lower decks. He will make his life better.

6

For the next two weeks, the Sickening Rose made its way toward the island city of Halitona. During that time, Remington made an effort to continue to build his relationships with his fellow crewmen, a new outlook on his life. He continued honing his skill with his blade with Nicky in the mornings, enjoying a lunch break with T'kocht who was able to change shifts to the day shift, and used the afternoons to learn the ins and outs of running the ship. At night, he became better acquainted with the captain, keeping her company, and learning the skills of the night.

One afternoon, as Remington was once again helping Glazzglek with minor repairs to the sails, he saw smoke rising off the horizon. He pointed this out to Glazzglek. "Thare is aye smoke rising fae th' island o' Halitona. Tis fae th' volcano. We wull likelie be making land in a day," Glazzglek explained. Halitona, thought Remington, He had not seen land in over a month now and he looked forward to it.

As he climbed down the mast, he ran into T'kocht. "Hey Remi!", T'kocht had taken to calling him Remi. Remington did not mind too much, but only because it was T'kocht. To everyone else, he was still Remington. "The captain says we should be making shore by noon tomorrow. Unfortunately, she does not quite trust you to be on your own yet and wants to keep you around so you will need an escort. But the good news is I volunteered, so hopefully your time on the island won't be too bad. Plus, you need someone to make sure you follow the Pirate King's rules. For being pirates, they are quite strict on Halitona."

Remington scoffed. Remington had thought about attempting to run when they made landfall, but he also knew this sort of thing might come up. He wondered what made the captain so interested in him. There were probably dozens of other men that she could take with her off the island, so why was he kept as her prisoner? Maybe he can try asking tonight. He turned towards T'kocht and put on a smile. "Who better to show me around the island than a local? I look forward to it!" He reached out his hand grasping T'kocht's forearm in appreciation, before heading to his hammock to attempt to get a few hours of sleep in.

Later that night, Remington made his way to the captain's quarters as he has every night since washing up on this boat. As he entered, he saw that the captain was still in her daytime uniform, a fire blazing in the only other chimney on the ship besides the one in the kitchen. "Is there something wrong Captain? Would you like me to leave?" Remington asked cautiously. She turned toward him, the feathers in her hat swaying with the movement. He immediately noticed the stern look in her face, not the usual mischievous smile she wore.

"No, don't leave. As you know we are making port tomorrow. I am not sure why, but even with my eagle as your escort, I have a sneaking suspicion that you are going to try to escape."

"I would ne-" Remington tried to cut in, but she stopped him.

"I am not stupid. I know you feel like a prisoner, though I wish that feeling would stop for you. I oh so very much enjoy our time together," she began brushing her hands across his shoulders, slowly working his shirt off. "And I see a lot of potential in you. You have... pleased me in ways that many have not, and I don't want to lose that. I do sincerely hope you have found some enjoyment in your time on my ship." She began to pull him closer to the fireplace, where some comforts were set up.

"So that is why you keep me around?" he asked. "I am sure there are many others that fit that description and I feel like a prisoner because I am. You force me to have an escort on the island to make sure I do not run off and threaten me with death if I do not do what you say. I don't know about you but that does not sound like freedom to me." Remington did not mean to speak so freely but he was angry. He was not satisfied with her comments.

She whipped her head around from the fireplace she was staring at, a hunger in her eyes. She dug her nails into his forearm and pulled him closer, her eyes not but an inch from his. "I knew you were smart," she responded. "You want to know the truth? I will tell you." Her eyebrows lowered her eyes into a squint, a cruel anger entering into her eyes, "The truth, is that you are a challenge. I have discovered in my years enjoyment in breaking those I can and found joy with the power it creates. And usually, they break quickly which is boring. But you, there is a fire that burns in you still, that even though you do your best to convince me otherwise, your spirit is still your own. I want to see how long you can last, what it will take for you to be mine, what it takes to break you."

As Remington watched her face, absorbing the honesty she threw at him, he felt a searing pain shoot from his chest. As he screamed in agony, attempting to pull away, he looked down to see Captain Atrigul pressing a burning brand into his chest. As she pulled it away, he saw forever marked onto his skin, a wilted rose with poison dripping from its petals. He dropped to his knees, the pain in his chest causing him to begin to lose sight and he felt dizzy. Captain Atrigul threw the brand back into the fire and grabbed

Remington. Throwing him towards the bed she said, "That is so you will always remember that you belong to me, no matter what you may think. Now, let's not let this little escapade ruin a decent last night at sea."

Remington did not remember much more from that night, the pain from the brand causing him to fall in and out of consciousness. He awoke in the morning, exhausted and still in pain. He could hear the excited chatter coming from the deck of the ship, they must be near port. He sat up and felt a sticky burning on his chest. He looked down at the brand, still raw and sizzling from the initial wound. He started to put his shirt back on, but the fabric stuck to the wound, causing it to burn even worse than before. He sharply inhaled, but forced his way through the pain, attempting to look as though nothing happened. Remington went outside.

The midmorning sun blinded Remington as he emerged. He could hear the sounds of seagulls flying around overhead and the excited chatter of the crew. As his eyesight cleared, Remington caught his first glimpse at Halitona. A large volcano emerged from the center of the island, smoke billowing from its crater. The island itself covered with colorful tropical plants, barely a bare spot could be seen except for on the slopes of the volcano. He saw up ahead the town, named after the island and home to the Pirate King. Already there were at least 10 large ships docked in its port, though there was room for many more. The beach was lined with buildings upon stilts, painted in many bright colors of blues, pinks, and yellows. Much of the city continued on into the tree line, various roofs sticking out above the canopy. Remington could not tell how far into the island the city went.

He winced, his knees buckling slightly as a hand slapped down on his shoulder. He looked over and saw T'kocht quickly withdrawing his hand, a look of concern rushing over his face. "I know well enough not to ask," T'kocht admitted, "but I can take you somewhere to get some healing if you need it. But first, let's get our payment and enjoy shore."

Remington looked at T'kocht, "yeah, that would be good." They stood together on the deck of the ship, watching as the docks got closer and closer. Eventually, the ship slowed and many hands on the docks worked to grab ropes and tie up the Sickening Rose. The gang plank was lowered and the crew began to line up. One by one, the crew approached Captain Atrigul who was waiting by the plank and she handed them their share of the spoils won during this trip. Most of it seemed to be various forms of coin, but amongst the pile were also jewels, weapons, and armor.

Eventually, it was Remington's turn. As he approached, Captain Atrigul smiled at him. "I hope you are feeling well this morning. As you may have noticed, whenever we make for port, I see that my crew is duly paid. You are now part of this crew, here is your share. Enjoy your time in the city! Remember, we make sail again in 10 days." She handed him a small bag of pre-portioned goods. From the sound of it, it seemed to mostly be coin. He made his way down to the wooden docks, his body swaying trying to recover his land legs. Shortly after, T'kocht joined him. "Come on, let's see what mischief we can get up to. But first let's do something about that shoulder of yours."

Remington followed T'kocht down the docks toward the city, his chest still screaming with pain, but the sight ahead of him distracted him. All around people were walking and mingling with the newcomers. The clothing they wore was as brightly colored as their buildings, the women wearing extravagant hats and the men with just as extravagant sashes around their waists. Many were calling out trying to catch his attention as they walked by, shoving various fliers advertising establishments into his hand. Above, brightly colored birds and seagulls flew, occasionally swooping down to steal food from an unsuspecting passerby. This was so different from the proud, posh society Remington was familiar with in the Saxe Empire. Everyone here seemed more relaxed, carefree, and yet very dangerous. He noticed almost every single person they passed carried a weapon on them, some advertised it out in the open, while other attempted to hide it on their bodies.

T'kocht continued to drag Remington through the crowds, weaving his way through the streets with ease and familiarity. Eventually, they made their way into the tree line where many buildings were structured around the trees. Remington thought this city could have almost been hidden if the walls were not so brightly colored. Many of the buildings here were smaller and more run down than the buildings closer to the docks. T'kocht stopped in front of a pale blue hovel, the outside of it weathered and faded. There was a decent size hole in the side of the wall, and it looked like there were probably many other holes along the roof.

As T'kocht opened the door and moved inside he called out, "Ma? Ma I'm home. I brought a friend with me. He might need your help." So, this was T'kocht's home, thought Remington. Eager to see what awaited him, Remington followed T'kocht inside. The inside of the house was not much nicer than the outside. Modest furniture was laid out around the main room that the door opened to. Much of it seemed old, though a few pieces such as the table seem to have been updated fairly recently. A staircase led to a second story. Remington could smell the smoke of a small fire burning somewhere in the house. He started gagging at the smell of the fire, the memory of the previous night and the pain in his chest still very fresh in his thoughts.

T'kocht turned around in concern, but Remington waved him off. Shortly after entering the house, a soft voice rang out from around a corner, "T'kocht? Sweetie? Is that you?" The source of the voice finally came into view. Remington saw a human woman in her mid-30's quickly walking toward them, attempting to quickly clean her hands on a not much cleaner apron. Her long red hair was tied behind her with a bright pink ribbon. Her small frame was a strong contrast to the pride and strength she held in her expression. The resemblance to his friend was undeniable.

The woman and T'kocht embraced. T'kocht lifted her into the air and spun her around, laughing with happiness in their reunion. Putting her down, T'kocht turned toward Remington, "Remi, this is my mother, Elianne. Ma, this is my friend Remington." Remington reached out his left hand in greeting, the right side of his body hurting too much for a proper greeting. Elianne brushed his hand away, instead embracing him in a hug. While Remington appreciated the welcome, he let out a grunt of pain as pressure was applied to the brand. She quickly pulled away looking at him with concern, "Are you alright sweetie? Did you get injured in battle?"

Remington immediately felt awkward. He did not like the feeling of needing help, nor the feeling that the wound is not a badge of honor. It was a mark of ownership and shame. "No, not battle," was all that Remington said.

Elianne changed her expression to a caring smile. "No worries my dear, come over here so I can get a better look at it. T'kocht, there is some soup in the kitchen. Why don't you grab a bowl for yourself and your friend to enjoy? It must have been months since you've had a homemade meal." She draped her hand over Remington's left arm and led him over to the side room she was in, which he now saw had a wide variety of plants, herbs, and medicinal supplies.

She motioned for him to sit down in the light of the fire, which he did hesitantly. "Can you show me?" she asked. Remington took a deep breath and winced as he peeled the fabric away from his wound and removed his shirt, revealing the decaying rose burned into his skin. She quietly examined it, not bothering to ask him questions. Remington appreciated that. After a minute, she looked up and said, "Well, luckily for you it looks worse than it is. Though it is bad enough that it will probably be permanent, I'm sorry dear. Let me go get you something for the pain and to help with the healing." She stood up and walked to her cabinet to start rummaging around.

T'kocht exited the kitchen, carefully carrying two bowls of steaming soup. Remington could smell the variety of herbs in the broth and many fresh vegetables that made his mouth water. As he placed the bowl in front of Remington, T'kocht let out a slight growl under his breath at the sight of the brand on Remington's chest. "I didn't think she would go this far. I should have said something, helped you if I could. Argh!" T'kocht smashed his fist against the mantle of the fireplace, the thunk of the hit mixing with a bit of cracking of knuckles echoed across the room.

Remington quickly looked toward his friend, surprised by the rage in his voice. For the almost a month that he had known T'kocht, he had always been calm, never once raising his voice besides to joke. This was the first time he had seen T'kocht's orcish ancestry take over.

"Hey, don't worry. I am okay, really. Captain Atrigul is a dangerous person. If you said something you would have been beaten or thrown overboard, and I would still be in this situation." Remington looked down, not wanting to make eye contact. He continued, "She said she is trying to break me, but I will not let that happen. You are my friend, trust me when I say I have a plan. It is going to take time though, and I will probably have to face things worse than this." Remington meant what he said about T'kocht being a good friend, and while he requested his trust, Remington did not know if it was wise to tell T'kocht everything. He wanted to share his idea to gain the captain's favor, to somehow get rid of Brend, and eventually overthrow Atrigul. If she planned on trying to take everything from him, well two can play at that game.

T'kocht looked back at him and nodded, his temper disappearing as fast as it appeared. "When you need my help," he said, "I will be ready. Just, be careful will you? Revenge can lead you down a path that you can get lost on."

At this time, Elianne returned with some silk cloth, a knife, and a spiky green plant. She looked at the two of them before kneeling back down next to Remington. Using the knife she extracted a viscous gel from the plant and placed it into a container. "All right sweetie, this should help soothe the burn. Make sure to reapply this every 8 hours until it heals." She rubbed some of the gel on the wound and he immediately felt the burn cool. He let out a relieved sigh. Elianne smiled at his relief before wrapping the silk fabric around the wound. The smooth fabric did not stick as badly to the wound as the linen shirt.

Elianne stood up looking at the two men in front of her. "I'll go make up some beds for you boys, you look exhausted. Eat your soup, you're too thin, especially you Remington. It's so nice to have you back home." She gave T'kocht a tight hug and a kiss on the cheek before making her way up stairs. Remington could not help but smile at her genuine kindness and motherly affection. That must be where T'kocht got his personality from, he thought to himself. Now that the pain in his chest was numbed, Remington began to feel the full force of the sleepless night before. Before Remington had a chance to say anything, T'kocht stood up as well. "I better go see what repairs are needed around here. You go get some sleep, we have a busy week ahead of us." With a slight smile, T'kocht made his way back into the kitchen.

Remington waited a few more minutes by the fire, before getting up and walking up the stairs. He ran into Elianne who showed him to a smaller room with two beds made up with basic blankets and a pillow each. She apologized, "I'm sorry you have to share a room. We don't have much here, but what we have is yours. Make yourself comfortable." She left Remington alone in the room, his sword at his waist and his bag of rewards from Captain Atrigul in his hand. He would have to count that and get some belongings soon he thought to himself. He walked over to the first bed and laid down. It was not soft, though it was better than the floor. Remington did not care too much as his eyes closed and he quickly drifted off to sleep.

7

Remington awoke to the setting sun glaring through the window in the room. He guessed he must have been asleep for at least 3 or 4 hours by this time. It did not take him long to remember the dull pain in his chest. He slowly unwrapped the silk and examined the wound. He could see that some of the blisters had already started to heal, though the burn was still in bad shape. He grabbed some of the gel given to him by Elianne and applied it to his chest, the cold numbing feeling finding its way deep into his muscles.

He re-wrapped his chest and as he stood up, he saw a fresh set of clothes folded at the foot of the bed. He gratefully put them on and began to head toward the stairs. As he reached the top of the staircase he could hear a discussion below; he stopped.

"Ma, you really need to take care of yourself first," T'kocht seemed to be pleading. "I know you want to help out the women in town, but there are holes in the roof, you are barely keeping afloat."

The soft voice of Elianne responded, "I don't need much, their lives are much more difficult than mine. I left that way of living over 10 years ago, and I want to help them if I can."

He could hear T'kocht sigh. "Ma, I am not always going to be around to help. I want to make sure you are okay, and that I can help provide for you, as you did for me. I don't know how long this next journey will be, nor if I will return."

Remington heard a slight knock, it almost sounded like a head getting flicked. "Don't you dare talk like that my boy. You will return, I know you will, you always do. I wish you wouldn't go out on the ships though, especially with Captain Atrigul. Can't you just get a job at the port and stay here, where it's safe? Or at least find a vessel that does not go to the Feylands?"

The Feylands, Remington thought to himself. He had heard that name before. Back in Rivenport, he had heard stories of the Feylands from those who had visited Cairnnathoul. The Feylands was an enchanted land on a separate plane of existence, home to a wide variety of strange creatures. Many of the creatures lure those who visit to their deaths by enchanting them. Within this land though, lies many mysteries and strong powers if you have the strength to find them. Remington never wanted to go there, it always sounded too dangerous. He couldn't help but wonder what Captain Atrigul was looking for there.

"She pays well and it gives me a job," he heard T'kocht respond. "You know most of the people here won't hire me, they don't like my kind."

At this point Remington realized he probably should not be listening to this conversation. It was private, and he had no right to listen. Attempting to make as much noise as possible, Remington made his way down the stairs to find them.

He found the two of them sitting across from each other, sharing a pot of tea. Though they both greeted him with the same smile, he could feel the tension that was in the room. "Did you rest well dearie?" Elianne broke the silence in the room.

"Yes ma'am, I feel a lot better already," Remington responded.

"Well, I am glad to hear that. I will want to check it tomorrow, make sure it does not get infected. And please, you don't need to call me ma'am. I'm not that old yet!" she said with a slight laugh. She poured a cup of tea for Remington, who gladly accepted it and joined them at the table.

"So, what crazy adventures did you get up to this time?" she asked, the majority of the question for T'kocht.

For the rest of the evening T'kocht shared the happenings of the Sickening Rose before Remington joined the crew. Both Remington and Elianne were listening intently as T'kocht talked about exploring the Tengroto Rainforest in Sokya and of the dangerous encounter with the locals there. He explained how the natives had the innate ability to transform themselves into snakes and laced all of their weapons with poison. They laughed hysterically as T'kocht told of how Brend accidentally touched a poisonous frog that caused him to start uncontrollably covering himself in mud. Remington learned that this past voyage was a short one, the crew being out at sea for only 4 months.

Long after the sun had set and the moon had risen high into the night sky, the trio eventually found the relaxation of sleep. Remington was the first to wake up in the morning, T'kocht still sound asleep and snoring in the bed across the room. As he applied more of the gel onto the wound, which has now started to crust up, Remington stared at the door. He could leave if he wanted to, right now and disappear into the forest, away from Captain Atrigul. He stared at the brand, now permanently apart of him and thought over the month he had spent in her company.

He hated the cruel words she spoke to him in the night, trying to convince him that he was nothing, that he had no life outside of her. He felt his body was no longer his own, ripped away from his soul by her teeth to be used for her pleasure and as tool for keeping the ship afloat. Though he would deny it to anyone who asked, Remington already felt himself being broken down into a husk of a man. Only 17 years old, he had lost much of his positive outlook on life having faced hardships from a tender age.

He could run, he thought to himself again. But where would he go. He had no connections, no way to survive, and no way off the island. Captain Atrigul offered employment, adventure, excitement, but also pain, misery, and entrapment. He hated this feeling that his only chance at succeeding in life was connected to her, that he needed her if he was to make anything out of his life. Her words to him echoed into his head, "what it takes to break you." Remington felt his tears beginning to run down his face. Had she succeeded? Was the branding of his body the final key to breaking him? Was he really that weak?

"No," he said out loud. He quickly looked over at T'kocht, fearful he might have woken him up, but he was sound asleep. He couldn't leave, he thought to himself. What would the cruel captain do to T'kocht had he slipped out under his watch. Who would be the next poor soul to face her empty wrath, to be emptied to the point of being thrown out with the rest of the trash? No, he wouldn't allow it.

Remington strengthened his resolve. He was not about to allow Captain Atrigul to destroy him, no matter the pain he felt now. He knew he had the strength to turn the tides, to do what was necessary to end her reign for good, to have the support to end her reign. But it will take time, and right now, time was all that Remington had. Wiping the tears from his face, he steeled his resolve, more determined than ever to keep himself whole.

Remington was working on patching a hole in a blanket downstairs when T'kocht finally came down. Having woken up earlier than everyone else, Remington wanted to make himself useful. He had found the blanket draped over a chair with a large hole in the center of it. It took him a while to find the thread and needle, but he decided it would be a good time to practice his sail mending on the fabric.

T'kocht let out a laugh as he saw Remington's terrible needle work. "Don't let Glazzglek see that work," T'kocht teased. Remington rolled his eyes as he put his work down, joining T'kocht for some tea and breakfast.

"Since you are my tour guide, what is the plan for today?" asked Remington through a bite of toast.

"Well first, I am tired of you borrowing my clothes, so we are going to take you shopping. Then, since we have only 10 days, I am heading to the tattoo parlor to update my arm. After that, I can show you around the island if that sounds alright to you." T'kocht responded, seemingly quite excited for the day.

Remington nodded in approval. He agreed he needed to get some personal items. He had been wearing the same shirt and pants for the past month, and they were looking worn and ragged. Though he will probably pass on getting a tattoo himself, he wouldn't mind having the time to watch people walking past the shop. Remington loved people watching. He believed the fastest way to get to know a new place is to watch its people. They finished their breakfast and made their way into town.

8

By noon, Remington and T'kocht had finished their shopping. Each carrying multitudes of bags of items, it was a successful morning. Remington was now wearing a simple black tricorne hat to help keep the sun off his face, which made him look even more handsome with his long hair tied back with a blue ribbon that matched his eyes.

As they headed to their next destination, the tattoo parlor, Remington noticed they seemed to be heading towards the more dangerous part of town. T'kocht seemed unphased by this transition in atmosphere, though they both held their bags a little closer to their bodies. Eventually, T'kocht seemed to find what he was looking for. Before them stood a small shop with a ragged sign on the outside that read *Isodira's Tattoo Emporium*.

A bell on the door rang as they entered and quickly running out from behind the front desk was a small woman, no taller than 3'2", half of her head shaved to reveal her pointed ears, the other half having long blonde wavey hair reaching down to her waist. Her own skin covered almost completely with tattoos of all sorts.

"T'kocht!" the woman shouted. "Welcome back! How is your mother doing is she alright?" She was quickly asking these questions as she ran to hug him, while T'kocht kneeled down to meet her.

"Aye, she is doing just fine, though the house needs some repairs," responded T'kocht.

At this point she noticed Remington, who had gotten distracted by the various artwork that hung on the wall. He was examining a drawing of some squid like creature that had wrapped its tentacles around a ship, dragging it to its doom when he heard her voice addressing him.

"You like what you see? I know I do." Remington quickly spun around, jumping instinctively in nervousness at the voice so similar in tone to Captain Atrigul.

"Uh, its uh well drawn," Remington stuttered out, slightly backing away from the gnomish woman. T'kocht stepped between them at this point, "Let him be Isodira, he is... not available. Atrigul already laid claim to him." There was a slight tone of pity in his voice but was yet very forceful. "Anyways," T'kocht continued, "We are not here for him. I need some more art on my arms, got anything exciting?"

Isodira looked at Remington with disappointment. "Well better not mess with Atrigul, she's got the favor of the King. I have some ideas for you that I think you will like, follow me," she said. T'kocht led Isodira away from Remington to discuss some of her ideas, leaving Remington to continue to browse the art, and lower his heart rate.

Out of the corner of his eye, Remington caught a glint of something across the street. He turned to look to see what it was, and he saw an old woman standing in a shop across the street looking at him. Her white hair was matted and tangled and her nose was long and crooked. When she smiled, Remington could see even from this distance that her teeth were yellowed and falling out. What disturbed him most were her eyes which seemed to be entirely white, besides the black pupils that now stared unblinking. He watched as she raised a boney finger in his direction, and he heard a voice that was not his own enter his head.

"You hold secrets that you do not know. Come to me and I will reveal them to you." The voice was old and shaky but had a wisdom hidden within. Remington did not trust this woman, but for some reason he felt compelled to go to her, to hear what she had to say. He looked over his shoulder to find T'kocht but did not see him. Curiosity overtook Remington and he exited the tattoo parlor and made his way across the street.

As he entered the shop, Remington could see all sorts of strange trinkets hanging about. A shrunken head spun hanging from the ceiling and various smells of rotten egg and incense filled his lungs. He saw the woman waiting for him at a desk in the back of the shop. He approached cautiously.

"Welcome my child, you carry a fate with you which I can reveal if you would like," her hoarse voice made his own throat scratchy.

"What's your price?" asked Remington. Everything had a price, especially here.

The woman let out a sickening cackle and gave him a wide smile, "The price is knowledge. Knowing your fate is a harsh price to pay."

Remington considered her words. He felt she was telling him the truth, though he yearned to know where his life will lead. He toyed with his sword at his side, contemplating if this was some sort of trick when he noticed the woman eying it.

"What do you know about this blade?" he asked. Remington had heard enough stories to know that when a blade has a name it usually means that it has a history behind it.

She waved her hands inviting him to lay it out on the table. He placed the sword and watched her carefully as she began to circle it. She reached her hands over the blade and began whispering in a language foreign to Remington. He saw her eyes flash briefly with a bright light before she once again began to chuckle.

"This blade dearie is named Fortune Teller. What a fitting blade for someone tied so closely to fate. Crafted by those who walk in the wilds of the fey, there is magic woven into its folds. If it deems you worthy, you can command this blade to influence your fate and the fate of those around you. It has the will to briefly see into the future and change it if needed. But be warned, by changing your future, it might not always change for the better."

Remington picked up the blade and examined its curves and writing. Now his curiosity was stronger than ever. Putting it back in its sheath, he looked back at the woman who was still smiling with a look on her face as if she knew something he didn't. "What do you know of my fortune, please I must know," he asked accepting of any consequences.

She took his hand into hers and pressed her other hand into his forehead. He began to feel a searing pain shoot through his head. He tried to back away but felt his entire body paralyzed unable to move. Remington started to panic when the pain began to subside and he could feel his legs again. Immediately he backed away, separating himself from this mysterious woman.

"What did you do to me," demanded Remington, feeling his forehead for any sign of damage though he did not find any.

"I looked into your future and saw your fate. Your course leads you to a woman who you will betray. This betrayal will leave you with power beyond your imagination, but nothing will satisfy the void that is left behind."

Remington gulped, immediately thinking of Captain Atrigul. That must be the woman she mentioned, he thought to himself, but what does that mean for him? He looked back at the old woman who was watching him carefully. Remington did not know what to say, but he did not like the look she gave him. It almost appeared as if she knew, that even if he tried to avoid it, this future will still come to him. Shaken, he turned around and exited the shop. He needed to get back before T'kocht noticed he was gone. As he crossed the street, he looked over his shoulder only to find the shop no longer there. Now, there was only an abandoned building, the windows boarded up. He picked up his pace almost running into the tattoo parlor. What did he just do?

He found his way to the back of the shop, face still pale from the unexplainable encounter. There he had found T'kocht who seemed to have settled on a nautical star being pulled up his arm by a rope attached to a grand eagle. The design drawn out was intricate and beautiful with fine details throughout, but most importantly to T'kocht, covered a large area of his arm, blocking out the pale green beneath. T'kocht noticed Remington's pale face but did not say anything about it. Remington hoped T'kocht just attributed it to his interaction with Isodira.

"What do you think Remi?" T'kocht asked indicating to the design, "You sure you don't want something?"

Remington knew T'kocht was just trying to distract him but he appreciated the out. "Looks good," he responded, "quite fitting for the eagle of the seas." Remington looked around and spotted an ear-ring that hooped under the earlobe with a small chain connecting it to a clip that attached to the upper part of the ear. He turned toward Isodira holding up the earring, "Do you do piercings as well?"

"Of course, we do all sorts of... modifications here. And just for you, since you are a new customer and a friend to one of my favorites," she pinched T'kocht's cheek who then swatted it away, "it will be on the house." So before she started the lengthy work of T'kocht's tattoo, she made quick work on Remington's left ear expertly installing the earring. Remington looked in the mirror. It looked quite nice, he thought. The platinum color of the earring creating a sparkle that drew the viewer to his face, and then to his eyes. Remington did not have much ownership of his body of late, but knowing that this modification was his decision, he felt a bit of strength and confidence return to him.

Throughout the rest of the afternoon and into the early hours of the night, Remington waited in the tattoo parlor. Much of the time he spent talking with his friend, but he also spent parts of it reading or grabbing food for the two of them. He was doing everything he could to not think about his conversation with the old woman. Finally, when the art was finished, the two stumbled back exhausted to T'kocht's home having completed a successful first day on land.

Over the course of the next nine days, Remington got to know the island and his friend much better. They spent their days touring some of T'kocht's favorite spots on the island, repairing the home, and helping Elianne when they could. Remington liked Elianne, she felt like the mother he never had. She took him in without question and gave him the support he never knew he needed.

During one particularly rainy day, she told Remington of her past, how she worked in her youth as an escort down at the docks, her occupation giving her "the greatest gift the gods could bring" with the birth of T'kocht. It was difficult raising him in such an environment, but she did everything she could to keep him safe. T'kocht grew up fast, quickly becoming a keen shot, learning to hunt to keep them fed and moving quietly so as to be unseen.

Not all children of the docks are as lucky. She explained that now days since her retirement, she continues to try to support the girls down by the docks by bringing them any extra money she has. Some of them have had a particularly hard life and she aids them in protecting and raising any children that come to the world as a result of their jobs. She keeps what she needs to survive, but she did not need to live lavishly, no matter how much T'kocht protests.

Remington listened to her story carefully, feeling the full impact of the care that Elianne gave to these women, appreciating the selflessness that came so naturally to her. Before their last day, Remington ended up giving her a large portion of his remaining funds, feeling he won't need much of it in this next journey, to help in her endeavors.

"You are always welcome here sweetie, no matter the circumstance. Our family is your family. Now you two be safe and hurry back here alright? Take care of yourselves!" She gave each of them a kiss on the cheek in farewell, walking them to the docks where the Sickening Rose awaited them.

The anxiety and fear he felt during his time on the Sickening Rose rushed back to Remington. After that first day, his time on Halitona had been relaxing, an escape from the harsh realities that he was still a slave to Captain Atrigul. He thought back to the prophecy given to him by the mysterious woman and shivered. He had not told T'kocht about that encounter and had no plans to. He still was not sure if it was real.

He took a deep breath in an attempt to calm himself and felt T'kocht's hand on his shoulder. "If things get too much, let me know. Remember the crew is a family, and families help each other. Don't try to face this yourself," T'kocht said sternly, turning Remington to look him in the eyes. "Do you understand?" T'kocht almost demanded.

All Remington could do was nod his head in affirmation. He turned back toward the ship and holding his head high, walked determinedly towards his fate.

9

As Remington walked the gangway, T'kocht closely following, he was greeted by the smiling face of Captain Atrigul. Remington almost gagged as the strong scent of her rose perfume hit his nostrils, one that he will never forget. He saw that he was not the only one who benefited from their time on shore. Captain Atrigul took the time to clean up, the sweat that all sailors carried gone from her hair and clothing, her skin dulled to a light bronze having had time to stay out of the sun. Upon her jacket which had been mended and the color refreshed, she now adorned a small medallion with the familiar skull and crossbones symbol that Remington learned indicated someone had the favor of the Pirate King.

"Welcome back aboard gentlemen," she welcomed them. "I am glad to see my eagle has as keen eyes on shore as he does on the sea. Your duties this trip will be the same as the last so go get settled, we make sail in 2 hours." She gave them both a wink as they continued on board.

Remington swallowed hard as he walked past her, hoping that she couldn't read his thoughts and hoping he would survive this trip. He walked with T'kocht down to the lower decks and began securing their belongings underneath their hammocks.

As the time grew closer to casting off, Remington and T'kocht made their way to the top deck where apparently Captain Atrigul always gave a rallying speech on new journeys. Remington saw many familiar faces, Nicky and Glazzglek talking with each other, Brend standing at the righthand side of the captain. But he also saw a few new faces in the crowd. He wondered if they knew whose ship they just set foot on and if any of them would feel the same pain he did. He hoped not.

Remington felt the ground shift beneath his feet and knew the last of the docking ropes had been released. As the ship drifted away from the docks, he heard Brend yell out, "Al'ight all ye listen close, your new captain's got something to say." As the deep voice echoed across the deck, the crew fell silent.

"Thank you, Brend," the captain started, her voice as clear and calm as the seas themselves. "To all my returning crew, welcome back. Loyalty is always rewarded here. To our new crew members, welcome aboard the Sickening Rose. Every man and woman on this ship is like family to each other and I hope you will feel the same way as I do."

Lies, Remington thought to himself, not everyone.

"During your time on the Sickening Rose, you shall enjoy all the pleasures that pirating life brings, but do not think you are completely free of rules. A ship requires order to function with efficiency. We live free of the laws of government, but while you walk her decks, you will listen to my orders. My rules keep you alive, I have not been on the seas for 15 years without learning a thing or two. Disobedience will be met with punishment, and if you disobey any orders that results in harm to your new family, expect that harm back in return."

Her voice had dropped in tone. Remington knew her threats were well founded and saw that everyone else noticed the cruel look in her eyes. The same look he saw every night. She continued, her voice returning to a calmer note.

"If you do not yet have a job on the ship, please talk to my first mate Brend. You will obey his orders as if you were obeying my own. Our destination is the Feylands, one which few captains know how to reach. We are about a month out from the jump, so take care and smooth sailings."

With the loud cheer of the crew in the background, Remington remained silent, watching as Captain Atrigul carefully turned on her heals and took up her spot at the helm. He flinched as Brend's voice cut through the cheers ordering everyone to get to work.

Remington made his way up to Brend, unsure of what his next rotation was planned to be. He braced himself for the whirl of insults that Brend sends at everyone when he was intercepted by Captain Atrigul. She placed her hand on his chest where the burn scar remained, though it was fully healed. She smiled at him, "I see some shore rest has done well for you. Let's hope you haven't forgotten everything in those 10 days."

"No captain," Remington responded briefly, making a point to make direct eye contact with her. "I do need orders as to where you want me to work."

"Oh yes, of course. Until we make the jump, I want you to continue your practices with Nicky, then work with Rodan the ships navigator. I think you could pick up a skill or two from him unlike most on this ship. And of course, your nightly duties are still the same." She gave him a wink, slightly brushing his cheek to send him on his way.

"As you say, captain," Remington responded, a little harsher than he intended. Captain Atrigul looked back over her shoulder at him with a questioning look before returning to the wheel. Remington immediately regretted it, anticipating the response he will receive when they are alone.

That night Captain Atrigul made sure that Remington remembered the full power she held over him. Remington did his best to ignore her words of his uselessness, of reminding him of his abandonment but how she would never let him go. She could make him useful. The arguments she made, the soft whispers in his ear as their bodies intertwined, were hard to shut out. She twisted his own thoughts, trying to take possession of them, the same way she took his body. It took everything in Remington to not fight back, to not run, for he would only run into the arms of death.

For the next month, Remington's days went by much the same as they have been. He spent the early hours of the morning with Rodan learning how to navigate by the stars, then the rest of the morning sparring with Nicky, perfecting his skill with his blade. He had become a good blades man by this time, even occasionally getting a hit against Nicky. At night, he was subjected to the ownership of Captain Atrigul, each week the mental torture slowly wearing him down. He had begun to almost forget his plans for revenge, forget the prophecy spoken to him. Her technique was working, for how could he betray her. The crew would never follow him, he was a nobody. No, he needed her, she was helping him. The lies that she constantly spoke wove their way into his head, planting and nourishing the seed of obedience and self-doubt.

The Sickening Rose had made its way south to the Gulf of Rossbalt which separated the two major continents. They had stopped off the coast of Ivorham of the Saxe Empire directly above the Lumduff Trench. It was all hands-on deck on the ship, preparing for the jump to the Feylands. All loose items were secured below deck, sails were lowered, and ropes tied down. Five crystals were carefully placed around the ship by Captain Atrigul. Around each one she drew an arcane circle with chalk, chanting in a language Remington did not recognize.

As her chanting continued, the seas around the Sickening Rose grew rougher. Large swells rocked the boat back and forth almost to the point of capsizing the large vessel. Clouds seemed to form out of nowhere, spiraling overhead the center of the storm directly over the main mast. Without hesitation, Captain Atrigul continued while many who had not participated in the jump before ran below decks. The arcane circles now radiated with light, burning into the deck, the light flowing into the crystals. The sky above them grew as dark as night, the crystals now the only source of light.

Remington thought he could see off in the distance a massive rogue wave heading towards them and began to panic. He prayed to the gods that Captain Atrigul knew what she was doing, though he knew the gods would not help.

The light from the five crystals shot towards the center of the ship, intersecting each other simultaneously. From this center point of light, the glow seemed to grow and spread. The beams wove themselves together, reaching upwards and branching out forming the shape of a gleaming silver tree.

By this time, the rogue wave was not but 20 seconds from impact with the ship. Many of the crew braced for impact while Captain Atrigul stood strong in the center of the deck, not stopping her chanting for a second, a deep focus on her face. The silver tree began to form blossoms which with a final shout from Captain Atrigul, burst asunder shedding its gleaming petals over the ship. Just as the wave reached them, the ship already sitting at a 30-degree angle, a bright light washed over all of them, causing momentary blindness.

Suddenly everything was calm. Remington wondered if this was the end if he had entered the Halls of Mirtis to pass her judgement and live in the afterlife. His eyes were closed as he squatted on the ground, hands over his head providing useless protection. Then he felt a slight breeze and the gentle swaying of the ocean. He opened his eyes to an unbelievable sight.

Above him the cloudless sky was a spectacular display of pinks, blues, purples, and oranges. Though there was no sun in the sky, the way these colors blended reminded Remington of a sunset, though he had never seen one so beautiful. Throughout the air, a soft breeze flowed bringing with it an intoxicating scent of sweet flowers and comforting aromas. As he stood up, he looked over the side of the ship to see crystal clear blue waters. He could count the fish that swam by, none of them bothered by the sudden appearance of the ship.

He looked back towards the deck of the ship. The crystals were no longer glowing and he saw Captain Atrigul kneeling on the deck, shaking. He looked for Brend, who he saw thrusting people out from below deck, some of whom looked as if they were going to be sick. One person he shoved a little too harshly and he tripped and smacked his face on the deck, causing blood to flow from his nose. Brend only laughed.

Remington made his way over to Captain Atrigul wanting to make sure she was okay. Did he want her to be okay, Remington thought to himself. If she was not, he could be free of her manipulation, but free to go where? As much as it still pained him to say it, he needed her. Even if to just make it back to the Prime Realm he called home. He approached.

"Are you alright Captain?" he asked kneeling down beside her. He could see now she was shaking, her arms helping her legs to support the weight of her body. Of what Remington could see of her face, hidden by a mess of hair whipped up from the storm, he could see that it was very pale. She took a deep breath and turned towards him. He could see a small stream of blood draining from her left nostril, curving around her lips before dropping to the deck. Her eyes were sharp, her face still contorted in concentration, though it was slowly starting to relax. She turned her body to sit on the deck, back resting against the main mast. Wiping the blood away from her face, she looked toward Remington and smiled.

"Hello Remington," she said shakily, "we made it." Remington was perplexed by this simple gesture. Her voice, usually so filled with deceit, with ulterior motives and veiled threats, was soft and gentle. Her smile, usually teasing and marked with malice seemed genuine and caring. What did this mean, he wondered? Was this just another one of her games to bring his guard down? He didn't think so. Maybe in this fragile state of weakness, she unintentionally let down her façade shown a different personality, one that she hid from the crew and Remington.

Remington reached to his belt and pulled out his water flask, handing it to her. She took a small sip, before handing it back and reaching for his arm, looking for support. Remington slowly helped her up, taking care that she did not stand up too quickly, for the captain still looked faint. He helped her walk to her quarters, where she laid down on her bed.

As Remington turned to leave, preparing himself for the miserable day to be had with Brend in charge while the captain was out, he felt Captain Atrigul reach out and grab his hand. "Please, stay," she whispered, her voice barely audible. Remington looked toward the door, knowing Brend would make him pay for skipping duties when all hands were required on deck right now. However, Atrigul was the captain, and he dared not disobey her orders, even in her current state. Turning around, he let her pull him towards her and crawled into bed next to her.

He braced himself for the words of torment, to shut out her voice and allow his body to be hers. Instead, she carefully shifted herself so that her head rested on his chest, using his shoulder as a pillow. Her arm wrapped around him as if she just wanted to know that he was there. He felt her hair brushing over his arm and he felt a slight chill run over his body. Her eyes fluttered close. Remington tilted his head to look at her. She seemed to have lost years on her face, now looking young and innocent, the strain of completing the jump washing the cruelty away. Remington almost felt pity for her, for whatever need drove her to be controlling of those around her. Almost.

For the rest of the day, Remington remained by her side, unable to move, not wanting to wake her. He spent the time he had alone, thinking about how this all affected his plan. Was she as broken as she was trying to make him? Probably. Did she have any chance at redemption? Perhaps, Remington decided he needed more data before deciding on that one. Could he still go through with his plan for revenge? Depends on the answer to the previous question, he thought. Either way, this threw a wrench in his opinion of Captain Atrigul. Tired, he too found himself drifting off to sleep, his head falling to rest on hers, the scent of sea salt in her hair bringing him a strange comfort.

10

Remington woke up some time later alone. He was not sure how long he had been asleep for, the light from the window looked the same as before. He made his way outside to the deck of the ship and saw that the sky had the same sense of sunset, it appeared as though time did not pass. He heard the loud crunching footsteps of Brend coming up behind him.

"Well looky here boys, the princess has finally gotten up from her beauty sleep," Brend let out a hearty chuckle. All Remington could do was resist the urge to roll his eyes.

"I was completing a special request from the captain," Remington responded coolly, making a point to maintain eye contact.

"Of course you were," Brend responded some what sarcastically. "Either way you missed your shift, so you'll pay for that. Get to work, you're doing a double shift today, go work the ropes!"

Remington sighed, but did not feel like arguing so he got to work. He looked over to see Captain Atrigul back at the helm, her usual expression back on her face, though Remington could tell she was still exhausted. He wondered if anyone else noticed the slight change in behavior, the serenity in her eyes, if anyone else saw the fragile person she was just this morning. He turned his mind back to his work.

Remington had been hauling the heavy ropes for a few hours but found the sky had not changed in color. Taking a few minutes for a break, Remington went off to find Nicky to plan his next training session, since he slept through the usual time, or at least he thought he did. Remington quickly learned that it was difficult to keep time in the Feylands, since the sky was always constant. Nicky explained to him that the local folklore believes that the sky was a fabric woven by the Moon King to fill the lands with everlasting light.

"Who is the Moon King?" Remington asked her.

"He is one of the Fey Lords of course," she responded. Seeing the confusion on Remington's face she continued, "In the Feylands, there are 8 Fey Lords and Ladies that rule over the Summer Court, well technically only 7 are part of the court. The Night Queen got banished a long time ago. Anyways not the point. The seven that remain split up the land and they each rule a bit, though they get together often to make group decisions. The Moon King acts as the leader of them, often making the final decisions. They say he is the most powerful, after the Night Queen."

"So are we in the Moon King's domain now?" asked Remington.

"No silly," replied Nicky, "we are sailing in the River King's domain. He controls all the water in the Feylands and rules over all the creatures that live there. Though I don't think the captain would want him to know we are here."

"Why not?" Remington's curiosity suddenly peaked.

Nicky looked around, confirming the two of them were alone. "Do you know why we are here?" she asked, a sudden seriousness entering her tone. Remington shook his head. He always imagined there was some wealth she was looking for here, or in search of strange creatures. He continued listening.

"The same legends that tell of the Moon King weaving the sky, tell of other creations by members of the Summer Court. They say that the River King created an item called the Jung Brunnen, the Fountain of Youth. They say the waters from this fountain can cure all diseases, remove any curse, and bring extended life to the drinker. The River King hid this somewhere, and there are always those seeking to find it. And that is what we are here to do. To find the key to everlasting life."

Remington sat in silence for a bit, pondering this quest. Remington knew little about the Feylands, but one thing he did know was bargains like that always came with a price. He wondered if the captain knew what the price would be and if she would be willing to pay it. It didn't matter anyways he thought to himself. Captain Atrigul will be dead if his plan goes accordingly. Could he pay the price? Did he have the strength to do it?

That night, exhausted, Remington made his way to the captain's quarters to fulfill his nightly duties. He was curious to see which side of Captain Atrigul he would meet, maybe there was a change in the winds coming. His hopes were crushed immediately. Captain Atrigul acted as if the previous day had not occurred. If anything, Remington thought her to be even more malicious than before as if to make up for her moment of weakness. However, even through the torture, the words of hate and demeaning, Remington thought he could feel something else behind them. Was it sadness, guilt, pity? He was not sure, but there was something. He wondered if somewhere deep within, if she cared for him. Whatever feelings the captain hid behind her mask, did not excuse the pain she placed upon Remington. He must not let his humanity get in the way of his freedom.

For the next month and a half, activities on the Sickening Rose continued as they always did. Remington and the rest of the crew were warned to stay away from the edges of the ship, as there were many creatures that lurked in the depths waiting to lure an unsuspecting person to their death. Remington was not sure if this was just the older crewmen messing with the new guys, but he was not ready to take that risk. They passed a few smaller islands during the journey, which Remington learned had already been explored by the captain and crew.

One afternoon, the booming voice of Brend echoed once again across the deck, indicating an announcement to be made. Captain Atrigul took her place directly in front of the helm, her vantage point allowing her to look over the entire deck. Remington could see in the faces of those around him that she had earned the respect of his fellow crewmen. He understood why. When she was on duty, she showed discipline to keep people in line and an intellect to lead the crew to success. She was stern and unmoving, but did everything for a reason, for a higher plan. He wondered if she held a higher plan for him, if there was something more than just the savage infliction of pain. There had to be.

"I am sure by now most of you know why we are here. For those of you who are good and don't ask questions, I will explain. There is powerful magic that resides in these lands, magic that if found can heal any hurt, extend your life beyond that of the elves, and bring wealth beyond your wildest dreams."

The crew cheered. Remington saw Nicky touch her scarred face out of the corner of his eye. He pretended not to notice. Captain Atrigul continued.

"Over the years, we have searched many of these islands already. We have found many treasures to take home but the ultimate find, the Fountain of Youth, continues to evade us. We are approaching an island that we have yet to explore. We may get lucky and it contains the fountain, its location lost to all but the River King. I will be taking a small group to traverse the island, the rest I leave in charge of watching the ship. Do not feel upset if you are not chosen, for you may face more dangers here than on the island. I expect to return to my ship in the same condition I left her. Do not disappoint me. We will arrive at the island tomorrow morning. I will have Brend notify those who are to be the landing party this evening."

As her speech ended and she turned to leave, the crew immediately went up in a chatter. They wondered who would be a part of the landing party, what they might find on the island, and what they would do if the fountain was found.

Remington listened to them all curiously. He liked the idea of the fountain. He wondered if the wounds its waters cured went deeper than physical wounds, if the scars of memories could be purified. He doubted it. He looked back over at Nicky expecting the same excitement he saw in everyone else, but only saw a look of disappointment. He knew from his conversations that Nicky had been a part of this crew for close to 5 years now, joining when Atrigul first rose to the rank of captain. After years of failure, she must be keeping her expectations low, Remington thought. He always wondered where she got her scars but knew better than to ask. He made his way back to his duties.

By the evening, the landing crew was decided on. It consisted of Captain Atrigul, Brend, Nicky, Rinva the platinum blonde woman who found the crystal ball, a wood elf man named Aldwin, and surprising to everyone, Remington. Remington was disappointed T'kocht was not part of the crew, but figured with his keen eyesight, T'kocht would probably be better off keeping watch on the ship.

In the early hours of the morning, Remington was roughly woken by Brend. They must have arrived. Sleepily walking to the top deck, Remington caught sight of the dense vegetation that covered this island. Soft white sand rimmed the island before the tree line started about 15 feet from shore. The trees were so dense, he could not see what secrets lay within.

On the starboard side of the boat, Remington saw the others starting to gather around and packing supplies. He heard Captain Atrigul explaining, "We need enough to last us a month and a half.

Aquila has been instructed to presume us dead if we do not return in 5 weeks without word from Rinva."

Remington had only talked with Aquila a few times. A shy woman with pale blue skin that always seemed dampened, she oversaw the night crew. She was nice enough, Remington liked her. Captain Atrigul must have left her in charge while they were gone. Within the next half hour, the group had everything they thought they would need prepared. Finished loading the dingy, they made their way to land, to the unknown.

II

The moment Remington set foot on the white sandy beach he felt like he was being watched. It was a similar feeling to the way Captain Atrigul looked at him, as if he was an item of prey. Remington saw that the others also seemed to have this feeling of uneasiness, though Captain Atrigul made a point to try to hide it. They unloaded the boat, carrying what they could and headed towards the tree line, no one saying a word.

The forest that covered this island was thick and marshy. Tall slender trees bunched together, many of the trunks growing from the various pools of water and mud that scattered the land. Between the trees, various brightly colored bushes filled out the foliage, preventing the party from being able to see more than 20 feet in front of them. The island itself seemed to be radiating off an intense heat. Remington estimated the temperature must be at least 30 or 40 degrees warmer than on the ship. It was uncomfortable.

It did not take long for them to notice the most distinct property of this island. The entire forest reeked of death. The smell of rotting meat penetrated their senses, causing Rinva to start throwing up. Almost all of the others were gagging from the smell as well except for Nicky who seemed more panicked than sickened. After the initial shock of the stench worked its way through their system, the party attempted to regrouped themselves. Remington was struggling to focus on anything besides keeping last night's rations down.

Captain Atrigul spoke up, "We knew we were entering unknown lands. This smell will not keep us from our goals. Let's not forget why we are here. Keep your eyes peeled, for even now there are eyes on us."

Remington quickly scanned the area around them, looking for signs of these watchful eyes, but saw nothing. He felt the adrenaline surging through his body, frightened about what may lie ahead. He did not want to show this weakness to the others, he felt the need to prove his worth to them and to his captain. So, he straightened himself out and followed the captain deeper into the forest.

After a short time, Aldwin took over the lead using a large machete to help clear the way for the others following. Captain Atrigul remained close behind Aldwin while Remington and Brend covered the rear, constantly looking back in case they were being followed. Even with Aldwin clearing a path, the hiking was difficult, their feet often getting stuck in the thick sludge like mud.

Remington heard a scream as Nicky's left foot slipped on the log she was attempting to cross. He watched as she fell into a deep pit of mud and quickly started sinking beneath the surface almost as if she was getting pulled. Even before he could finish that thought, he heard Nicky manage to get out, "Something has my leg!" before he saw her head dip under the mud, only her small arm reaching out searching for help.

Faster than Remington had ever seen him move before, Brend leapt toward the mud pit, reaching his hand in where Nicky's was disappearing. Brend let out a long grunt in concentration as he used all of his strength to start to pull at something beneath the mud. He was struggling to find solid footing, the ground was too slippery and even Brend in all his weight began sliding towards the pit.

Remington looked around, trying to find a way to help, and saw off to his right a large broken tree branch. Grabbing it, Remington leapt over to Brend and jammed the branch into the mud in front of him. Brend immediately put his foot against it, which was holding firmly in place and used this added traction to begin to pull backwards. Remington held his breath. For a few seconds, time seemed to slow as Brend pulled attempting to return to a full standing position. Then suddenly, a hand appeared out of the mud clutched to Brend's arm. An audible sigh could be heard from the group, but she was not out of trouble yet. Captain Atrigul stooped down next to Brend and grabbed onto Nicky's arm and helped to continue to pull her from the force that was trying to drag her under.

With the two of them pulling, Nicky's other arm appeared, which Remington and Rinva grabbed and began pulling. This last bit of extra strength gave them the force needed to completely free Nicky from her sticky prison. As Nicky shot out of the pit, unrecognizable from the mud, Remington thought he could see some sort of tentacle slithering back into the pit. He did not want to know what it was.

Captain Atrigul made the decision to rest for a bit, to allow Nicky to recover, for she was still gasping for air and coughing up mud. They had already been traveling through the forest for 5 hours, so no one complained. They took the time to rehydrate and eat for a bit to recover their strength. Remington was concerned about their water supply. None of the water on the island seemed safe to drink and with the high heat, they would go through what they had very quickly. He mentioned this to Captain Atrigul who let out a small chuckle.

"I thought you already knew about everyone on board," she replied with a bit of teasing in her voice. Remington's confused look told her otherwise. She called Rinva over and placed an empty jug next to him. "There is a reason Rinva is a trusted member of both my crew and of this landing party. You see, Rinva is a devout follower of Valtameri, and that grants her special favors from him. One of which, gives us water." At this cue, Rinva quietly whispered some words that Remington was unable to catch. He saw a small necklace that she wore around her neck glow for a brief second. Before Remington realized what was happening, the jug on the ground began to fill with fresh clean water.

Remington had never seen the power of the gods in action. He knew of their existence and their roles in the world, but never believed they ever did anything to help. There were 13 gods that people worshiped, Valtameri being the god of the oceans. Growing up in a port city, Remington saw many sailors worship Valtameri, though he did not know of any that were granted special favor. The only other god that Remington actively noticed people looking to in his small circle was Lannwit, the goddess of the night. They say she watches over the thieves and those who live in the shadows. Remington let out a small chuckle, thinking about how neither god has done anything for him, besides bring him pain.

He was not going to say no to this gift now though and accepted some of this newly created water gratefully. Remington did not talk to Rinva much before. He always thought her even soothing voice hid a much more dangerous person underneath. Knowing now that she followed Valtameri, he decided his analysis was probably correct.

After about 15 minutes, Nicky seemed to have recovered so they continued into the forest. They were heading towards a large hill that stood at the center of the island. Captain Atrigul wanted to have a high vantage point to see what the lay of the island looked like and to determine where to start their search. It was going to take at least a couple of days to get to the top and it was not going to be easy.

On the third day of travel, the party had almost reached the peak of the hill. All throughout, they had carefully moved along narrow edges that overlooked deep ravines that stood as a natural barrier protecting this hill. They had been traveling single file for the majority of this leg of the journey, the ledge just wide enough for Brend to feel comfortable.

Remington was once again in the back of the group, directly in front of Brend who was watching the rear. They had already been walking for over 9 hours on this day and everyone was growing tired. There was no room to safely rest on this ledge so they kept pushing forward, hoping to find a good resting point soon. Remington was focusing only on placing one foot in front of the other and keeping his eyes open. The continuous heat was only growing stronger the higher they went.

Up ahead, Aldwin motioned for the group to stop. Remington heard Aldwin whisper that he heard voices somewhere above them. Remington barely had time to look up before he saw the first rock come tumbling down, the head of a small creature made of flames poking out from the ledge above. Remington started to run, hoping to escape the growing avalanche that was now approaching. He could hear Brend at his heals. He did not dare look back up in fear of losing his footing.

He saw the first small pebble roll past his foot as panic set into his eyes. He saw the others in front of him had just reach a small overhang, giving them shelter from the rocks. Remington was not far from it, only 5 more feet when a large rock smashed into his head knocking him off the ledge. He could see a hand reaching out to grab his, though it was just out of reach. As he began to fall, he thought he heard Captain Atrigul scream his name before the rumble of the surrounding rocks drowned out all other noise. Out of the corner of his eye he thought he saw Brend also tumbling with him and attempted to reach out. Before he could call out to Brend, he felt his body crash against the mountain side, his head hitting hard against the ground, and his vision faded into blackness.

12

Remington felt something wet touching the tip of his nose. His head was spinning as he attempted to open his eyes. The little bit of light that got in caused a searing pain to shoot through his head and he immediately closed them again. He felt his nose get tapped again, almost as if something was licking it. This time, he opened his eyes slower allowing them time to adjust. Looking down his nose, he saw a small lizard like creature staring back at him, occasionally sticking its tongue out and hitting his nose.

Remington smiled at the small creature and attempted to move it off his face. However, as he went to lift his right arm, he felt pain spread throughout his body like wildfire and found his arm was pinned under a rock. He immediately remembered the events that led to his current predicament. He could see now looking up, the hill side in which he tumbled down. It was a miracle he was even alive, he thought to himself.

Remington had no idea how long he had been out for, with no sunrise or sunset in the Feylands, time was almost non-existent. The dryness in his throat told him it must have been at least a day, if not longer. Taking a moment to try to calm his panic he took an inventory of the rest of his body. His head hurt like never before and he could feel a wetness in his hair, most likely from his own blood. He tried to shift his body and found that his legs and left arm were not pinned. However, he was fairly certain his ankle was broken and suspected he might have cracked a rib or two.

Grunting through the pain, Remington attempted to position himself to move the large rock that current sat on his arm. He shoved his weight against the rock, but there was too much pain. He let out a small yelp as tears began streaming down his face. Remington sat for another 5 minutes, trying to ready himself for another attempt. He knew he could not stay here. The death that would cause would be much more painful than another attempt to get free. Taking a deep breath, he dug his uninjured foot into the ground and pushed with all his might. He felt the rock begin to shift and using the trapped arm, levered the rock to roll off. He let out a rough sigh of relief, he was free.

Taking a bit of time to examine his arm, he was fairly certain it too was broken, though he was unsure of the extent of the damage. Remington fought to hold back the panic setting in. He had no idea how he was going to get back to the ship, nor any idea where he was. As he laid on his back, deciding whether he should even try, memory shot through his brain. He was not the only one caught in the rockslide. Maybe Brend was okay. As much as Remington hated Brend, he knew he had a much greater chance of making it out with two people instead of one. With a renewed vigor, Remington got up, trying his best to not put weight on his ankle. His entire body screamed with pain, but he blocked it out.

Remington looked for 30 minutes, calling out Brend's name, hoping to hear a response. He was leaning against one of the larger rocks, catching his breath from the effort when at last he heard something. A quiet groan from not but 15 feet away. Quickly Remington hobbled over to the sound where he found Brend's large hand twitching underneath some rocks. Remington worked to uncover Brend, hoping to find him in better condition than himself. It took about 10 minutes to completely release Brend, even with Brend helping.

Brend indeed had fared better than Remington. Many bruises covered his body, shown from under tattered clothing, and his left arm was bent in the opposite direction than it should, but he otherwise seemed alright. Brend stood up, clasping onto Remington's shoulder, which caused Remington to let out an involuntary gasp of pain.

Brend chuckled, "Looks like the gods on our side. Milas decided to show her mercy. Though how you lived with that twig of a body is a miracle."

Remington knew an insult had to be in there somewhere but was glad to see Brend was in high spirits. Remington responded, "I think the rocks hit your head a little harder than mine with that compliment." Remington smiled at the frown that now resided on Brend's face. He continued, "We should try to get back to the ship and find help, though it will be slow going." He gestured to his ankle, "Do you know if any of the others fell down too?"

Brend shook his head. They were the only two. At least the others made it safely to cover. Remington saw Brend staring at his ankle, a look of internal debate on his face. Remington wondered if Brend was deciding whether or not to leave him here alone, before Brend pulled out a small vial of red liquid that somehow did not get crushed in the fall.

Remington began attempting to crawl away, thinking Brend was going to end him mercifully with a quick poison. Remington was not able to get far in his condition before Brend placed his large foot on Remington's chest, pinning him in place. Remington stared Brend in the eye, daring him to do it, and face his victim head on. He could tell Brend recognized the look in his face but was shocked when Brend only let out an exasperated sigh and rolled his eyes before shifting to kneel on his chest, the weight excruciating against his cracked ribs.

"Focus on your damn ankle you idiot," commanded Brend as he forced Remington's mouth open. In this moment of confusion, Remington obeyed and thought of his ankle. There was not much else he could do. Brend pulled the cork out of the vial and began to dump the red liquid down Remington's throat.

The liquid was warm as it entered his stomach, similar in feeling to a strong liquor. He coughed a bit as some of it went down his windpipe, his body rejecting this forceful introduction of a foreign substance. He felt the warmth travel through his stomach and down toward his leg, stopping at his injured ankle. He felt a slight tingle in the area before an even worse pain shot through his body as he felt the bones in his ankle shift to their correct location and mend together. Then there was no pain in his ankle, it felt as healthy as before.

Remington stared at Brend in shock. "It's healed! I don't feel a thing, what was that?"

Brend snorted, "It was a healing potion. Can fix up any injury if you focus on it. If you had any brains in that thick skull of yours you would have gotten one at port, but instead I had to use mine. You owe me 50 gold pieces for that."

Remington was even more confused now. "Now don't take this the wrong way, thank you for helping me, but why? You could have just left me here; we both know you do not like me very much."

Brend grumbled, his knee still pressing down on Remington's chest. "Capt'n would have killed me if I let you die without putting at least a little effort in," he responded curtly. Remington wanted him to explain, but decided not to press the issue.

Remington attempted to stand, only to have Brend push him to the ground one last time for good measure. He knew Brend would hold this over him for the rest of his life, but it did not matter, he was alive. Taking inventory of what they had, they found they had a decent number of rations, though their water supply would likely run out quickly. They would have to find some fresh water somewhere on this island.

Not sure of their location, Brend made Remington climb a tree. Remington was a lot lighter than Brend and could make it to the higher branches to hopefully spot the Sickening Rose. It was slow going trying to pick his way through the branches with only one arm, but eventually he was able to poke his head above the canopy. He gazed about, seeing they were surrounded by forest. As he took in the full 360 view, he thought he could make out the upper flag of the Sickening Rose, just to the left of the large hill they were scaling before. It was at least a week away if not more at the pace they were going. With a bit of hope, Remington climbed down, paying extra attention to keep the direction they need to go in his mind. They had to make it back to the boat before the captain.

For two days they traveled slowly through the forest. Every once in a while, Remington would climb a tree and confirm they were still heading in the right direction. On one occasion Remington found they had been heading in the wrong direction for four hours. Brend made sure he felt the consequences of that by pressing in on his remaining broken bones causing the pain to return with ferocity.

On the third day, Remington and Brend had reached the wet part of the forest filled with large mud puddles. They slowed their already slow pace. Once again Remington could not shake the feeling that something was watching them, following them. He tried not to think about it.

The days had been quiet with neither man saying anything to the other besides directions. There was an unspoken acceptance of needing the other to make it out, both injured badly. The electrified tension between them was strong, animosity towards both sides as powerful as ever, but they endured.

Brend was leading the way, his large sword cutting through the brush easier than Remington's sword. Remington had the Fortune Teller drawn as a guard ready to strike at what ever may be following them. Up ahead he saw a large clearing that appeared to be solid ground. He hoped for a bit of salvation from the careful movements around the mud pits.

As Brend reached the clearing, Remington felt time around him slow. He watched as an echo of himself walked forward toward the clearing, following closely behind Brend who also seemed ghostly in nature. He felt his sword burning hot in his hand, but he held on tightly. Remington watched as his echo and the ghostly figure of Brend stepped into the clearing sinking into a concealed mud pit that spanned the whole clearing. He watched as his echo immediately dipped beneath the surface while Brend hung on to the ledge, barely staying afloat.

Just as soon as the echoes appeared, they vanished as if no time had passed. Remington quickly attempted to process what had happened when he heard Brend's sword cut through the plants again. Remington snapped out of his thoughts and shouted, "Brend, no!" but it was too late. Just as his words left his mouth, Brend stepped forward into the clearing, his body immediately sinking into the hidden mud, covering him up to his shoulders.

Remington rushed forward to stand at the entrance to the clearing, still struggling to understand what had just happened. Brend's sword had already sunk through the mud, while Brend had his forearms clasped to the dry ground attempting to pull himself up, but with one arm broken was struggling. Brend had a look of determination on his face, and shouted at Remington, "Don't just stand there ye idiot help me out!"

Remington hesitated. Remington owed it to Brend to help him, to save his life like he did to Remington. But, in the back of his mind, a dark thought had always been growing in Remington. His thoughts turned towards Brend's cruelty towards those on the ship, towards the potential for Captain Atrigul's death, like grip on his soul, and towards his plan for revenge. Remington wondered if this was a sign, Vengo the god of revenge telling him now was the time to make his move. Could he go through with this, he wondered, just watch as Brend died a terrible death after having helped him thus far?

His thoughts were broken by Brend shouting again, this time with more desperation, "Remington, *please*, it's pulling me down. Help me!"

Please. Such a simple word and yet Remington had not once heard it pass Brend's lips. Until now. Remington took the smallest of steps forward, pity filling his mind to help this man doomed to a terrible death. Then the terrible thoughts flooded his mind. There was no room for pity in a quest for revenge, no room for helping those who stood in his path to freedom. If he let Brend live, he would die before he found freedom.

Hiding his indecision behind a face of indifference, Remington quietly whispered, "I'm sorry," as he watched Brend get dragged below. Brend's one good hand made a final desperate reach for anything that could save him but found nothing. The mud went still and no sign of Brend ever being there was to be seen.

13

As Remington turned to walk away, his pace was slow, each placement of his footsteps methodically chosen. His mind was in shock. He still had not fully processed what had just happened, how he just stood there watching. He could have helped; it would not have been too difficult to find solid footing and pulled Brend out. Instead he stood unmoving and unfeeling. No, not unfeeling. Remington remembered the hatred running through his vanes, the icy chill of anger and vengeance filling his soul. It was a terrible feeling; one Remington did not want to feel again.

Brend's face flashed in Remington's mind, his final moments plastered with the realization of betrayal and death. Remington broke out into a run, not caring if he was heading in the right direction or not. He just wanted to escape this reality, but the image only followed him, reminding him that he murdered Brend.

Remington, exhausted, slumped against a tree and began to cry. He had killed only one other time, and that was in self-defense. It was either him or her, and he needed to live. This was not self-defense; it was a choice. It was a moment when Remington allowed darkness to influence who he was and push him over the edge of destruction. There was no need for this death, or was there?

Remington through his hysteric tears, began trying to reason to himself that it was needed. He was still a captive of Captain Atrigul. Even if he stayed on this island, faking his death, her existence was carved into his being, literally. Her poisoned words and acts of torture and ownership of his body remain as a scar on his soul. He knew he would always be haunted by his actions today, but he could not let them be in vain. His plan must continue forward, he must find his freedom and healing through betrayal and vengeance.

He remembered what T'kocht told him, that vengeance can lead down a path that he will lose himself on. Had he started down that path? The tears on his face, now running dry, convinced him otherwise. If he could hold on to his humanity, to his present guilt over his actions, then maybe he could find his way back, to heal from the hurts dealt. He did not want to be cold and heartless, but the old woman's warning still rang in his mind, sending a shiver down his back. He will not let that happen; he will not be broken.

Taking a deep breath, Remington stood up. He realized in his blind running he had no idea where he was. It was sheer luck that he did not crash into a mud pit himself. Luck seemed to be following him around quite a lot recently. He began to make his way up a tree to see where he was and found that he had run in the exact opposite direction he needed to go. Remington needed to hurry. He needed to catch that boat.

Remington began to make his way through the jungle, always keeping an eye out for fresh water, which was scarce. The heat of the island unwavering and every minute he could not shake the feeling that something was watching him, following him. His arm and ribs were feeling worse each day, and his wrist was red and hot. Infection may have set in, but he needed to press on. Each day, moving a bit slower, exhaustion setting in earlier and earlier.

On the fourth day of his travels to the ship without Brend, Remington finally caught sight of the owners of the watchful eyes.

As he was settling down for a rest out of the corner of his eye, he saw a flicker of flame behind a tree. Concerned that the forest might have caught fire, Remington quickly shifted to get a better look. He only saw it for a second, but it was no forest fire. It appeared to be a bipedal salamander like creature wreathed in flames. It fled as soon as it noticed Remington, but he feared it did not go too far.

Remington wondered why they had not approached or attacked. Were they waiting for him to weaken more, were they just curious? He tried speaking to them on occasion as he walked, the mindless chatter a needed break from the deafening silence that he felt without Brend. He immediately locked out that thought, not wanting to remember.

Remington's days of peace did not last long after that. He estimated he still had 3 days before reaching the shoreline, where hopefully he would be able to catch up with the rest of the landing party. He had been very careful with his path, making sure to stay as far away from the mud pits as possible. Remington was not sure what he did or said to cause a change, but as he was nearing the end of his travel for that day, the salamander like creatures revealed themselves.

There were about 4 of these creatures in total, each seeming to be made from flames as their light flickered. They were all armed with crude weapons and were shouting something at Remington. He did not understand their language, but he could tell they were angry. Remington raised his hands in the air, hoping to show he was not a threat. He spoke as calmly as he could, "Hello, my name is Remington. I mean you no harm, I am just trying to leave your island."

The creatures looked intelligent, though it was abundantly clear they had no understanding of the common tongue. The largest one in the center, who appeared to be their leader, let out a signal that sounded like a high-pitched whoop. The other three readied their weapons, as the leader spit a fireball heading directly towards Remington's head.

Remington quickly ducked out of the way, but not nearly quickly enough. The edge of the blaze grazed his left side, causing an intense burning sensation, and his shirt to catch on fire. Remington frantically ripped the shirt off preventing the flames from spreading. He saw the other three closing in on him, fast.

Deciding that he could not outrun them, Remington drew his sword and prepared to stand his ground. The salamander on his right reached him first and swung its own sword at him. Trying to remember all the techniques that Nicky had taught him, he dodged out of the way, parrying back and catching part of its side. As the creature fell back, Remington felt a slice across the back of his thigh as the second creature attacked as he was busy with the first.

He could feel the blood beginning to flow down his leg, as he spun around, narrowly missing the creature. The third one now sprang from the ground and grabbed onto Remington's shoulders and hung on. The heat of the flaming body burning into his skin. He cried out in pain. Now losing all technique Remington started swinging wildly, attempting to both hit anything and knock the creature off his shoulders to no use.

Remington took a second to regain his focus. Using this little bit of time to think, he took another attack to his leg, but he had a strategy. He made a false swipe at the one attacking his leg and continued his sword in a wide arc around his body, heading towards his back where it made direct contact with the creature there. He heard the pained yelp as the Fortune Teller dug into its flesh, the grip on his shoulder going limp.

The creature fell to the ground dead. The other two immediately backed away, looking distraught at the loss of their comrade. Remington took this moment of hesitation and ran into the forest, hoping that the death of one of their people would be enough to get these creatures to leave him alone.

He continued running for 2 hours, seeing no sign of being followed before his injured leg gave out from underneath him. Forced to stop, Remington stretched out his leg to examine the damage. Luckily, the wound did not look too bad, but the bleeding would need to be stopped. Using his dagger, he cut away part of his pants and wrapped his leg in the fabric, applying as much pressure as he could with only one arm.

Though Remington knew he only had two more days until he reached the shore, he worried he might not make it. This island was dangerous, and his new wounds would only slow him down. Even worse, his wrist was deteriorating, the bright red now turning towards a shade of black. Even with the extreme heat, he felt chills along his body; a fever must have set in.

Remington forced himself to get up. He had to keep moving if he wanted any hope of getting off this island. Climbing another tree showed he was heading in the correct direction, and that the Sickening Rose had not left yet. The exertion left him dizzy, but he continued to stumble forward, unable to focus on anything besides move.

Remington lost track of how long he had been traveling, the endless twilight of the Feylands showing no signs of the passage of time. The fever caused him to start to be delirious and hallucinations followed in his footsteps. He saw Brend walking besides him, the constant echo of his final words, "please" passing his lips, torturing Remington. Images of his younger self starving on the streets, begging for food as older Remington walked by. The whispers of Captain Atrigul ordering him to meet her, to do her bidding, to need her. He clasped his hands to his ears, attempting to block out the noise, the painful reminder of his past. It only caused more pain.

Remington could now smell the salt of the sea, a refreshing

change from the decaying flesh that had been following him. He could barely continue walking, the bleeding in his leg never truly stopping and the fever blazing as hot as ever. Remington was determined to keep going, to make it to the shore in hopes that someone would see him.

His legs gave out from underneath him. He could see the sandy beach teasing him just out of reach, so close but he felt as though it was miles away. Throwing his good arm in front of him, Remington began to pull and crawl his way to the sand. He felt one final surge of energy pulse through him, his body's last attempt at self-preservation. It took Remington almost an hour to move the last 300 feet needed to get to the shore, but at last he felt the cool sand move through his fingertips. The wet sand was refreshing. He could feel a cold breeze coming off the water. His goal completed, Remington let his exhaustion crash over him like a wave on the beach. This was a good place to die, he thought. His eyes closed as the comforts of the sea eased him into unconsciousness and peace. Finally, he could rest.

14

Remington felt a warmth begin to spread through his body. It was comforting and he felt all his muscles relax in complete content. He let out a sigh before the warmth began to fade and was replaced by pain and the sigh turned into a groan. He felt cold water being poured down his throat and coughed at the unexpected liquid.

He could hear voices around him now, familiar ones of his fellow landing party. The first clear voice he heard was Captain Atrigul, her intense tone sending a shiver down his spine. "You are going to be fine, did Brend make it?"

The memories that he remembered of the past week flooded back to Remington. So he was alive, he did not die on the beach. Remington was too tired to let the emotions wash over him again. He slowly shook his head. Brend did not make it, and he was to blame.

He heard Captain Atrigul let out a disappointed sigh, and he felt her hand on his shoulder. The tips of her fingers, usually soft, now felt rough against his bare skin. Her fingers lightly brushed over his arm before taking hold of his hand. Giving it a quick squeeze, she let it go.

He felt the sand move near him as she stood up. With a

commanding steady voice she ordered, "Get him to the boat and let's leave this cursed island. It has brought us nothing but loss."

Remington groaned as he felt someone pick him up off the sand and began carrying him. He was tired and began to feel himself drifting off, his head lulling onto the lower back of whomever was carrying him. The darkness was once again returning, Remington welcomed it to ease the pain.

He felt a tight grip on his face, shaking off the darkness, and forcing his eyes to open directly into the face of Captain Atrigul, her eyes blazing with intense focus on his. Bringing her face right up to his ear, she whispered, "No, you stay awake. I have brought you back from death once, and I am not doing it again. Always remember you would be decaying right now without me." She dropped his head which swung down to be hanging. He did not have the strength to lift it himself.

He was trying to ponder the words she spoke, but he was not able to maintain focus on anything. He felt his body get flung onto the small boat they landed with, the wooden floor sending small splinters into his unprotected back. He felt the boat begin to rock with the waves as they pushed off towards the Sickening Rose.

Remington felt something cold get pressed into his hand and reflexively curled his fingers around it. He immediately recognized the grip as that of the Fortune Teller. He heard Nicky's voice off to his left, "You forgot rule number 8, never let your sword leave your hands!" Her always friendly teasing voice brought a faint smile to his face. He could picture the massive grin she had on her face, though his eyes refused to open to confirm it. He was glad she made it back.

About an hour later, Remington felt the boat get hauled into the air, so that its passengers may disembark. As the dingy, jerked to a halt, Remington could hear the chatter from the rest of the crew of the Sickening Rose as they took in the sight before them. On occasion he could hear Brend's name and each time he winced.

He heard Captain Atrigul call out, "Give us some room please. I know you want answers, and I will give them to you in a minute. Until then, bring the treasures we got below deck and I will make an announcement in 20 minutes. The rest of you, raise the anchor and make sail, our journey is not over yet."

The voices quickly quieted down and were replaced with scurrying footsteps as people rushed to their stations. He heard Captain Atrigul say, "Taking him to my room, I know you are tapped. Thanks for everything."

"Yes, Captain. It is only with the blessing of Valtameri that I can help in our noble cause," responded Rinva. He felt her left him up, not a hint of strain in her muscles. He let his body go limp as he folded into a cradled like position. As she walked with him across the deck, he heard someone shout his name in a concerned voice. "Remi!" It was T'kocht, Remington opened his eyes, looking for his friend, but could not see anything from his buried angle. He heard Captain Atrigul order T'kocht back to his station, saying he can visit when his shift is over.

Rinva laid him down onto a soft bed before immediately leaving the room. Her breathing was more difficult, and he could hear her footsteps slowing. She must have been putting on a show of strength out there, he thought. Just like Remington, she did not like to show weakness.

Remington tried to sit up, but the pain was strong, and his muscles felt very weak. He gave up his attempts and tried to sleep. His time to himself did not last long as the door opened once again. He just wanted rest, why would no one give this to him. He shut his eyes even harder, which only made his head hurt more. He heard whoever entered rustling in the cabinets, the sound of glasses clinking against each other echoing through the room. A satisfied, "There it is" came from that direction from Captain Atrigul.

He watched her hurry over to him carrying a vial of red liquid, similar to the one Brend had. She sat on the bed next to him and ordered him to drink. Not able to grab the bottle himself, she helped pour it into his mouth, gently stroking his hair as he swallowed. Once again, the warmth entered his stomach, this time spreading to all parts of his body. He cried out as the pain of the accelerated healing hit, but it left as quickly as it came. He felt much better though the exhaustion was still there.

"Now that the immediate threat of death is out of the way, tell me what happened out there. What happened to Brend?" Her voice, while urgent, had a slight tinge of relief in it.

Remington paused, thinking about what he wanted to say, for this was not the time for truth. He began, "Well, after the rockslide, I woke up buried under some boulders." He paused again. "I looked around to see if any of the others fell with me. I found Brend's body a short time later, he wasn't as lucky." He looked up to Captain Atrigul's face, looking for any sign that she did not believe him waiting for her hand to grip his throat, demanding the truth. It never came. She looked saddened.

"He was a good first mate, a little dull, but he listened well. We will hold service for him tonight. How did you make it out of the forest by yourself? The locals were much more aggressive than we anticipated."

Remington looked at her in surprise. Noticing now for the first time, Captain Atrigul was not in decent shape, she looked tired. Her usually clean smooth skin, was now coated in mud and blood. She had done her best to clean it off, but the wounds were still there, and she had missed many spots in her haste.

Remington continued his story, this time keeping it as faithful as he can, leaving out any mention of Brend and leaving out the mysterious vision he had. He was not yet ready to tell someone about that. He ended his tale not remembering much of the last days and his acceptance on the sand. Captain Atrigul listened carefully, not giving out a single sign of what she was thinking.

When he concluded, he asked, "What about you, what happened to you all after the rockslide?"

"That's none of your concern for now," she responded. "You were lucky we returned when we did. We found you barely breathing on that beach mere hours from death. I made Rinva use the last of her powers today to pull you back a little bit. You are alive because of me, and I hope you never forget that. I guess you are not as weak as I thought you were."

She leaned down and kissed him, pressing her fingers purposefully into his wounds that had not been healed by the potion. The pain was unbearable, and he passed out, her lips still locked onto his.

Remington woke up sometime later in his own hammock. He could feel the tight bandages around his wounds, protecting them from the outside world. His hammock rocked as someone pressed down on the side, using it to help them stand up. Remington looked over to see T'kocht quickly scrambling to stand. "Hey," Remington said weakly, still waking up and still exhausted.

T'kocht let out a faint chuckle, that was filled with both concern and relief. "You are okay," T'kocht finally said. "The captain told us briefly what happened on the island. It's a miracle you made it out of there, but I am glad you did. You are going to have to tell me everything when you are ready, but first, I need to let the captain know you are awake. Sorry, I can wait a few minutes to give you time to yourself if you want?"

Remington did not answer for a bit. He did not feel like talking, the guilt from his actions on that island still sinking in, and the fear of the truth getting out growing. He could tell that T'kocht noticed this change but was thankful that he did not press the issue.

Eventually he answered, "A few minutes would be most welcome. How long have I been out this time?"

T'kocht handed him a glass of water, "About 14 hours. They brought you down here not long after Rinva carried your body on board. I honestly thought you were dead with how limp you were in her arms. You haven't missed much though. There was a ceremony for Brend last night, and Captain Atrigul gave the overview of what happened and what they found. Sadly, no fountain and the whole trip was only 20 days, but sounds like the treasure is going to make us some decent pay."

T'kocht patted Remington softly on the shoulder in support before turning to leave. Remington did not want to wait around, lying in his hammock. He began the effort to climb out and see what was happening on the ship. He was still in his torn clothing, and looking to find something fresh to put on, he saw that T'kocht had already laid a new set out under the hammock. Apparently T'kocht knew Remington was not just going to wait around. His muscles were stiff, but eventually he made himself look presentable and began to head up the stairs.

Remington's path to the deck was intercepted by the return of T'kocht, and trailing behind him Captain Atrigul. "Thank you, my Eagle, you can go now," Captain Atrigul said calmly yet firmly. T'kocht hesitated for a bit but seeing the look in her eyes gave a nod and headed back to the deck of the ship.

She approached Remington, her long stride closing the distance between them very quickly. Her outstretched arm pushing Remington forcefully against the nearby wall, pinning him in place. The scent of roses on her was stronger than usual causing Remington to hold his breath. She smiled at him brushing the hair that had fallen into his face behind his ear. Her thumb stroked the base of his neck, running over his Adam's apple, the hand threatening to choke him.

Her hand still lingering there, she stepped even closer, her hot breath blazing against his cheek. Remington did his best to remain motionless, to fight the need to push her as far away from him as possible, to fight the hint of comfort creeping into the back of his mind.

In a soft whisper she said, "Twice now I have saved your life, a life still in its youth, too short to be taken. Know that it was never out of the kindness in my heart, it was out of utility." Her grip began to tighten around his throat. "You had something that I desired, and even now you continue to provide a pleasure that most cannot. You owe me two lifetimes of gratitude, of obedience. You have and always will belong to me, to follow my commands and do my biddings. You would never do anything to hurt me right?"

Her eyes bore into his, searching for an answer, daring him to lie to her. Remington stared back, feeling the grip of her fingers on his throat. She had saved him twice, but she killed his innocence by doing so. He was not who he used to be just 4 months ago, or even just a week ago. He questioned if he could do the same thing to her that he did to Brend. He thought about his answer, and to his surprise, he answered truthfully, "I could not hurt you."

Her grip on his throat loosened, allowing air and the smell of roses to fill his lungs. She leaned in, kissing him on the forehead, "Good. That is all I needed to hear. Follow me to the deck, I have an announcement to make."

Remington took her offered hand and followed her silently. Did he really mean that? He imagined Captain Atrigul in the mud pit instead of Brend, her calling out his name, begging to be saved. Over and over he ran this scene through his head, telling himself to let her fall, to free himself of the pain she has caused. Each time without fail, he rescued her, pulling her free of the mud, letting the key that bound him to her to sink forever to the bottom.

Eventually they reached the deck of the ship. Remington felt a few pats on his shoulder and back in support of his recovery on his way there, but any words said to him did not register. She left Remington on the deck with the rest of the crew, making her way to the helm. Captain Atrigul's voice sang across the deck of the ship causing everyone to pause and listen. She waited until the crew gathered underneath, looking down upon them with grace and power.

"My crew, my family. On this journey we have lost one of our own. Every person here knew that the life of a pirate was a dangerous one and was willing to put forth the risk to reap rewards beyond their wildest dreams. Brend was a good friend, and an even better first mate. His absence will be most dearly noticed. However, we still have 3 more months before we return to the Prime Realm. Order must be maintained if we are all to make it out of here. I have discussed with some of the more senior crew members and have come to a decision. I am pleased to announce that the position of first mate will be given to Remington Darkwalker."

Immediately, the crowd started chattering. Many were congratulating Remington, giving him pats on his back and compliments. Others were discussing amongst themselves whether someone so new and young should be given such high ranks. Remington just stood in shock, unable to move or speak, wondering if this was some cruel prank.

Captain Atrigul continued, "If anyone has objections to this choice, you can bring it up to me or leave at the next landfall. I do not want whispers of dissent around my ship, and if I hear rumors of people questioning my decisions as captain, just know you have been warned once. I expect all of you to listen to Remington, for his commands come from me. Now get back to your stations, we have islands to explore."

15

Remington did not have much time to process what had happened before Captain Atrigul began listing his new tasks aboard. He did his best to try to remember all of them, but the instructions were coming in too quickly. His mind was also busy trying to understand this decision. Why would she choose him? Who were the senior crew members she was referring to? There were plenty of sailors on board with more experience than he had, who were more qualified than he was. The guilt of knowing he murdered Brend and yet took his place in leadership weighed heavily.

Since he was still recovering from his injuries, Remington's first task was to inventory the loot that was taken from the island. He was to meet Nicky who would help sort the items for future use. It was a welcome break, and Remington soon learned that Nicky was one of the senior crew members that the captain mentioned.

Nicky explained that there were 3 crew members and Captain Atrigul in the meeting to select Brend's replacement. Nicky was the first to be suggested to take over, but she rejected it, not wanting that responsibility. She explained she prefers having fun and going where the wind blows versus having to make decisions and give orders. There were a few other names thrown around before Nicky herself recommended Remington.

"The other two laughed, but I was serious," she said a little bit of frustration leaking out. "The captain put her hand up, which of course immediately quieted the other two. It's amazing she can do that. Anyways, she then asked me 'why do you recommend Remington?' her voice all steady as always."

Remington could not help but chuckle a bit at Nicky's poor attempt at Captain Atrigul's voice. It was very cartoonish, but still respectful.

"Well I thought you seemed to have a head on you, and though you were still new, you know everyone on the ship really well and people seem to like you. Plus, I think that with a bit more experience, you could do well. That's what I told her anyways. She seemed a bit hesitant, maybe she still missed Brend, I don't know, but after a bit more thinking, she came around to the idea. The other two protested, questioning your loyalty, but captain said not to worry about that. Then here we are, and you are first mate!"

Nicky always talked so quickly and with such a bubbly voice that Remington felt a bit happier after any conversation with her. He was grateful for the high praise that she gave, but not everything in her tale was good news. If his loyalty was questionable, he would have to work hard to prove otherwise. He thought back to the question Captain Atrigul posed to him this morning. Would he really have to fake his loyalty? One thing was certain, the truth of Brend's death must never be known.

"Thank you, Nicky," Remington stated, giving her a hug, "I won't let you down." He meant what he said. He would prove he was worthy of this position. He had to.

The two of them chatted throughout the rest of the day as they took inventory. It turns out the rest of the landing party had found quiet a lot of goods on the island including many pieces of gold, exotic fruits and herbs, some strange gems and pearls that Nicky says change color with one's mood, and in a bag, a body of one of the salamander creatures no longer lit aflame. It was perfectly preserved, with no sign of decay. Nicky explained that bodies and parts of fey creatures fetch a high price to rich noble men in search of exotic items, and that Rinva had preserved the body until it could be placed in storage.

Before Remington could ask what storage meant, Nicky pulled out a medium sized satchel that seemed empty. "This is one of the well-kept secrets aboard the ship. Only a few of us know about it. This is the captain's endless bag. You can put whatever you want in it and it will never go bad, and the bag will never be full. Always looks like it is empty you see. Then whenever you want something, you just name it and pull it out! It is one of the coolest things on this ship, but the captain keeps it hidden, except during inventory. Here, help me get it in!"

With a lot of pushing and prodding, Remington and Nicky were finally able to get the body into the bag, and just as Nicky said, the bag looked completely empty. She handed the bag to Remington, and with a friendly farewell he left to bring the bag back to the captain.

For the next two months, the Sickening Rose continued to explore the seas of the Feylands. They visited one other island, which was empty of life except for strange crabs that Remington learned the hard way blocked any form of speech when they clamped down on him. The captain collected about twenty of them to sell back on the Prime Realm. Though Captain Atrigul wanted to stay longer, the crew were beginning to run low on supplies. They had not had the fortune to encounter another ship which they could *borrow* from, nor had they found any friendly civilization on either island they visited.

The day before the jump back to the Prime Realm, Remington was dressing after spending the night with the captain, always at her request. Remington had hoped this abuse would have ended when he became first mate, but it had not. In fact, in the few weeks after his promotion, the captain became less inclined to hide his involvement. She began having him stay well into the morning, exiting to a full deck instead of sneaking back to his hammock before the main shift.

Many of the lower members of the crew now stared at him in anger and contempt. The first day they saw him exit the room in the morning, they all assumed it was he who was manipulating the captain, using his youth and beauty to further his station. They began to resent him, whispering to each other rumors of enchantment spells and of his sleeping his way to the top. Hearing these words only added to Captain Atrigul's breakdown of his soul and pride.

He dared not correct them, for the truth that he was a captive, a slave was far more humiliating, and Captain Atrigul would deny it. He knew the crew would side with her and he shuttered to think what his punishment might be, and this time the punishment would not be in private as it always has been. The careful drownings, the nonlethal poisons added to his drinks, the cruel words constant in his ear, the forced use of his body. Always torture and punishment for existing, but never visible the next day, all in the name of breaking him, of hurting him for her own enjoyment.

Remington found some peace in his friends. During times of quiet, he sought refuge with T'kocht who understood what Remington was going through. He knew he could trust T'kocht to not say anything to anyone, so he talked to him. T'kocht always listened, never judged, and constantly offered help where Remington saw fit. Remington still had not told T'kocht about the truth behind Brend, but these small talks helped him to not hold in his pain like a bomb waiting to burst. He never said everything, but even little things here and there helped. T'kocht could tell that Remington was holding back, but never pressed him further.

Remington's other friends on the ship helped to shut down the rumors spread by the rest of the crew. While they did not know the truth, more senior members like Nicky and Glazzglek would explain that the captain knew what she was doing and not question decisions. They always lingered a light threat of informing the captain of the insubordination against her first mate. This threat usually worked.

There was one time about a month in, where one of the newer crewmembers from Halitona did not accept this threat. Captain Atrigul caught wind of his discomfort and confronted him about it on the deck. She gave him a chance to voice his disagreements, and he took the opportunity. He spewed his concerns of a deranged captain who got her first mate killed and only promoted his replacement because he was sleeping with her. Captain Atrigul listened unmoving before defending herself.

"Brend's death was a tragedy, but danger is something we all signed up for when we stepped onto this boat. He died as he would have wished, a free man making his own choices. In regard to his replacement, the decision to promote Remington was a group decision amongst those loyal to this ship, who have lived on her decks long enough to care for its safety. They all agreed that Remington had the wits to maintain that safety. What I do in my personal time with anyone on this ship is up to me and is none of your business. If you think you can captain better than myself, please challenge me."

With that last dare she drew her own sword, a fine rapier that shone with its own light, the tip sharpened to smaller than a needle. Still angry and feeling ambitious, the crewmember took up her offer and charged her with his sword. Remington watched the fight go down; the man did not last longer than 20 seconds before her blade had found his jugular leaving him to bleed out on the deck. Captain Atrigul had not even broken a sweat, easily moving and dodging his attacks with grace as the man swung wildly. Captain Atrigul had Remington tie the corpse to the main mast as a reminder to anyone else who challenged her authority. The blood was quickly cleaned from the deck.

Remington's mind was quickly snapped back to the present by his name being called by Captain Atrigul. He turned around to face her, his shirt only halfway buttoned.

"As you know, we are making the jump back to the Prime Realm tomorrow," she began. "As my first mate, it is your job to run this ship when I am unable to. This includes learning how to complete the jump. I had taught Brend, though I am not sure if he ever fully got the ritual down. You will trail me today and learn all you need. Come, we have a busy day ahead of us."

For the rest of the day, Remington followed Captain Atrigul around the ship as she prepared it for the jump. He learned the proper placing of the crystals which contained the magic needed to jump. He watched carefully as she showed him the arcane symbols that would be needed to activate the magic. She explained that to make the jump, one needed to be in the correct location to allow the crystals to absorb the energy around them.

The jump back was much smoother. Though no storm appeared, the ship rocked by dangerous amounts, constantly threatening to tip over and capsize. Before it could, the captain completed her ritual and Remington felt everything around him compress then expand as if his body was being torn apart causing him to drop to the ground.

When the feeling subsided, he looked up again to find the heat of the sun glaring down onto his face. The sun! He had not felt its warmth for over three months, and it comforted him. Looking around, he found Captain Atrigul collapsed onto the deck, the effort of the jump once again too much for her. He carefully picked her up and carried her to her room to rest. He always thought she looked so kind when she was asleep, so innocent. He wondered what haunted her mind to create the waking monster.

Remington did not stay with her, nor was she awake to make him. He now had responsibilities to take care of. Before the jump, Captain Atrigul informed him they were to head to Tortuga to sell their wares and potentially restock before heading to Halitona for a much-needed break. After confirming everyone on board safely made the jump, Remington gave the order to make sail, taking his place at the helm. Those who gazed upon Remington behind the wheel standing young and strong could see that there stood a man who could lead. They followed his orders without question.

It would be another month and a half before they reached Tortuga. During the journey, the Sickening Rose raided two merchant ships for supplies and treasures. Remington was thankful that these raids went smoother than his first. Both ships surrendered immediately, allowing the crew to take what they wanted. Remington always made sure the raided ship was left with just enough supplies to get to the next port.

16

The island of Tortuga was much different than Halitona. Having the separation from the Pirate King, Tortuga was more unruly. Many of the buildings were run down and leaking. Remington estimated that a third of the buildings were dedicated to bars. The people who roamed the unpaved streets were unsightly, many in filthy clothing and in desperate need for a bath. On occasion, Remington saw a group of people in nicer clothing go by, he assumed they are probably from one of the docked ships at the port.

The crew did not spend much time in Tortuga, only two days. Captain Atrigul explained that while the island is much more unfriendly than Halitona, she typically gets a better price for items here. The black market is stronger, and many buyers will deal under the counter without notifying the Pirate King. She introduced Remington to her usual contact on the island, a dark-skinned half elven man named Vanhorn.

Captain Atrigul explained that Vanhorn was the island's liaison for the black market in Cairnnathoul. The market there was one of the largest in the world, especially for items from the Feylands. It was run by a man known only as The Master and he was very good at keeping the market up. The captain sold their collection from the Feylands including the salamander body and the strange crabs.

Remington was shocked at the price they fetched and made note of it in his mind.

Remington was glad to leave Tortuga. The atmosphere about it gave him the chills. He did not trust anyone on the island for they answered to no one. Compared to Halitona, this island proved to be what everyone thought pirates were and worse.

It would be another 3 weeks to navigate the islands between Tortuga and Halitona. Many of the crew were excited to reach land again, to enjoy a few weeks off and see their friends and family on the island. Remington was looking forward to seeing Elianne again and to spend some time by himself, but he was also nervous.

Captain Atrigul informed him that as her new first mate, he would have to be presented to the Pirate King. The Pirate King watched over the seas in this area and worked to keep some order within the community. It was his duty therefore, to know who ran the ships that sailed into his port, so that he may keep eyes on those who dare to cross him.

Upon arriving in Halitona, Remington helped Captain Atrigul distribute the funds to the crew before following her ashore. She led him through the colorful winding streets towards a large mansion that stood high atop a hill overlooking the city. The King's palace was guarded by many men each keeping a close eye on the two of them as they passed through the gates.

Before they were allowed to enter, Remington and Captain Atrigul were stripped of all weapons. Remington felt uneasy not entering armed, but a forceful look from the captain made him comply. He was curious to meet this man that everyone seemed to hold to high respects but viewed him with fear. They entered the massive gates into the gleaming palace.

Inside, a grand entrance welcomed them, the marble stone walls decorated with black glass like stone, treasures from the sea, and various portraits of past kings. There were many people of all races moving in and about the inside, many of whom were well dressed. Remington dressed in his finest clothes at the request of Captain Atrigul, who also presented herself in high fashion, thought he still felt very out of place.

They worked their way towards the King's Hall, where they could seek audience with the king. Along the way, Captain Atrigul stopped to make small talk with many of her friends, introducing Remington to all of them. Remington tried to remember all the names, but it was difficult, another captain here and there, some first mates, others who worked within the palace. Many of them congratulated Remington upon news of his promotion, gave condolences when they heard about the loss of Brend. However, after the initial introduction, most ignored him, focusing their attention on their conversation with Atrigul. Remington did not mind, he preferred not being seen by these people.

Eventually they reached the King's Hall. Upon confirming their permission to enter with the guard at the door, Captain Atrigul pushed open the gate, leading Remington in. The hall was magnificent, the large columns held up a painted roof of marble, depicting scenes from the seas and the blessings of Valtameri. The room was entirely empty of people, save for a singular man sitting on a throne at the end of the room.

The throne was well forged from iron, sea creatures and kelp carved into the scenery giving the illusion they are at the command of the person who sat upon it. The man sitting tall and proud wore a platinum crown upon his head that perfectly contrasted the long black hair that was braided along the sides. His sea blue skin was coated with a thin layer of water, looking as if he had just exited the waves. His left hand wielded a large trident, prepared to strike at any moment, while his right hand rested upon his knee, his legs crossed in a scene of relaxation.

Captain Atrigul walked towards the king before stopping to bow deeply. Remington copied. "Greetings Your Majesty," she said with great splendor. Remington thought he detected a bit of sarcasm within her voice but said nothing. "My loyalty is pledged to you and to the seas." She stood up and faced the King.

"Areliel, welcome back. It has been sometime." His voice was smooth and calming, his tone rose and fell like the tides, reminding Remington of the ocean. "I am so sorry to hear about the loss of Brend, he was always a loyal member of your crew. I see that you have brought someone new. Please introduce yourself."

"My name is Remington Darkwalker, Your Majesty," Remington responded, holding his head high and speaking clearly.

"You are quite young aren't you. Come here boy, I want to take a look at you."

Remington stepped forward toward the throne. The king stood up and began circling Remington like a vulture examining every inch. He paused in front of Remington, looking at him with a quizzical look before grabbing Remington forcing his shirt aside to reveal the brand he bore on his chest. Remington reflexively pushed the king's hand away from him and backed up.

The king looked shocked for a second at the act of aggression before letting out a deep laugh. "The pup has got a bite. I never thought you would think so highly of one of your pets Areliel, especially one who is barely even a man. Has your crew fallen to such low standards?"

"My crew is as strong as ever, Your Majesty," she responded, a sharpness in her voice. "Remington has shown himself to be quite capable, I am sure whispers to prove me right will eventually reach your ears."

Remington's face twisted in annoyance. His captain did not even try to deny the insult, though she did defend his worth. He was not anyone's pet; he did not belong to anyone but himself. He felt he was lying to himself.

The king tilted his head slightly in analysis, his face wearing a grin that screamed he knew the truth, but what truth that was, Remington did not know. "Well he does seem to have some spirit, and enough wits to not talk too much. Maybe he will prove to be good to you." He turned to look at Remington. "Welcome to my domain boy. Now that you have entered it, you must swear fealty to me if you wish to leave it. If this fealty is broken, know that all who are loyal to me will hunt you down and your name will be forgotten."

Remington swallowed hard and dropped to one knee. Staring into the eyes of the king he stated as he rehearsed, "I, Remington Darkwalker, here pledge my allegiance and loyalty to the King of the Pirates and the seas that he rules over."

The king smiled and bid him to rise. "Very good. I hope that you do not forget it or may Valtameri bring his wrath upon you. It appears now our business is done here. Areliel, please drop your journey updates off with my secretary and do enjoy your stay on Halitona."

Remington stood and exited the chamber, hoping to be able to enjoy what time he had on the island with T'kocht and Elianne as much as he could.

17

"Captain, Remi, are you alright?" T'kocht's voice brought Remington out of his reminiscing of the past. Remington instinctively moved his hands to brush his hair out of his face, only to remember that it has not been long in over 3 years. Instead he rubbed his eyes, his hand brushing the starfish attached to his ear and turned to look at T'kocht. He saw T'kocht staring at the broken glass in the corner and tracing his eyes to the torn-up portrait.

"I'm fine, just thinking about the past, back to when things were better. For all of us." Remington trailed off at the end in thought.

T'kocht gave Remington a reproachful look, "Remi, you know even better than I do, that time before you became Captain was torture for you. Literally. Whether the rest of the crew knew it or not Captain Atrigul was poison to those aboard the ship."

"And I'm not?" Remington snapped back. "Look at me, look at yourself, and everyone else on this boat. Cursed! You would all be off living your best lives if it were not for my decisions." Remington did not mean to yell but he was angry.

T'kocht calmly walked over and sat next to Remington, resting his hand on Remington's shoulder. "So, what if we got scales or tentacles. Actually, I think most of the crew likes that aspect." He chuckled lightly. "Look, I miss feeling, and I am tired of always being hungry and thirsty, but this is not all on you. We followed you and continue to follow you because we believe in you. If we did not agree with pirating in the Feylands, then we would never have set foot on this ship, but we did. If we hadn't been cursed, many of us would still be serving the Pirate King and his stupid treaty with the Saxe Empire. We thrive on bringing chaos to the seas and on exploration. It would not be possible without you. I would not even be alive without you."

Remington listened, moving to rest his head on his friend's shoulder. He appreciated that T'kocht always knew what to say, how to bring him peace. In a quiet voice Remington asked, "Do you remember that day?"

"How could I forget," T'kocht responded, still gazing at the portrait.

The day in question occurred almost 9 years after Remington had become first mate. Remington was about to turn 26, having grown and matured from the young boy that he was when he took the position. He served faithfully under the command of Captain Atrigul, learning all that he could and growing as a leader. During those 9 long years, he also continued to suffer under her cruelty. At some point, Remington could never pin down when, he broke. Though the destructive words and wanton abuse continued, Remington grew dependent to her. His success, his life, his thoughts required her to be there. He loved her.

During that time as well, Remington grew closer with the returning crew of the Sickening Rose. Some people joined for singular trips, but many saw the ship as a home and its crew a family. They bonded, helping each other during raids of other ships, during downtime sailing, and during the many island explorations that occurred in the Feylands. All in search for the fountain of youth.

The Sickening Rose was once again sailing the crystal-clear waters of the Feylands. They had just found a new island to explore, hoping to find the fountain of youth, the eternal waters they had spent years searching for. The island seemed to be composed of a long series of tunnels that ran beneath the baren landscape above. The exploration crew consisted of Captain Atrigul, Remington, Nicky, T'kocht, a newer crew member Serafina, and Glazzglek, who as a dwarf, had a lot of experience with navigating tunnels.

The group had been traveling through the tunnels for 5 days before anything happened. Every step they took echoed through the eerily empty halls, no sign of life whatsoever. However, as evening approached, the usual narrow winding hallways finally opened up into a large cavern. The floor and ceiling were dotted with various stalagmites and stalactites formed from salt. A haunting howl continuously echoed throughout, sounding as though thousands of voices were all screaming at once. Within the center of the cavern, stood a dried-up fountain carved from an impossibly smooth grey stone. Along the fountain, there were messages written throughout in a language that Remington did not recognize.

Captain Atrigul let out a small gasp before rushing over to it. The rest of the crew quickly followed, eager to discover if this is what they have been looking for. As they reached it Captain Atrigul said, "This is it, the fountain, the key to my success." Her voice was barely audible, spoken in a low whisper.

Serafina was the first to speak the obvious, "Captain, it's dried up Are we too late? Is there nothing to be found?"

Remington watched as Captain Atrigul remained silent, quietly examining the carvings on the fountain He noticed that the initial joy had left her face, and now her brow furrowed in concentration. Everyone else stood back, allowing her the space she needed to think. After circling the fountain many times, reading, and re-reading the symbols, Captain Atrigul stopped and leaned over the fountain staring into the empty basin. Her hair fell over her face, covering any emotions she might have be feeling.

She stayed there for 5 minutes, unmoving. No one dared approach or interrupt her until she chose to address them. Captain Atrigul stood up, and in a steady voice she whispered, "I'm sorry." A flash appeared in Remington's eyes as time seemed to stop. He had felt this a few times before, the first being the death of Brend. As all of his friends remained motionless, frozen in time, he watched as an echo of Captain Atrigul turned around drawing her rapier. It only took a second for the echo to reach T'kocht, the point driving itself through his body. An echo of T'kocht moved from the body falling to the ground before being dragged away by Captain Atrigul's echo. The bleeding out echo was thrown into the fountain bed before the vision started fading.

Fear and confusion flooded Remington's mind, unable to process what he had seen. But he knew he did not have much time to react. When the future showed itself to him like this in the past, it always played out in truth only seconds later. His captain, his savior, his love, killing his best friend with no hesitation. Time was up. Captain Atrigul spun around lunging toward T'kocht. Remington did not think. His body and sword moved automatically, blocking the trajectory of Captain Atrigul, parrying the blade to skim just over T'kocht's shoulder.

T'kocht could only let out a mumbled "What the..." before quickly backing away out of the reach of Captain Atrigul's blade which was still locked with Remington's. Remington stood between them his eyes locked with Captain Atrigul's. The whites of his eyes were clearly visible, fear and panic had set in now that he had a clearer look at his captain. He could see a madness had taken over, anger and a hunger set deep within her green eyes. Her lips were twisted into a scowl. She was not looking at Remington. Her gaze continued past him toward the target of her strike.

"Move out of the way, Remington. This is not your business." Her voice was lower, a guttural growl present behind the strong authority of her tone. Remington flinched at the aggression in her voice but did not move. He could see the others frozen in place, unable to decide what to do next.

"No," Remington responded. "You just tried to kill one of our own, with no explanation. You are not yourself. Just put your blade away and we will figure this out. We always do."

Captain Atrigul lowered her blade, but the determination never left her eyes. She explained, "I read the scripts and confirmed what I already knew, this is the Jung Brunnen. The fountain requires payment. The life and healing must come from somewhere, be transferred from someone to the drinker. I must make the difficult choices as a captain, and this is a sacrifice I am willing to make. Now move out of the way Remington." She one again raised her blade, her eyes gazing past him toward her prey.

Remington shook his head, attempting to wake himself up from a reality that could only be a nightmare. It did not work. Remington had to try to find his captain, his love, again, for the woman who stood before him was a stranger. "Captain, we found the fountain. If it truly requires a sacrifice, let us find someone else. We know where it is, we have time. Areliel, please."

"No, I do not have time," she responded, her voice becoming even harsher, a dark echo filling the room. "This island may move; we may never find it again. I need this power; I need the extended life. I have searched my whole life waiting for this moment, and you deny me. I trusted you to stand by my side Remington, no matter what. It appears I was wrong. If you are so determined to protect these pawns in my game, then I have no choice. The fountain needs a life and you are offering yours."

Captain Atrigul lunged at Remington, the tip of her blade aimed at his neck. Adrenaline still rushing through Remington's veins, he quickly stepped to the side dodging her first attack. He faintly heard a small commotion, and only taking a brief time to look, saw that

Nicky had Serafina in a choke hold. Serafina's blade had clattered to the ground as Nicky prevented her from joining in the fight.

Remington felt a burn of pain as the captain's sword nicked part of his arm, blood welling up. He focused, keeping watch, and dodging her attacks. He played defense, not wanting to hurt her. How could he hurt the woman who gave him everything? But this person, this monster, attacking him was not her. Some horrible greed had possessed her, made her forget who she was. All that was left was a lust for blood and death, no matter who it was. He wondered if she even recognized him, if she cared.

Remington continuously begged and pleaded for her to stop, to think rationally, but it fell on deaf ears. He realized that she was going to kill him, it was life or death now. Her swings were deteriorating, transitioning from her highly technical footwork to swinging with abandon, attempting to hit anything that stood before her. Remington used this opportunity to try to disarm her, to place his hits that would stop her as safely as possible. He had landed a few blows, slashing at her arms and legs, but never any lethal attacks. None of it stopped her. The rage that flowed through her prevented her from even acknowledging her wounds.

The fight continued, the rest of the crew staying back, not involving themselves in this duel between two people who used to trust each other without question. Captain Atrigul ran past Remington, her wanton charge missing as Remington once again side stepped out of the way.

His back now turned to her, Remington spun around his blade stretched out, preparing to parry the upcoming rebuke. He had misjudged the time it would take for her to attempt the second charge. Attempting to only knock her rapier out of the way, his blade swung in an upward diagonal, but the rapier was not there. Instead he felt his blade cleave through flesh, the warm blood splattering against his face, and the audible gasp released by Captain Atrigul drowned his ears. His blade had caught just below her rib cage, moving upward before intersecting with her heart.

He froze horrified as her body collapsed onto the ground, her chest heaving heavily gasping for air as blood drained out of the wound. He dropped to the floor, cradling her body into his lap. His hands moved to the wound, helplessly attempting to apply pressure, wishing the gash to close. Her blood was soaking into his clothing, but he hardly noticed. He began scrambling through his pack, hoping to find a healing potion, anything to save her. Desperately he searched but found nothing.

He looked up, throwing his bag across the room and saw his friends staring at him, concern plastered on their faces. He felt Captain Atrigul cough and seize in his lap. He clutched onto her harder. Through a choked voice he shouted to anyone who would hear, "Please, somebody, help me! I... I can't help her. I didn't mean..." He was barely coherent, trying everything he could to stop the bleeding that was pumping directly from her heart. No one moved, understanding the truth. He knew there was nothing that could be done to save her, but he had to try. His hands were drenched in her blood.

Remington felt a hand wet with blood touch the side of his face. He looked down to see Captain Atrigul looking up at him. She was pale, her life draining with every fading heartbeat. The barbaric rage that had once possessed her was replaced with a softness that Remington had only rarely seen but craved every second. She spoke, her voice barely a whisper as she used the last of her energy, "Remington, it's okay. It's okay." Her eyes closed, hand falling down to her side.

Remington broke, tears streaming down his face. Then he looked up, an idea forming in his mind. His eyes shifted from Captain Atrigul, to the Fortune Teller, to the fountain. He reached for his sword as he dove toward the fountain. Remington was barely on his feet before he was tackled back to the ground by T'kocht. "No, Remi, don't. There is nothing you can do. She's gone, don't throw your own life away."

Remington tried to fight against his friend, punching and kicking him, struggling to break free from his grip. T'kocht was strong though, and easily kept Remington pinned down. Serafina was frozen in place, unable to process the chaos around her. Nicky and Glazzglek were quietly talking with each other. Remington could not hear what they were saying, nor did he care. He had just committed mutiny, killing his captain and the person that meant the most to him.

He stopped struggling against T'kocht, who finally released him. Remington crawled his way over to Captain Atrigul's lifeless body, once again cradling it in his arms and rocked back and forth. His head resting against hers, trying to take in the last of her warmth that was quickly fading. He was whispering, repeating over and over again, "I'm so sorry. She was right." He heard T'kocht asking him who she was, what he meant, but Remington did not listen. He did not want to accept reality.

He felt T'kocht leave his side to join in conversation with Nicky and Glazzglek. Remington wondered what they were discussing, what punishment they were coming up with to deal with his mutiny. His curiosity faded quickly, and he remained on the floor of the cavern, clutching her body. He quickly ran out of tears.

Remington was unsure how long he remained there, his mind too distraught to think clearly or to move. He jumped as a hand fell on his shoulder. He looked up with red irritated eyes, expecting a blade at his throat, but instead found T'kocht kneeling next to him.

"Come on Remi, we need to go. We should return to the ship, this place is not safe." T'kocht tried to pull him up, but Remington resisted.

"If you are going to kill me just kill me now. End it. I know

I deserve it." Remington's voice was still shaky, but he spoke with a commanding voice. There was no point in returning to the ship, they are just going to kill him there anyways. It would be better to end his misery and distribute his punishment now.

Another voice came from his other side, "Shut up, you idiot. We aren't going to kill you." Nicky was also now grabbing at his arm to pull him up. She reached to shift the body off Remington's lap, but he slapped her hand out of the way. "Remington, come on, let's leave here. We won't leave her, T'kocht can carry her. Get up, I can't carry you too, it would ruin my outfit."

Remington couldn't find the strength to even chuckle at her poor attempt at a joke. His muscles resisted movement, having stayed in one place for so long. He shook his head, lifting the body with him as he got up. He saw his clothing was drenched in blood, he wondered how so much came from a person. "No. If we must leave, I will carry her. I owe her that much. This is my weight to bear."

18

Remington could not remember much of the next 3 days that they walked through the tunnels. Sleep rarely came to him. All that had happened had shut down his thoughts as he walked in silence, the weight of her body unnoticed. The others traveling with him did not speak to him, giving him room to be alone. Occasionally he remembered hearing their voices talking quietly to each other, but he never bothered to try to listen.

The way back had been much faster since they were not aimlessly wandering the tunnels. They returned to the Sickening Rose much sooner than the rest of the crew had anticipated. Chatter and gasps of shock erupted immediately upon the party boarding the ship. All eyes were turned to Remington, clothes still coated in the blood of Captain Atrigul who he carried in his arms.

A cacophony of questions were thrown at him, what had happened, how did she die, who is the next captain. Remington ignored the hounding as he moved across the deck, to lay her body to rest near the helm, to be where she belonged one last time. Remington looked out over the crew, feeling the daggers of their stares at him, begging for answers he could not give. He opened his mouth to speak, to announce his horrible act of mutiny, but no words came out. They caught in the back of his throat choking him such that he could not breath.

Remington could feel his legs telling him to run, to jump overboard and let the sea drown him like it should have 9 years ago. He felt an arm slide around his shoulders in a comforting hug and looked up to find Nicky standing by his side. "Don't worry I got this," she whispered to him, giving his upper arm a friendly squeeze before letting go. Remington only nodded. Now that Captain Atrigul was dead, Nicky was the most senior member of the ship, having now served for 15 years on the Sickening Rose. All of the crew respected her and shifted their attention to her as she walked to the front of the helm.

"Alright everyone, listen up. Yes, it is true, our captain has paid the ultimate price and is dead. Now, we all talked, and we don't want any rumors spreading about what may or may not have happened, so we are going to give it to you straight." Nicky looked towards the landing party, then at Remington, and back to the crew. "We did not find the fountain."

Remington looked up in shock. He looked toward T'kocht preparing to correct her. T'kocht shook his head discretely, warning Remington to stay quiet, so he did.

"Instead, we encountered a cruel trick of the Feylands. We all know that there is always a danger here of the fey playing with your mind, turning you into something you are not. The six of us had come across a strange cavern with runes written along the wall. The captain was the first to enter, and as she did, a madness fell over her. She turned her back on us and attempted to murder one of our own. We tried to free her of whatever evil possessed her, but nothing worked. Under some unfortunate circumstances, a misplaced blade dealt a fatal wound leading to her death."

Murmurs erupted across the crew once more at this, trying to make sense of what Nicky was saying. One man shouted out, "We ain't got a captain, whats we supposed to do now. We stuck here forever?" Many panicked conversations picked up with that and many people were talking over one another.

A loud whistle from Nicky quieted them down again. "Everyone calm yourselves, geez." Nicky let out an exasperated sigh. "The Sickening Rose will have a captain, and you will return home. Have you forgotten who has stood by her side for the past 9 years learning from the best? Captain Atrigul trusted Remington to be her right-hand man, and I hope now you can honor her by following him as your captain."

That was not what Remington expected her to say. He was preparing himself to walk the plank, to be the subject of execution, anything but that. He did not deserve that. He waited for the rest of the crew to object, for someone to try to dig deeper into Nicky's descriptions of the event in question, but none came. Instead, he heard T'kocht's deep voice shout clear, "To Captain Darkwalker!" Then one by one the rest of the crew joined in on the welcome. Remington looked towards Nicky, waiting for a turn of events, but she only smiled at him, raising a glass of her own in his direction.

She turned back towards the crew. "We have all suffered a great sorrow with the loss of Captain Atrigul. We shall give her a proper send off this evening. Captain Darkwalker was closer to her than any of us here and needs time to mourn. We all need time to mourn, but we must keep moving. Get back to your stations and set sail. We are going home."

As the crew dispersed, many talking amongst themselves of the announcement, Nicky moved over to Remington, who still stood in disbelief. "I'm sorry to drop this on you," she said, "let's get you inside, then we can talk, okay?"

Remington took her outstretched hand and followed her towards the captain's chambers, his chambers now. T'kocht and Glazzglek followed behind, keeping away crewmembers that were trying to sneak into the discussion. T'kocht locked the door behind him, and the four friends were alone. Remington looked over each one of them, waiting to wake up from this dream he must be in, but he never did.

"Why?" His question was barely comprehendible, he was not sure he wanted the answer.

"Seriously Remington, snap out of it." Nicky gave Remington a solid slap across his face, knocking him off his feet. He could feel the heat growing where her hand made contact. Remington turned toward her in surprise, he had never heard her raise her voice like that.

"Look, I am sorry. I know you are still mourning; the captain meant a lot to you. She meant a lot to us, so don't think you are the only one who is upset. We can all see you carry her death on your shoulders. It wasn't your fault so stop blaming yourself and come back to the real world."

"She's right you know," T'kocht stepped in. "Without you, I'd be dead back there. You almost were too. Atrigul was driven mad by the power of the fountain. You tried everything to not hurt her."

"Aye, that wis th' best finesse wi' a blade ah hae ever seen, 'n' Nicky is standing richt 'ere. Thare wis no else ye cuid hae dane. 'twas ye or her." Added in Glazzglek, who got an accusatory glance from Nicky. "Tis true."

Nicky rolled her eyes before turning back to Remington. "We all agreed, that even though the fountain was the one thing we were looking for, the one thing giving many of us hope for the future, the price to use it was too much. It's best if we keep its location secret, it would cause chaos if the others knew. So, we told them only what they needed to know. Don't worry, Scrafina has been... properly warned about opening her mouth."

"We also know a ship is nothing without a captain," continued T'kocht. "You have been learning from Atrigul for the past 9 years.

There is no one on this ship more qualified. So, we made the executive decision to announce you as captain. We will make sure the crew follows your orders don't you worry about that. Plus, you got to get us back home remember. You are the only one now that knows how to do it."

Remington stood in silence, absorbing this flood of support from his friends. He shifted his arms which caused the dried blood on his clothes to crackle with the movement. The guilt still stained his soul like the blood on his shirt, but he was comforted. He swallowed hard before lifting his chin high to meet the gaze of those surrounding him. "You are right," said Remington, strength returning to his voice. "What is done, is done, and we cannot change that. The ship needs a leader. If you all truly think I am the best person for the position, then I will accept. We all need time to heal, then we must figure out what we are to do next. I do not think the Pirate King will be pleased by this news. First, let's lay her to rest, as a proper captain."

The strength that he started the speech with began to die towards the end as Remington felt his own lies sink in. Remington brought his hand up to his chest and ran his fingers over the scar that was there. His revenge he had planned so long ago was complete, but he did not want it to be. Remington's love for her was forged from abuse and lies, and it only made the chains that bound him to her stronger. Now that the chains were broken, Remington struggled to see his place in this world, aboard this ship. But he had to appear strong. He let Areliel down; he failed her. He could not do fail his friends too. He had to at least pretend.

"That's the spirit," shouted Nicky. "Now get some sleep and clean up, you look like a walking zombie, and trust me I've seen one." Nicky exited the quarters, leaving Remington trying to make note to ask her what she meant by that at some point. Glazzglek followed after her, giving Remington a pat on the shoulder before leaving.

As T'kocht prepared to leave, he embraced Remington, giving him the support needed without other eyes or ears to notice. T'kocht released him and looked Remington in the eyes, "I know you are hurting, and I know you don't believe us though I wish you would. Her poison has slowly eaten away at you until you forgot the poison was even there. I know you have tolerated more than you ever should, and it caused you to be blind to her cruelty. But I still saw it. Every day. You may not believe me now, but just give it time. You will heal, and the poison will leave your body, though the scars may remain."

T'kocht left, leaving Remington to think over everything that was said. He walked over to the small pile of clothes she kept in the corner of the cabin and picked up one of her shirts. He could still smell her perfume on it. He paced around the room, keeping the shirt to his nose trying to maintain the connection to her, to convince himself that he could walk out those doors and she would be there. But she won't.

Eventually, Remington gave up wishing. He searched the room for a bit, finding a change of clothes he had left there and replaced the blood-soaked garments he was wearing. Remington ran some water through his hair, combing the knots from his hair and tying it tightly back with a ribbon in his typical ponytail. As the blood and mud washed off, Remington slowly felt lighter, as the weight that the dirt carried lifted the emotional turmoil from his mind.

He turned to return to the deck when something caught his eye. One of Captain Atrigul's large trifold hats was leaning against a bottle of rum. He picked it up and placed it on his head before exiting the room. As Remington stepped out into the light of the Feylands, all eyes turned toward him. Much of the ship's activities halted as the crew sized up their new captain. Remington made a point to look each person in the eye as he passed them on the way to the helm.

He saw Nicky currently at the helm. She did not immediately see him, her back turned to him as she battled with a rope that did not want to cooperate. Remington unhooked the rope from the peg it was wrapped around, causing it to fall all at once onto her, burying her under close to 30 feet of rope. As she pushed the rope off, releasing every curse in her vocabulary, she finally noticed Remington. He was chuckling at her misfortune. Remington saw her take a moment, still covered in rope, to give him a quick visual inspection before she broke into a massive grin.

"I kept the helm warm for you captain," she said finally getting the last of the rope off of her. "Take your place, you deserve it. Not to mention, you look the part now. Glad to see you clean up well."

Remington reached down a hand to help her up, before dropping her half-way, causing her to burst out laughing. He turned toward the wheel, stroking his hand over the smooth wood of the spokes. As he took hold, he looked out over the deck, out over everyone that now looked to him, that he has known as a family.

"What are you all staring at, back to work. We have a ship to run. Raise the port sails, make ready to head west. Let's go home." Remington's voice commanded across the deck causing everyone to immediately break into their work. Nicky patted his back in support before moving to her own responsibilities. As he watched her leave, he saw the white fabric draped over the body still lying on the deck. He quickly looked away, not wanting to think about it.

That night they gave Captain Areliel Atrigul a proper send off. They had set her body in one of the spare row boats, before lighting it in a funeral pyre as it floated into the open waters of the Feylands. Remington remained like stone through the whole ceremony, he did not want to look weak now that he was their leader. It would be years before the continuous nightmares he kept private would stop.

19

During their journey back to the Prime Realm, Remington made some changes around the ship. Within the first couple of days, Remington chose his first mate. Initially, he had asked Nicky as she had the most experience and helped him get this far. She cackled until she realized he was being serious. Remington was slightly disappointed but understood that she did not want the responsibilities that were involved with it. Nicky was never the responsible type unless it came to combat.

Nicky however, did give her approval for his other choice, which was T'kocht. He needed someone he could trust one hundred percent to have his back, and that person has always been T'kocht. His first instinct was to pick T'kocht but was worried that he would be seen as playing favoritism. Nicky was quick to remind him that's the whole point of a first mate, and that he should follow his instincts, not his brain.

T'kocht gladly accepted the position, and he was officially promoted that evening. The two of them working together became an unstoppable duo, causing the ship to run smoother than it had in a long time. Remington continued to keep the appearance of a strong captain to the entire crew including T'kocht, doing his best to keep his misery and regret a secret. He suspected that T'kocht saw through the mask, but T'kocht never confronted him.

A few weeks later, Remington performed his first jump to the Prime Realm without the assistance of Areliel by his side. Remington took extra care in each step, making sure everything was perfect. He remembered starting the ritual, clearly speaking the arcane words, drawing the correct symbols, then the world going black.

Remington awoke to T'kocht shaking him awake. His head hurt and his vision was blurred. He could hear mumbled voices but was unable to make out any words. It would be a few hours before he was coherent enough to learn that it was a success.

A month after their return to the Prime Realm, the Sickening Rose made port in Halitona. Remington was nervous about this landing. Landing here meant he would have to give notice to the Pirate King, to relive those moments and open wounds that were just beginning to heal. He would have to present T'kocht to him, but that part he was less worried about. He was glad to have T'kocht by his side for this.

Trying to keep his breathing steady, he walked with T'kocht to the king's palace. T'kocht seemed more concerned about Remington rather than himself, giving him an encouraging smile. Remington could not understand how T'kocht was so calm but appreciated him being a rock at his side.

They walked through the gates of the palace greeted by curious glances from those that they passed. Many of the folks Remington had met over the past nine years attempted to talk to him, asking where Areliel was. Remington only shook his head and ignored them. Some of those that were closer to him got a mumbled, "Tell you later."

Remington stopped in front of the double doors, his hand on the handles to push inward. He turned to T'kocht for one last glance before entering. The King's Hall was once again emptied besides the king who watched them enter with an intense look. His eyes darted between the two men searching for something that was not there. His gaze finally rested on Remington.

"Is the little pet lost?" the king asked mockingly, "or did Areliel finally abandon you like she does all of her pets. If you think you are going to find help here, then you are dumber than I thought."

Remington felt himself starting to shrink, to want to be as small as possible to be unseen. That was not possible, he was captain now and had to earn some respect from the king. He returned the eye contact with the king speaking slowly so that the king would hear, and to hide the shaking he felt inside, "Captain Areliel Atrigul is dead. I have taken over leadership of the Sickening Rose."

The king immediately sat upright, shifting his weight to the front of the throne. He examined Remington, trying to decide if this was the truth before a smile crept over his face. "You killed her, didn't you?" The question was stated more as a fact than a question as if he already knew the answer.

Remington thought about lying or being vague, but he was in a dangerous situation. One wrong move could cost him his life. "Yes, I did," Remington responded. Those three words were the only ones he was able to choke out.

The king's smile broke into a sickening laugh that echoed through the empty hall. "I warned Areliel that if she beat her dog enough times it would eventually bite. And bite you did, little pup." He stood up from his throne, his massive trident moving with his footfalls, the clang of metal on stone ringing out with each step. He approached Remington, who was now frozen in place, not daring to move.

The king stopped in front of Remington, glancing slightly upward to meet Remington's towering presence. The tips of the trident pointed at his throat, mere inches from death. "The seas are unforgiving Remington," the king stated, "the currents are constantly changing. You never know what direction they will go. Areliel had a blind spot for you, though I never understood why, and did not see the tides change against her. I will admit that I am disappointed to see Areliel gone, but I accept your declaration as captain."

The trident moved to be pointed upright, no longer threatening. Remington let out a small sigh of relief. The king continued, "I do not expect you to amount to much, or to last very long out there, but I look forward to your loyalty. Now, introduce your first mate here, I don't believe we've met."

Remington introduced T'kocht to the king. T'kocht moved pass him to present himself. The Pirate King looked at T'kocht before shifting his glance over to Remington, before starting to chuckle. Remington watched as the king leaned into T'kocht and whispered something to him. He was unable to make out what was said, but he could tell it greatly upset T'kocht. T'kocht only clenched his fist, gritting his tusked teeth taking whatever was being said in stride.

The king backed up and dismissed them, ordering Remington to fill out the necessary paperwork. As they were about to leave, the king stated, "Oh and Remington? Be sure to rename your ship, its bad luck to keep a dead name."

Remington attempted to press T'kocht to learn what the king told him, but T'kocht refused to answer, insisting it was not important. Remington could tell that T'kocht was still affected by whatever was said and seemed to be more distant. Returning the favor that his friend had granted him all those years, Remington let it go. The curiosity was still overwhelming.

During the remainder of their stay on Halitona, Remington and T'kocht stayed with Elianne and worked on selling the small grouping of treasure that they acquired before the trip was cut short. They assembled replacement crew for those that decided to leave and after a lot of brainstorming decided on a new name for the ship, The Fey's Fortune.

20

"You know you never did tell me what the Pirate King said to you the first time you met," Remington stated, remembering back to that day.

"I don't even remember it now," was all that T'kocht replied, refusing to make eye contact. Remington could tell that T'kocht was lying. He always was when it came to that topic. It did not matter now anyways. He held no respect for the Pirate King, and most sailors seemed to believe they were at war. Remington was at war, but not just against the Pirate King. He was pledged to cause chaos, to have no peace in retribution for his actions. The sea was unforgiving, and so must he be.

The Fey's Fortune found its way to Tortuga a week later. The dock that the ship pulled into cleared out immediately. Many gathered at the surrounding docks to get a glimpse of the ghost ship and her crew. They knew to stay out of the crew's way, for though they remain peaceful on land, the rumors of their ruthlessness remain. Remington never went ashore after being cursed, he never wanted to.

T'kocht acted in his stead for exchanging goods and gathering information on the happenings in the world. He was interested in the activities of the Pirate King and his dealings with the Saxe

Empire, and more importantly, anyone looking for him. Typically, no one ever was, for he made sure that his name never passed the lips of those who were not his crew. The name Remington died that faithful day with the River King, and he made sure it passed out of history. Remington worked hard to make sure no one knew who he really was, and those that did knew better than to say. It was the only way to separate himself from his actions, from the monster that was born from the waves.

A few days after making port, as Remington attempted to relax reading from one of the few books on board, he heard a knock on the door. A few seconds later T'kocht entered, his footsteps as quiet as ever. Remington saw T'kocht seemed nervous and concerned. He quickly closed the door behind him.

"Remi," T'kocht started, "There are some people here I think you will want to speak to. I found them at one of the taverns, they were asking for you."

"People ask for the Drowned Captain all the time, what makes these folks special?" Remington asked. He knew people were constantly wanting to meet him, but what did they say that T'kocht thinks he should oblige?

"No Remi, they asked for *you*. By name. They said they had critical information you would want to hear. I tried to tell them whatever info they had, they could just tell me, but they insisted. Said you would regret not hearing it. I know you don't want to talk to them, but I figured we could take care of them if they prove useless." T'kocht had his hand resting on his pistol at his side. Not his favorite, but easily concealable.

Remington thought about it. Even if they were lying, they knew his name, and were willing to speak it. He could not let that progress. "Very well, let them in."

Remington sat behind his desk as T'kocht brought the visitors. Entering into his chambers were two humanoids. One was a dwarvish man with a roughed-up face and scars lining his arms. The other was a half-elven woman with very light blonde, almost silver, hair. While the man kept a stoic demeanor, the woman seemed very flighty, skipping her way into the room with a smile on her face. Remington did not trust her, there was something off putting about her smile.

Remington stood up to greet them. "So, I hear you have been looking for me. Well congratulations, you found me. How can I help you?"

The two strangers looked at each other in agreement before turning their attention back on Remington. The man spoke first "So, it is true then, the real name of the Drowned Captain is Remington Darkwalker? You don't look nearly as dangerous as everyone says you are."

Remington cut him off, he did not appreciate the man's unwarranted arrogance. "I don't take kindly to insults. Say what you came here for, and depending on the results, I might forgive your indiscretion. I don't play games."

The man shifted nervously, the swagger he came in with was torn apart by Remington's icy voice. "Of course, it was meant as a compliment. I have some information I think you would like to hear, but a reward is to be expected."

Remington eyed the man, "I will give reward if I believe the information is worth it. Now speak, my patience is wearing thin." He moved his hand toward the hilt of the Fortune Teller. Remington was getting annoyed, who is this man to think he could prance about spilling his name to the world and acting like he is in charge and not face any consequences.

"I am sure you will find this information well worth it. I come bearing news of a young lady who I recently helped cross the Gulf of Rossbalt. She was asking for information on a sea captain under the name Remington Darkwalker, captain of a boat referred to as the Fortune. Now, I got brains along with brawn, and I made the connection she might be looking for you, though the name was new. Sounds like she'd been asking around a lot of folks searching for you. I've been around a bit, and if I know anything, it's the scorn of a woman. So, as a loyal follower of the Nautilus, I thought it was my duty to inform our esteemed leader of any misgivings that might face him."

The man gave a mischievous knowing smile and an exaggerated bow. Remington's curiosity was peaked, it was rare to hear of someone so openly looking for him, and not know of his fate. "Did you get her name?" he asked, keeping his voice level but glancing over toward T'kocht.

The woman finally brought her attention to the conversation and answered, "She called herself Maeve. Was a real feisty one, I liked her."

Remington stopped in his tracks, and abruptly turned towards the strangers. "Are you sure that was the name?" His question came out more eager and interested than he intended, but he was unable to hide his surprise.

"Aye, it was Maeve," the man confirmed. "She was traveling with a few others; it was a strange bunch to be sure. She said you took something from her, and she wants it back."

Remington poured a glass of rum, uselessly hoping it would help. It never did. He turned back towards them, casually taking a sip of the alcohol using the time to regain his composure. "Well, that was some interesting information. I will reward you justly. T'kocht, please put some coin together for these lovely folks. In the meantime..." Before Remington could finish his sentence, Remington flicked his wrist, using the arcane powers granted to him with his curse to freeze the two strangers in place. He could see their panicked eyes darting back and forth, struggling to move any part of their body. Remington approached looking both in the eye.

"You will not speak of my name, nor this conversation to anyone. If I hear you do, and trust me I will, know that there are fates worse than death. I am a harbinger of chaos. No matter where your loyalties lie, if you cross me, I will bring about a punishment more horrible than your worst nightmare. You have been warned. Now get off my ship."

He released them from his hold, both stumbling to catch their balance as they regained use of their limbs. T'kocht shoved a small bag of gold into their hands. Without further debate, the two rushed out of the cabin taking the threat very seriously.

As soon as the strangers were gone, Remington collapsed onto the floor, clutching at the seal skin that hung over his shoulders. Maeve. He had not heard that name in over 3 years, and yet he thought of her almost every day. She was here, in the Prime Realm, looking for him, hating him.

T'kocht carefully approached, kneeling onto the floor next to him. "Remi, it's okay. Those scoundrels might not even be telling the truth. This could just be a ruse by the Pirate King."

Remington looked up at him, trying to hold in the panic that was setting in. "No, not even he knew her name. Only you and I. She is here, I have to see."

He scrambled over to the loose floorboards that hid the bag that he inherited from Areliel. From the bag he pulled out the crystal ball, an item he quickly learned could be used to see people from very far away. He pictured in his mind the Maeve he once knew, the fiery spirit of the woman he met in the Feylands.

Remington felt his mind extend out of him, blackness filling his vision before reforming. He was now looking at long grasslands, still wet with moisture. It did not take him long to recognize the terrain as that belonging to the country of Alba. His vision dialed in on the face of a young woman, hiking with determination. He saw the unmistakable hints of teal throughout her hair and in her eyes. She occasionally turned to the side, to talk to a younger boy, barely 17 next to her. It looked like she was teasing him, which caused Remington to instinctively smile. He could see the forms and shadows of a few others traveling with her, though he could not make them out clearly. He felt the vision fade out, returning his mind to the floor of the Fey's Fortune.

"She's here," Remington said. His eyes still focused on the crystal ball in his lap. If she found him, how could he face her after all that he's done, after how much pain he must have caused her. After how much pain she has caused him.

21

Three years after becoming captain of the newly named Fey's Fortune, Remington had grown to be an excellent leader. Though the Fey's Fortune remained low on most sailor's radar, it became well known for its dealings in fey creatures and items. It was extremely rare to find anyone who knew how to complete the jump into the Feylands, so items from there were valuable. Especially items that could not be obtained legally through the city of Cairnnathoul.

T'kocht had grown skilled in the use of a new deadly technology created by the Saxe empire that they called guns. Much more accurate and powerful than a crossbow, it proved to be a valuable asset to the Saxe army. He acquired a prototype pistol during a raid of a Saxe naval ship, and spent his shore leave creating his own more powerful version.

Remington and his crew had gone to the Feylands a few times through those years, always bringing back strange animals and enchanting items. His reputation on Tortuga grew and his dealings with Vanhorn increase exponentially. Along with his success, his arrogance and greed followed closely behind.

Though Remington still felt the pains and the loss of Areliel, he found some healing in her absence. He recognized the poison that she continually poured into him and accepted that he was better off on his own. But the internal scars she left continued to influence him and a hole remained within. He sought relief from the loneliness that still plagued him through endless flirtations and constant manipulation of those around him. He could get what he wanted through well placed words and the wink of an eye. He felt unstoppable.

Remington had gotten word that some high paying customer in the Saxe Empire were looking for a particular item from the Feylands. Many had refused the offer, for what they were looking for was the skins of a Selkie. Remington had heard of Selkies and had met one in the past. Selkies were fey creatures that lived in the River King's domain. Often times they spent their times in the form of a seal, frolicking in the waves of the island they called home. However, when they felt the need to interact with humanoids, they could shed their seal skin to take the form of a human. They were known for their extraordinary beauty and have caused many sailors to fall in love, only to be gone the next day.

Though pirates often fought and killed for treasures on the high seas, no one was willing to take on the contract. For to have a Selkie skin retain its magical abilities, its original owner must be kept alive. Most Selkies were very protective of their skins as well, as their skins were a part of them and meant everything to them. They were also favored creatures of the River King. No one who knew how to get one was willing to take on such a difficult challenge, the risk was too high.

Remington saw this as an opportunity of a lifetime. The reward per skin being offered was enough to live an extravagant life with an early retirement. So, taking it up with his usual crew, they made the decision to head to the Feylands in search of Selkie skins.

It did not take long after the jump for them to find their first Selkie. They had gotten word that there was one living on a nearby island, who did not often see visitors. The Fey's Fortune made its way to the island where it docked a few hundred yards offshore.

Knowing the tendency of these creatures toward seduction, it was determined that the best plan of attack was to use their own games against them. While the rest of the landing party would search the rest of the island for small trinkets, Remington would approach the Selkie alone. His looks and charismatic personality were the perfect choice for luring these creatures into his trap.

It only took a week for the plan to work. After finding the creature, Remington used his charm and wits, all of the skills he had learned from Arcliel, to slowly break down the creature's guards. He gave her a constant flow of words of affirmation, shared false secrets with her, did all the right things to build her trust. He learned where she hid her skin and was gone the next morning taking it with him, without even a word of goodbye.

Remington felt no remorse over his actions. It was purely a business transaction, with a poor naïve girl stuck on the losing end. The crew celebrated the success, actively looking forward to how many they could get, entranced by the prospect of a rich life. It was also discovered that anyone who wears the skin can transform into a seal themselves. Many saw the possibilities this ability holds and wanted to use it, but Remington knew better. This was a dangerous item to be flaunting off and if they were to be caught, it would spell trouble. So, he hid it in his satchel out of view of everyone but himself.

The crew visited 4 more islands this way. Each encounter, Remington became more skilled in his art. It only took 3 days to get the last skin. In celebration of their success, Remington decided to stop in the city of Vauxquet on one of the large islands in the River King's domain. It was a bustling city home to mostly sea elves along with a wide variety of fey creatures. Vauxquet was known for being a relaxed city, often a popular destination for tourist who make their way from Cairnnathoul. This time of year, there were no tourist as the city of Cairnnathoul resided in the Prime Realm for half the year. This meant that many of the creatures that avoided the outsiders took the opportunity to enjoy their city without any threat.

Remington was enjoying some time to himself on one of the secluded beaches, taking a moment to be alone with his thoughts. He had chosen a spot that hid him from prying eyes but allowed him clear view of the crashing waves. As he enjoyed the calming sounds of the crashing waves, he heard splashing coming from the water. Opening his eyes to see the cause he noticed a seal playfully leaping through the waves, making its way to shore. Upon reaching the sand, the seal began to transform into a woman, the skin of the seal folding onto her shoulders.

She was a Selkie. Remington remained still, as to not draw attention to himself. Maybe the crew could get one final skin before leaving the Feylands. He watched as she made her way along the beach and smiled. It would not be difficult to find her in town. Her dark tanned skin seemed to shine with golden undertones, still glistening with ocean water. Her deep brown hair hung down to her waist and he swore he could see subtle streaks of teal interwoven, as striking as the sea itself.

She did not notice him as she passed, heading in the direction of town. Remington waited a few minutes before packing up himself to follow her. It was an hour walk back to the city center, and he made sure to keep his distance staying in the cover of the trees. By the time they reached town he was able to blend in with the small crowds making their way through the streets. He watched her confidently stride up to a local bar and sit down for a drink. Her voice was loud and clear, bellowing with an air of confidence and self-assurance. She was complaining of the lack of waves today, calling them smaller than any pixie she'd seen.

Remington took a short moment to straighten himself out

before striding over and taking a seat next to her. Putting on his best smile he leaned over towards her and said, "I thought I had seen all the beautiful wonders of the Feylands but clearly I missed one." She turned to him, a teasingly questioning look to her eyes, which he now noticed were a brilliant gold with flecks of teal that matched her hair.

"Is that really what you are going with? Really? Why don't you try that again?" She smiled at him before going back to her drink.

Remington chuckled, intrigued by her feisty yet collected movements. He very loudly cleared his throat, purposefully overacting every movement. "Excuse me my lady," he gave her a very deep bow, "but would you please permit me to purchase you a drink?"

She burst out laughing unable to control it, "Wow I think that might have been worse than the first one, but I am not one to say no to a free drink. What's your name, you aren't from around here are you."

"Understandable," Remington laughed, "my name is Remington. And you are right, I am not from around here, I am visiting with my ship the Fortune. But maybe I could get a tour with a local. You know its rude for you to know my name when I do not know yours."

"Name's Maeve. I usually don't interact with tourists Remington, but I think I can make an exception. I am going to need a few more drinks first though." Her smile was comforting and genuine. Though she teased, he felt no malice from her words. He felt a little guilty of his plan for her, but quickly brushed the doubt aside. It's not his fault she is young and naïve.

They talked over the next few hours, time melting away into their conversation. Remington offered to walk her home, but she refused. She did agree to meet him back in town the next day to show him around a bit. He could see his plan taking hold. Remington predicted that he would leave the island with his prize within a week.

Remington returned to the Fey's Fortune and updated T'kocht on the day's events, excited at the prospect of another victory. T'kocht seemed skeptical, "Are you sure you want to go for one more Remi? I am concerned about you; you don't seem yourself lately. I know what we came here to do and accepted the choices we would have to make to accomplish it but it's affecting you, I see it. If I may be so blunt you are starting to sound like Atrigul."

Remington snapped at T'kocht, "Don't ever compare me to her. I am not her and I never will be. This is purely business. I take no pleasure in this. Don't you want to give Elianne a comfortable life? This is how we do it."

"Don't bring Ma into this, she will be fine with or without this mission. Maybe it started as purely business, but you can't lie to me. We have been best friends for the last 12 years; I know my best friend. You are starting to enjoy this. The unnecessary games that you play with them, it's the exact same games Atrigul played with you. Check yourself or you will become a monster too."

"Just because you look like a monster, doesn't mean you have to project that onto me!"

Remington regretted the words as soon as they came out of his mouth. He knew T'kocht's orcish heritage was a sensitive topic, but he was angry. He saw T'kocht was shocked and pained by his words. T'kocht shook his head and clenched his fists causing his knuckles to pale.

"Can't you hear yourself. I only wanted to help because I care about you, because I love you. I just hope you figure it out before you really mess up." His face flushed, the deep red of blood rushing up darkened his cheeks. T'kocht turned around and stormed out of the room.

Remington moved to go after him but decided against it. They both needed time to cool off. T'kocht was wrong, this was purely business, he never tortured the women, never destroyed them bit by bit until they were nothing. No, it was simple deception for profit. He found no joy in the scheme. At least that is what he kept telling himself for the rest of the night.

22

The next day Remington left for town early in the morning. He had not slept at all that night, haunted by the words said in the heat of anger. He returned to the bar for an early morning drink, he needed it. As he stared into his drink, the town around him began to awaken. He felt someone was staring at him. Turning around he saw Maeve watching him, one eyebrow raised and a sly smile gracing her mouth.

"Drinking already? You sure like to get an early start to the fun. Move over, it's never fun drinking alone." Maeve moved to sit next to him and ordered a drink herself.

"Rough night," Remington responded, "doesn't matter now that you are here though." He put on his most dashing smile causing her to blush.

They finished their drinks before Maeve began their tour of the island. Throughout the day, he asked her many questions about herself. Each one designed to break down her guard, to build the trust that was needed for a Selkie to show another their skin.

It did not take long for her to talk about herself, and her life as a Selkie. He was surprised by her confidence, not even attempting to hide her identity and who she was. Remington was content to listen and stay close, answer her few questions curtly and vaguely, before redirecting the talk back to her. It was not difficult to do, and she grasped at any inch he gave.

Contrary to what Remington initially thought, this conquest was not as easy as expected. Two weeks had passed, with no signs of seeing the prize. While she shared much about herself, he found her to be quite protective of her identity. Though he would occasionally press to see it, she always denied him sight of her seal skin.

Though Remington was frustrated by her stubbornness, he also found himself hoping she wouldn't relent. He had grown fond of her company. He smiled at the sound of her voice, the salty smell of her hair, and the sight of her brilliant teal and gold eyes. He attempted to shut down these thoughts to no avail, they always returned.

Remington knew the crew agreed to one month on this island, to relax, to escape reality before returning to the Prime Realm. Yet, deep within him, he wanted more time. He wanted to talk to T'kocht, to get the truth from his friend on what he should do, but they were not talking. In fact, T'kocht and Remington had not talked since their fight two weeks ago. There had been many times when both would look at each other, wanting to make amends, but neither willing to forgive the other yet.

The next weeks flew by for Remington as he spent more and more time with Maeve. Each day that passed he felt his attachment toward Maeve grow stronger and stronger. Each day that passed he buried his feelings. He could not let himself fall again. Each time he felt his heart flutter, his mind went back to that fateful day at the fountain. If he let himself feel, all he would get is pain and he feared it would kill him. But no matter how hard he tried, he could feel himself falling and he hated himself for it.

On Remington's final day on Vauxquct, he once again met Maeve on the island. He was preparing to tell her he was leaving, that he couldn't stay. He saw her running towards him, shining bright as ever and she jumped into his arms in her normal fashion of greeting him. He could put off telling her until later, why should he ruin a perfectly good day.

Maeve looked like she was nervous, debating something in her mind. Remington rubbed her arm, trying to give her comfort for whatever was eating at her. Eventually she made up her mind. "Remington," she whispered looking him in the eye, "I have something I want to show you. Follow me?"

Remington gave her a comforting smile and took her hand, "Of course."

He let her lead him through the town towards an area of the island they had not been to before. She kept looking back toward him as if to make sure he was still there. Each time he gave her hand a tight squeeze in response. A few hours later they crested a small hill, where Remington saw a small hut hidden away on the edge of the beach.

"This is my home," Maeve stated. "That's not what I want to show you though."

Remington pulled her hand up to his mouth and kissed it before following her down to the beach. As they walked along the sand, Maeve suddenly stopped in front of a small boulder. She stooped down and began pushing away the sand, revealing a wooden chest that was buried beneath. She lifted it up, setting it on the beach. From around her neck, she pulled out a small key and inserted it into the lock. She watched his reaction as the chest opened up to reveal a carefully folded seal skin.

Remington could not help but let out a nervous laughter. On the last day of all days, she decides to show it to him. After a month of getting to know her, of caring for her. He realized he was hoping she would never show him, that he could just leave her with the fleeting memory of the man from out of town. He did not know if he could complete the mission now nor if he should.

He saw concern wash over her at his reaction and he quickly regained control over himself. "So, this is who you are? Thank you, for sharing this side of you, it only adds to your perfection."

"It's not something I share lightly," Maeve said quietly, "but I trust you, and I want you to see. Many people look at me differently when they learn of what I am, especially non-fey creatures. They look at me like I am some mystical creature that should be in a museum. I am a person, who happens to be able to become a seal. I wish more would see past my skin, like you have. Do you want to see my real form? I actually usually prefer to be in seal form."

Her voice began to rise into a passionate speech by the end, heated by the discrimination she felt in the past. Each word that she said felt like a dagger in Remington's chest. *No, you shouldn't trust me. I am exactly like the others. Why did it have to be you?* These thoughts raced through his head, the guilt settling deeper and deeper within him. The only reason he talked to her was because she was a Selkie, but how could he ever tell her that.

Before Remington could answer her question, she was already running towards the water. When the first wave washed over her feet, he watched as the water seemed to almost swirl around her and in her place a seal splashed down into the water. He smiled as he watched her play in the waves, gracefully flying through the water and soaking up the sun. Eventually with enough unspoken coaxing, she convinced Remington to join her in the water. He noticed the seal look at the scar that still marked his chest but was thankful when she quickly looked back at him.

They spent the entire day on the beach in each other's company. Maeve was in her seal form for most of it, only occasionally returning to her human form when she wanted to speak. Remington tried to push back the thoughts of what tomorrow may bring, and how he was going to break it to her. Each time he tried the words would not appear. Perhaps it would be easier to not say anything at all.

Though the sky never changed in the Feylands, they knew the day was ending. Remington laid on the beach wide awake with Maeve curled into his chest fast asleep. He was jealous of how peaceful she looked in her sleep, when so much turmoil ran in his mind. The Fey's Fortune was set to leave the island in just 5 hours, and it was at least 3 hours to get back to it. He would have to leave soon.

Remington looked at the seal skin draped over her body as if she were using it as a blanket. He would never return to this island, he thought. His life was on the Prime Realm where he could enjoy early retirement from the riches gained in this gamble. But what if he retired here? What if he handed control of the Fey's Fortune to T'kocht and stayed on this beach with Maeve forever?

The idea made him happy, he would give anything to be able to just run away. Remington knew he could not though. Eventually she would learn of his past. She would find out about the 5 other Selkies who he stripped of their identity, and she would never forgive him. He did not deserve her; he was too broken. He had only known the poison drip of Areliel's affections, and he feared he would inflict the same pain onto Maeve. He had to go.

He slowly stood up taking extra care to not wake her. He watched her for what felt like an eternity before making his decision. If he was to leave, he should complete the mission, that is what he came here to do. At least, then Maeve would believe that maybe none of this was real, and he was just another terrible human. Then she could move on from him, though he took a piece of her with him. She would eventually live on, continue her life on this piece of paradise. Why should he care if she hated him, as he told T'kocht, this was only business. Business that paid.

He lifted the skin from her shoulders and placed it into his bag before walking away, not daring to look back. It was a long walk back to his ship and he would have to make it alone.

23

Remington returned to his ship 3 hours later. It was still the early hours of the morning and most of the crew was asleep. He searched for T'kocht who would be one of the first ones up to prepare for leaving and found him working on undoing some of the ties.

Remington did not say anything, but motioned T'kocht to follow him into the captain's quarters. When the two were alone, Remington took the skin out of his bag and said, "You were right. I messed up. I am no different from her. I'm sorry." He could feel his voice choking up, tears filling his eyes as the feelings he held back on his walk were released. Remington slid to sit on the floor.

T'kocht was quiet for a while, trying to figure out what to say. He finally approached Remington putting his arm around Remington's shoulder. "No you are not. I was wrong to say those things and reopen that wound. But look we got another. We can live like kings."

Remington looked over at T'kocht and shook his head. "Maybe the others, but not me. How could I go living like a king knowing how completely I betrayed her. How completely I betrayed myself."

T'kocht leaned back. He looked very confused at Remington and picked the skin off the ground to examine it. "You didn't feel this way about the others. What's different about this one? Remember it's just business."

"Maybe initially it was," Remington respond, falling backwards until he was sprawled out on the floor, "but I messed up. You should have seen her eyes as teal as the ocean itself and with a fierceness stronger than any summer storm. She had so much life in her and she was so youthful and playful in the waves. I took all of that from her."

"So, you fell in love. You know, I'd miss you and Nicky would probably hunt you down, but you could stay. You don't have to do this." T'kocht suggested, joining Remington in staring at the ceiling. They could hear the rest of the crew waking up now and readying the boat for takeoff.

"No, I do. Like you said, this is just business. It's my fault for being weak, I have to grow stronger. I cannot let my emotions keep running unchecked, it will only be my undoing. Even if I did stay, she would find out about my past, and never forgive me. So, I might as well leave with my family and make a few gold from it. Let's head home."

Remington could feel the walls building in his mind, to block out the thoughts of Maeve, to block out the troubles of his past, and to strengthen his defenses for the future. A wall like that though came with its own faults and try as he may, there were still many cracks.

As he stepped out onto the deck, he barred his teeth in a large grin shouting, "Yet another victory for those who find their fortune in the Feylands!" He hoisted the skin into the air for all to see.

The crew that was on board turned to look and started cheering upon seeing the new bounty. Remington put it away into his bag with the rest of the items and the Fey's Fortune made sail, leaving the island of Vauxquet for the last time. Remington did not turn to watch the shoreline disappear over the horizon, his sight was set only on his future.

Remington had planned to sail 3 days to the nearest lay line intersection of arcane energy to make the jump back. However, on the second day of their journey, the Fey's Fortune was overrun by a powerful storm. The torrential rain and hurricane like winds came out of nowhere, forming over perfectly clear skies mere seconds before. Remington and the crew fought against the raging winds to no use. The ship was being pulled by the winds and the current as if they were willed by something or someone.

Eventually, Remington spotted what he believed the storm was bringing them to. He saw a large tower extending upwards from a small island surrounded by sheer cliffs. The tower itself rose upwards of 200 feet into the air. The stonework that created the walls were well worn by the pounding rains and salty air. Large groupings of moss, mollusks, and seaweed hung from sides seeming as though the tower rose from the depths of the ocean. The storm that was bringing them there and growing strong was spiraling around the pinnacle of the tower. Someone had summoned it.

The currents maneuvered the Fey's Fortune to within a stone's toss of the cliffs. Remington and the crew tried desperately to avoid collision and escape the storm. However as if by command the ship stopped just short of disaster remaining still and calm while the sea around them bashed against the rocks.

Remington took this moment of calmness to regather the crew and try to formulate a plan to get out of the situation. There were discussions of abandoning ship, which Remington refused with a passion before Nicky arrived from her duties below deck. Her swearing was so loud it could be heard well over the howling winds. He watched as she ran up, a look of terror in her eye.

"Oh no this is not good," she started staring up at the tower. "Don't any of you recognize what this is? Am I the only person who cared to read up on anything? That tower there is the River King's Tower and this storm means he is angry, most likely at us."

"So how do we get out of this?" Remington asked, looking for any escape for his crew.

"You hope he is willing to talk or forget." Nicky was interrupted by a large splashing sound as water erupted from the stern of the ship. It moved deliberately as the water formed itself into a set of stairs leading up into the tower.

Remington approached the stairs and tested out the first step, finding it able to hold his body weight. He turned around and shouted, "T'kocht, Nicky, and Rinva with me. The rest of you, don't worry I will get us out of this. I always do." Holding his head high Remington began the ascension up the stairs into the tower.

As the four of them reached the top of the stairs, drenched by the unrelenting rain, part of the wall of the smooth tower opened up before them. The water that formed the staircase suddenly rushed underneath of them dragging them deep into the tower. Remington struggled to breath each time his head was forced beneath the river, which it almost felt as though the water was doing purposefully.

After a few minutes of being dragged in circles, Remington felt the water drop out from underneath him and he plunged into a pool below. He felt the impact of the other three shortly after and they made for the first sign of dry land which was not too far away. As Remington pulled himself out of the water, he finally took a moment to gather his surroundings. All around this room were various pools of water with currents of water shooting out and away or flowing into the pools like three dimensional rivers. More of the moss and mollusks were growing on the inside of the tower and he could hear the clicking of crustaceans somewhere nearby.

Floating above one of the pools, held aloft by a whirlpool stood a very large humanoid creature. His long hair whipped in the wind, a deep cerulean that ended in pure white giving the impression of waves crashing over his shoulders. From beneath his hair long pointed ears extended far from his face. His eyes were pure white with no pupil to be seen but bearing an anger stronger than Remington had ever seen before. The man's armor was made from wrapped seaweed embezzled with various marine life and he wielded a large trident, more magnificent than that owned by the Pirate King.

Remington stared at this fey creature. The power that surrounded the creature told Remington this must be the River King. Remington walked towards the swirling mass of water calling out, "I believe my crew and I have unfortunately been caught in your storm. We are just trying to make our way home."

The swirling whirlpool rushed towards Remington before halting abruptly in front of him. The water dropped from the River King allowing him to tower over Remington standing at over 9 feet tall. "Do you not show respect for the King of this realm as you have disrespected his subjects? I see all that occurs within my realm, did you think you would pass unseen?"

Remington stared up meeting his eyes, not daring to look away. "I am unsure of what you speak," stated Remington his voice unfaltering. "We have been traveling your lands and enjoying the gifts it has to offer."

Remington felt the winds inside the chambers strengthen to a point of almost blowing him off balance. The River King rushed forward, placing himself within inches of Remington. "Do not toy with me mortal. You have taken the identities from my people, stealing who they are. I have seen you in my lands before, causing minor infractions that I could overlook. I know you have seen the waters of life and rejected them."

Remington swallowed hard as he refused to move. The River King was not one to be lied to, he must bargain his way out. "You are right," began Remington, "I have walked away from the Fountain of Youth, for the price was too much to pay. But you are wrong about what I have done. A man's identity is what is inside, what they feel.

I was shown a simple trinket that I relieved from them. They are still who they were before, it is not my fault they were too naive to let it out of their sight."

Remington immediately knew this was the wrong thing to say. He could feel his lungs filling with water, his vision beginning to darken as he struggled to breath and dropped to the floor. The River King's voice echoed through his ears, "Is the air you breathe a simple trinket? You have shown me disrespect that should not be forgiven, so why should I not let the water continue to fill the lungs of you and your kin?"

The water suddenly emptied from his chest, as Remington was finally able to cough the water out. He could hear the rest of his party also coughing fluids from their chests. He rose to one knee still too weak to fully stand. He needed to change tactics. "Apologies, I should have known better." He turned to look back at his friends who were still struggling. "If there is anyone to be punished, punish me alone. The rest of my crew were just following orders. I should not be forgiven; I know what those skins meant to them and I took them anyways without regret. Let them go home and place it on me."

Remington could hear the start of protests from behind him but held up his hand to silence them. They could go home, and he would be freed from his pain. As he braced himself for whatever punishment may come, a laughter erupted that sounded like the crushing of waves and looked up to see the River King laughing. The sudden shift in emotion was jarring. Remington felt himself being lifted from the ground by the water to face the River King.

"No, I see your pain. You feel a deep guilt and cannot take that guilt off of your people. Though I commend you for trying to protect them, they shall be punished as well. Very well then, I will allow you to return to your home, but I shall steal a piece of you as well. The guilt you will carry with you forever as a chain anchoring you to the depths of your own despair."

Remington felt his body freeze unable to move. He felt a lump form in his chest and move its way up his throat. He began to gag as it reached the back of his mouth but still his body refused to move. Remington watched in horror as a small ball of glowing light emerged from his mouth floating away from him toward the River King. The River King gripped the small ball between his fingers before absorbing it into his body.

"I release you now, holding a piece of your soul. You and your crew will never find relief from the constant want of something more, holding a greed that will never be satisfied. The skin that you stole be bound to you as a reminder of the pain it caused you and others. I grow tired of those like you who come and meddle so now you shall do the same. Return now to your lands and bring chaos to the seas as such the world has never seen before. I grant you aid to bring destruction to the world, use this power to do my will."

Remington felt the water surrounding him flow into his skin and a magical strength infuse into his veins. The remaining water lowered him onto the tower floor where Remington could not find the strength to stand. The River King continued, "If you do not follow my will, be warned for I will bring about a punishment worse than I have already provided. Now you and your people are banished from this plane, never to return. I will know and I will find you."

As the River King finished, Remington did not have time to react before water rushed all around him sending him flying out of the tower towards his ship. He landed hard against the rough wooden deck, the other members landing on top of him shortly after. The Fey's Fortune began spinning, trapped in a whirlpool. Soon the water was above the mast and the ship fell beneath the waves taking her crew with her.

24

The bright sunlight pierced Remington's eyelids as he lay on the deck of his ship. He reached for his forehead to itch and found his fingers running over what felt like rough scales. He could feel his clothing soaking wet and he shot upright, remembering the events mere seconds ago. As he opened his eyes, he stood up in horror at the sight around him. The once beautiful ship that he prided himself in keeping in pristine order was now covered in mosses and mollusks. The sails and planks were in disarray and barely holding together. His crew as they slowly started waking up seemed to be in the same condition. Some had scales on their skin, others had claws growing from their arms.

Remington thought he heard his name being called out, but the sound coming into his right ear sounded muffled. He turned around to find T'kocht staring at him. Remington could see short tentacles growing from T'kocht's chin and let out and involuntary gasp. His breathing was quickening as he took in the scene around him. This was all his fault.

Remington scrambled to the helm. He needed to talk to his crew, they deserved answers. He let out a sharp whistle to get their attention which he received immediately. Remington could see the fear and confusion on their face and the guilt began to wash over him. They deserved the truth.

"Attention!" he cried out. "I know you are confused, frightened, maybe angry, I understand. We set out on a mission that was high risk, that if we were able to pull off would have made us rich beyond our dreams. However, I got greedy. I made the decision to go after one more skin, one more payment. If we had left then, we might have been safe, we might have made it back. Instead, our exploits were discovered by the Fey Lord, the River King. I was unsuccessful in efforts to escape. He threatened you and suggested death, however he showed mercy. Instead, he placed his mark upon all of us, as a reminder of what took place. In exchange for our lives, the River King now holds a piece of my soul, and I must create chaos on this plane to repent for my actions."

Remington paused for a moment, still processing that once again he was a servant forced to do the will of another. He took a deep breath and continued, "I accept full responsibility for this failure. I am not fit to be your captain, and I understand if you want your revenge. I would too. I relinquish my position."

Murmurs spread through the crew though many were quiet. No one was quite sure what they were to do, and many were still processing what was said. The silence was broken by Nicky. She jumped atop a large barrel to gain attention, "Who amongst you disagreed with this plan? This ship has always been run under if someone disagrees, you speak up. We work as a team, right?"

A few cheers of agreement erupted from the crowd. "We all boarded this ship for our own reasons, some because we had nowhere else to go, some because we were rejected by our own people. We all came aboard because we said down with the rules!" Again, cheers were yelled, this time louder than before.

"We may have failed on our quest by getting caught, but Captain Darkwalker was brave enough to stare into the face of a Fey Lord and give us our lives at the cost of his. He has not once left any of us behind, do we abandon our captain now? After everything he has done for us? We are pirates because we want chaos. So let us bring chaos."

The crew roared with support shouting "Chaos for Captain Darkwalker!" Remington looked over towards Nicky, giving her a thanking nod. She was right and he needed to take his place as their leader. He could not abandon them to face this new curse. The crew broke out some bottles of rum in celebration, but it did not last long. Many spat out their first sip, others tried to shoot their way through it, but all found no comfort in the bottle. The rum tasted of salty water and there was no warmth flowing through their bodies. Over the next few hours they discovered that food did nothing to satiate their hunger, liquids did nothing to quench their thirst, and they were left always wanting more.

Remington eventually found a mirror to see the oceanic growth now peppering his face. He attempted to peel off the starfish that was dulling his hearing in his right ear, but it felt as though he was ripping part of his body off with it and had to stop. There was no getting rid of this mark now. He found a tattoo between his shoulder blades, an upside-down triangle with three curved lines extending from the base in a circular arc. It felt cold to the touch.

The confusion on board was broken by a distraction when a ship was spotted up ahead. It was flying the flag of the Pirate King. As Remington debated what to do, the scene around him faded until he was surrounded by darkness. He frantically looked around trying to see anything.

"Remington." A familiar voice came from behind causing him to freeze in his tracks. He very slowly turned around to confirm the voice and there standing in the void was Captain Areliel Atrigul. Her abdomen was still covered in blood and her face was pale and lifeless, though she still had her possessive smile.

"I thought this was the best way to communicate with you, someone you know very well," she said. "Or do you prefer this form?" The image of Areliel shifted until Maeve stood before him. Remington began to back away at the sight of her, the pain still fresh and worsening as old wounds were torn open. He realized this must be the River King playing his tricks. "No? Very well then," and the figure was once again Areliel.

"Now that you are back where you belong, it's time to start working off your side of the deal. Bring chaos to the seas, and what better way to bring chaos than to spread fear. And what do mortals fear most? As your good lover here knows, it's death. Bring it to others or I will bring something worse than that to you and your crew. Have fun."

Remington blinked and he was once again on the deck of his ship. He was breathing heavily, and his legs felt weak. A hand fell on his shoulder, and he turned to see T'kocht standing by his side glancing at him with a questioning look. Remington only nodded to indicate he was okay. Quickly composing himself, Remington bellowed out, "Prepare to attack, turn starboard and make for the enemy ship. Let's make this quick."

The crew cheered and rushed to their places. Remington took his place at the helm and they began their pursuit. When they were within range, Remington gave the order to begin firing cannons. Though the other ship attempted to defend itself, it was much smaller than the Fey's Fortune. Eventually, a solid hit from a cannon ball took out the enemy's sails, causing them to raise a white flag in surrender. The Fey's Fortune suffered minimal damage, with a few cannon shots through the hull.

Remington maneuvered the ship to pull up alongside their target before his crew lowered a plank to cross over. They waited for Remington to cross first as they always did. As he stepped down onto the ship, he felt a cold wind blow over his shoulder and the crew members before him began to quake with fear. He could see the captain of the ship was amongst them and Remington approached.

The captain seemed to shrink as Remington approached, as though he was absolutely terrified of Remington. "Show me your ledger. What do you have on this boat that could interest me?"

The man shook and tentatively asked, "Who are you? Your ship arose from the depths from nowhere and her crew with it. Please, we do not have much but take what you need and let us go."

Remington looked back over his shoulder at his crew. They truly were a terror to behold as they wove their way through the opposing ranks. "Go search below deck, take whatever you find and bring it aboard," Remington ordered. His crew immediately went into action grabbing what they could as Remington continued to circle around the surrendered crew, thinking about his vision.

After 15 minutes, his crew had finished and were awaiting Remington's next command. Remington once again approached the captain who stood up to meet him. In a calm but loud voice Remington said, "Kill all but one."

He could hear the hesitation in his crew behind him. He has never given an order like that before. They have killed men in the heat of battle, but if someone surrendered, he always let them go. He heard T'kocht question him, "Captain?"

"I said kill all but one. Now!" Remington took his sword and sliced through the captain in front of him. The man's body dropped like a stone as his blood soaked into the deck. The thud was like a bell to kick off the fight. Many scrambled to protect themselves or jump overboard to avoid the conflict. Remington's crew was much more skilled than the small crew of this ship; they did not stand a chance. T'kocht refused to fight.

Remington saw the look of judgement on T'kocht's face as he stayed away from the battle. He walked up and without saying a word, grabbed the pistol from T'kocht's hands. One by one he took out the sailors that had attempted to escape into the ocean, leaving the waters a dark red.

Remington saw many of his crew hesitating as their opponents begged for their lives, unarmed. Each time, Remington would end it when his crew could not. By the end, Remington had taken the lives of 20 of the original 35 crew members until there was only one still alive.

He was a young man, no more than 20 years of age, soaked in the blood of his comrades around him. Remington approached, wiping the blood off of the Fortune Teller before sheathing it. He knelt down before the man and grabbed his jaw forcing the man to look at him. Remington could see his wide pupils trying desperately to look anywhere else.

"What's your name son?" Remington asked, brushing some hair out of the boy's face.

"T-t-thomas," he stuttered out. Thomas was shaking hard, Remington's hand around his jaw the only thing keeping him still.

"Well Thomas," Remington said, "Congratulations, you get to live. I will let you take one of the row boats with a bit of water and hopefully you can find your way to shore or another boat. If you happen to survive this journey, let all those who will listen know that a new monster has awoken from the deep. No one is safe."

He pushed Thomas away and stood up. "Set the rest on fire, it is no longer needed." Thomas quickly scrambled away to the nearest stocked rowboat and plummeted into the water before desperately rowing away as the crew of the Fey's Fortune began to light the ship on fire.

Remington walked across the plank where T'kocht was awaiting him, arms crossed. T'kocht ripped his pistol back and hooked into his belt. "What the fuck was that Remi?" T'kocht did not even attempt to keep a level voice, allowing the whole crew to hear. They stopped to listen as the now flaming ship drifted away, the crackle fueling the flames of T'kocht's anger.

Remington looked at T'kocht then shifted his gaze to the rest of his crew who were all anxiously watching him, awaiting his response. He could clearly feel the blood of those men soaking through his clothes and he fought the image of Areliel's blood soaking into him. Remington moved to the edge of the boat so he could get a clearer view of his crew. As he climbed onto the rails of the ship, it was a fearsome scene of Remington standing tall and bloodied, the burning ship of his enemies behind him.

"Today was just a glimpse at what our new lives will be. I was told to cause chaos on the sea, to instill terror to those who encounter our sails. I was told to be a harbinger of death. Do not think for one second, one second, that I enjoyed what just went down." He looked toward T'kocht, meeting his gaze. He could see T'kocht still did not approve.

"I know many of you do not approve and despise me and my actions right now. Remember that at any point you are welcome to disembark from my leadership. Before you condemn me as an unnecessary monster, know that if I do not follow orders, if we do not follow orders, then the pain and fear we inflicted today would be brought upon us, but without the merciful end of death."

This statement caused a shift in tone amongst the crew. Many began to look frightened, and even T'kocht dropped his arms down to his side. Remington continued, "We are a cursed crew, created and shaped to be demons that haunt the seas. But we should not despair, for this will open opportunities for us. We may face an unknown future of violence and fear, but we only need to look next to us for hope, strength, and power. No longer must we answer to the bullshit lawfulness of the Pirate King. We run the seas now, as a family, and we will navigate this nightmare together."

Remington never raised his voice; he did not want this to be a motivational rally. He just wanted to tell them the truth, for them to know how this ship must be run. As he stepped down, many of the crew gave him nods of support or patted his shoulder. They stood with him, they understood. He approached T'kocht, whose eyes never drifted away from Remington. T'kocht gave him a smile before pulling him into an embrace. "We have navigated nightmares before," T'kocht whispered, "we will find our way home from this one too."

Remington walked to the helm and ran his hands along the wheel. Looking out over the deck to the open seas, Remington smiled. "To Tortuga."

25

As the months wore on, Remington and his crew continued to be merciless terrors of the sea. Each victory after the last numbed them to the monsters that they were becoming, and many began to enjoy it. Rumors of the undead captain and his ship began to spread far and wide. Sailors were warned to avoid the Fey's Fortune, lest they want to meet an unfortunate end themselves.

Remington found himself to be a source of chaos on the seas, giving into the monster he felt inside himself. For too long there had been rules in the pirate community on who to plunder and rules of surrender. Under Remington's reign, there were no rules except for one: leave none alive. Occasionally, Remington would choose a crew member to spare, leaving them adrift at sea to spread the tales of their terror. Other pirates began to admire this mythical monster they had nicknamed "The Drowned Captain" and followed his lead. They abandoned the Pirate King in favor of a more lawless way of life that Remington flaunted.

Tales of the Fey's Fortune eventually reached the ears of the Pirate King who did not take Remington's insubordination lightly. The Pirate King placed a large bounty on Remington's head and began a campaign to lessen the fear that Remington had dripped into his ranks. Remington knew knowledge of who the "Drowned

Captain" was would lessen the effects of his mission. He kept his eyes and ears open, punishing any who mention the name Remington, and keeping himself hidden only coming ashore under the cover of darkness. It only took a few months before the name Remington dropped out of existence; people too afraid to even whisper it in the shadows less he might hear. The only one outside of his crew who still used his name was the Pirate King, who refused to acknowledge the Drowned Captain.

Many ships hunted for the Drowned Captain, looking to cash in on the massive reward offered by the Pirate King. Those that found themselves lucky enough to find him, did not think themselves lucky for long. Remington and his crew were very skilled, and their powers granted to them by the River King grew day by day. He made sure that the Pirate King knew about each and every failure by sending the head of the captains back to the Pirate King. This only infuriated the Pirate King even more.

One captain sent knew about Remington's relationship with Elianne and threatened to find her in Rivenport if Remington did not come to meet her and surrender. They say Remington dragged this captain behind his boat for 5 days, making sure to keep her barely alive as the sharks that followed slowly ate away at her body. Only half of her was returned to the Pirate King and after that no one dared go near Elianne.

The ever-growing group of supporters began calling themselves The Nautilus. They made their base on Tortuga where the Pirate King had the weakest hold of the Northern Keys. The lawlessness that took root there created rising tensions between the Saxe Empire and the Pirate King, who held an unofficial peace treaty for over 6 years. Many even began to advocate for the Drowned Captain to overthrow the Pirate King. Remington always scoffed at that. He did not care to get involved with the politics of the seas.

During the next 3 years Remington's crew changed as well. They began to find enjoyment in the pain, the killings, the chaos. They grew numb to the constant feeling of thirst and hunger, though many were still disappointed that they could not feel the effects of alcohol anymore. Remington, however, could never find the enjoyment, though he became indifferent to the world around him. He let the Drowned Captain, the monster whose mask he wore, have all the fun.

The River King continued to plague him during the night with terrible visions. The nightmares rotated in their themes but most nights he relived a twisted version of the death of Areliel or the last night on the beach with Maeve. On occasion, the River King would surprise him, reliving the death of Brend. Remington often avoided sleep, staying up for upwards of 60 hours before T'kocht finally forced him to get sleep. When he did sleep, it was never satisfying and he often woke up screaming or crying, an intense pain radiating through his body. Not even T'kocht knew of the struggles that Remington went through at night. Remington went to great lengths to not show his suffering to his crew. He was content to know that those memories would be locked away in the Feylands, a place he would never return to.

These visions now were no longer memories. Remington could only stare at the crystal ball in his lap, the object that confirmed his fear that Maeve was now here, and he could have to face her.

T'kocht knelt down next to Remington, but Remington quickly scrambled up. He shoved the crystal ball back into the bag and threw it into its hold in the floorboards. "It doesn't matter," Remington started, his words coming out faster than he wanted. "It's not like she is going to find me. No one out there is dumb enough to tell her where to find me or take her to me. I have made sure of that. Go back ashore and enjoy your time. We are in no rush to leave."

T'kocht looked at Remington with concern. He opened his mouth to say something, then thought better of it. Instead, he gave

Remington a squeeze on the shoulder before turning to leave. He gave one last look over his shoulder before exiting Remington's quarters.

Remington paced the room, anxiety pulsing through his veins. He pulled the knife out of his painting and threw it as hard as he could back at it. With the precision of years of practice, it stuck right back into the same spot, but it did not help relieve the stress. The room felt small and restricting, he needed fresh air. Running full speed out of the room, Remington flew across the deck before diving over the railings.

Before he reached the water, Remington felt his body begin to shift as the selkie skin activated and he transformed into a magnificent seal. He felt the cool water rush over him and relax the muscles in his body. The open waters gave him the freedom he looked for, the fresh air clearing his mind. He made a running start to leap out of the waters to splash down, the thrill of the free fall embracing the adrenaline that was already pumping.

He rose to the surface to try to feel the warmth on his skin and saw T'kocht watching him from the pier. He could hear the faint echoes of T'kocht's joyful laughter. Remington pretended like he did not notice him there, he did not mind. But as he floated in the waves, his mind began to drift back to Maeve. He saw her playing in the waves like he was. He heard his own laughter as T'kocht's reached his ears. He saw her fiery eyes staring into his as the colors of the Feylands danced around her hair.

He felt himself sinking beneath the surface. She would never dance in the waves while he existed, while he carried her with him. He wanted to return it to her and often thought about it, but he never would be able to. His punishment glued it to him as though it was part of his body as a forever reminder of his cruelty.

Remington's thoughts turned towards his curse. He constantly thought of ways he could get out of it, but each idea was scratched.

Early on, he attempted to fulfill his name as the Drowned Captain and sunk beneath the waves. As the darkness began to fill his sight, he once again saw the River King appear before him. "Don't think you can get away that easily," the River King said, his voice coming through as Maeve's. "The curse upon you does not end with your death. Could you really abandon your crew like that? Are you as cowardly as you are cruel?" Remington suddenly felt air rush into his lungs though he was still sinking beneath the waves. He swam back to the surface and climbed aboard before anyone realized he was gone.

As he felt the sand touch his back, his mind was quickly brought back to his reality. He saw a fish swim right in front of his face, oblivious to the danger it was in if he was a true seal. Remington continued sitting on the seafloor for a long time, breathing the water as easily as the air. Another gift from the River King. He could see the sky darkening above him and decided it was time to return to his ship. Remington swam back up and returned into his human form before climbing aboard in preparation for what would probably be another sleepless night.

26

Though Remington searched for more information on where Maeve was heading, it would not be until a month and a half later when news of her reached him. They had been sailing the oceans just off the coast of Rivenport when Remington received a message from Elianne. He had given her a stone the last time he saw her in Rivenport that allowed her to telepathically send him a short message if trouble was stirring. It was extra precaution after she was threatened by the Pirate King.

Her voice was calm and soothing as it always was, but the message she bore was anything but. "A young woman stopped by," she said. "It was Maeve, she is asking about you, looking for you. I denied any relation as you asked. Be careful Remington, she seeks revenge."

Remington froze in his steps as the voice came to him, the name Maeve ringing through his mind. He mentally responded to the message, "Good, keep it secret. I don't want you to get hurt from my actions. We are just outside of Rivenport, I am coming now. Don't look for her."

Panic was beginning to set in as Remington wondered how Maeve had found Elianne and if she knew of their connection. Elianne was like a mother to him, and he would not see her tangled in the mess he had gotten himself into. In a moment of distress, he activated another one of his powers, an ability to message whomever he liked in the same way as Elianne's stone. He sent a message to Maeve.

"Stop, don't play games with me," was all that he said. He hoped the aggression in his voice, the shock of hearing his voice unexpectedly would be enough to get her to leave him alone. The voice that answered cut deep into him like a knife, "This is not a game." Her voice was angry and fiery, filled with a determination that Remington could see as if she were right in front of him.

Remington realized his mistake in sending the message. This would confirm for Maeve that he knew Elianne and that she was important to him. Racing to the helm he shouted to his crew, "Lower the sails, and make haste to Rivenport. Quickly!"

He began turning the wheel to steer the ship east when T'kocht flew up the steps to the helm. "What's wrong, why are we going to Rivenport? It's dangerous going that close to Empire land."

"Maeve found Elianne. I need to make sure she is safe. My nightmares should not haunt her as well."

T'kocht's face paled, "You don't really think Maeve would harm Ma? From all I have heard, I would not picture her as violent."

"I don't know what she would do," Remington responded. "Elianne said Maeve was angry, seeking vengeance. She has enough spirit that she would do anything to take back what is hers. I just need to make sure."

T'kocht only nodded his head before leaving Remington to his business. They were only 2 days from Rivenport, he only hoped they were not too late. He sent Elianne messages every now and then to make sure she was okay, and though she swore she was, Remington wanted to see for himself.

On their second day of travel, T'kocht spotted a Saxe Empire naval ship just off of starboard. Remington, feeling anxious himself and knowing his crew had not enjoyed a good raid in a while, made the decision to stop. He and the crew began to move into their positions as an abandoned ship, with Remington and 5 others taking to their seal forms in preparation for the surprise.

They waited for thirty minutes before the first signs of life began boarding the Fey's Fortune. A few privates climbed over the deck and began looking around. Remington chuckled to himself. This would be an easy assault, the Empire ship sending people over slowly one by one until they were outnumbered. His planning was halted as the final private climbed aboard. Her brown hair braided down the side reflected the all too familiar teal colors. Her loud cheerful voice filling the air as she looked directly at him. He could see the gears turning in her head as she processed the seal in front of her. He could not help but think how beautiful she looked in the sunlight, the salty air giving her dark skin an angelic glow.

He then remembered that T'kocht was in the crow's nest, taking aim at these visitors, waiting for a signal. Remington quickly slapped his tail indicating T'kocht to stand down and not fire. Unsure of what he wanted to do, Remington rolled over to better see her. As she turned towards one of her companions, Remington returned to his human shape saying, "Halt, don't attack."

The silence was deafening as Maeve froze in place slowly turning to the all too familiar voice. They stared into each other's eyes as his crew slowly emerged from their hiding places confused by his command. He could see her processing the situation and the recognition slowly building. He stepped forward saying, "Hello, Maeve."

He watched as her look of shock dissolved into uncontrollable anger as she yelled out, "You are wearing it!?" This opened the flood gates to a wide variety of insults and death threats as every bad thought she had began flowing out. Remington attempted to maintain a stoic outward appearance, but each flurry of words felt like a knife being stabbed in the chest. He did not say anything for a while, letting her say what she will. Remington faintly heard

Nicky ask, "Want me to take care of her, Captain?" He only shook his head; this was something that he needed to deal with.

His attention was brought away from Maeve when he heard one of her companions speak, addressing T'kocht who had returned to the deck by name. It was the younger boy that he had seen in his crystal ball. T'kocht himself seemed confused as to how this boy could know his name. Remington turned to the group, he wanted to talk, but not in front of his crew. "Welcome aboard the Fey's Fortune. Why don't all of you come into my office and we can talk like civilized people. T'kocht, come with me."

The group of strangers looking around at the crew surrounding them began to follow Remington into his office. As T'kocht was the last to enter, he closed the door behind them, separating them from the rest of the crew. Remington took a moment to look over this motley crew that Maeve seemed to be traveling with. Creatures of all shapes and sizes ranging from a small gnomish fellow to a tall goliath towering at close to 8 feet tall. All of them dressed in Saxe Empire naval uniforms. He could not imagine Maeve joining the army, it must be a disguise.

He turned toward Maeve, who for a moment had quieted down taking in the office around her. "What do you want Maeve?" he asked, already knowing the answer.

"What do I want? Are you kidding me?" Maeve responded with force, the flames of anger never dying down. "I want my skin back what did you think I want a tea party? You stole it from me, now give it back."

Remington sighed. He couldn't give it back, not with the curse that bound him to it. "I can't," he said firmly, "if that is all I suggest you leave this ship now and be thankful that the Drowned Captain showed mercy today for it does not happen often." He could feel the panic rising inside, though the outside remained stoic. He needed her to leave, before he did anything he would regret.

"You can't?" she asked incredulously. "What do you mean you can't? Or do you mean you don't want to. Of course, you would just keep it and not even sell it just to rub salt into the wound. I had hoped you at least took it for money, but no, you are just an ass. No you are worse than an ass, you are a monster. I have heard the stories. No survivors, how could you."

"I said I can't." Remington almost shouted back. His heart ached to see how low she thought of him, how much pain and anger she directed toward him. It was his fault. "I would think you would be happier to know it at least remained in my possession as reminder of my treachery. Do you think I want this life, to be killing without second thought, to be reminded day in and day out of my mistakes? If you want it back, take it up with the River King. He is the one that is preventing this, maybe he would listen to one of his subjects."

This seemed to cause some hesitation in Maeve, though he was not sure why. However, during the moment of silence the young half elven boy spoke up, "If you don't want to be killing people then why don't you stop? I mean it's not that hard."

Remington turned to the boy and chuckled at the question. "Because not causing chaos is worse than the nightmare I have created. There are fates worse than death that await if orders are not followed."

"So why don't you just kill yourself?" Maeve asked.

The question startled Remington. The command in her voice, the pure hatred in each word wishing him to be out of this world. "That is the coward's way out," was all that he replied.

"So why did you do it then? Why did you steal it, something I held so dear, that was a part of me?" she asked.

"It was only for the money," Remington responded. He spoke the truth but only a part of it. Even he did not fully understand why.

"Well then who were you going to sell it to? At least give me that." Her statement which started out strong dissolved into a plea.

"I do not give out the names of my clients," Remington lied. He did not know who put out the call, but he would not admit that. Her question was valid though, who was the person that led him down this path. He could see her getting frustrated.

"I am going to give you one last chance to leave my ship alive. I don't want to hurt you Maeve, please just leave."

Maeve looked at him with shock and disbelief but he could see the threat was finally starting to take hold. As she turned to leave she said, "You know, the only reason I am not killing you right now is because I don't want to hurt Elianne. Goodbye Remington."

T'kocht stepped forward stopping the half elf boy, "How is Elianne?" he asked in a whispered tone, though Remington could hear.

"She is doing good, she misses you," the boy responded. Remington called T'kocht over, these people were not their friends.

As the group was leaving, the large goliath woman turned to Remington and said, "You know, I think death would be the braver route," before turning and exiting the door. She was probably right.

Immediately after, Remington saw one of the companions, a wild half elven woman reach to try to pickpocket an item from his cabin. It was nothing of consequence, but he would not allow it. Reaching out his hand he froze them in place, grabbing the item out of her hand. "I would not try that again," he stated before releasing them from their hold. One by one they exited back onto the deck.

Remington could see the confusion in his crews' faces, he would deal with that later. As Maeve and her crew climbed over the edge of the ship, Remington said, "T'kocht give them a warning shot, just next to the last one's head." T'kocht drew his pistol and a shot rang out splintering the wood next to the hand of the half elf boy before his head disappeared over the side.

As soon as the little rowboat they arrived on was out of sight, Remington let out a shout as his fist made contact with the hull. He could feel the bones crack in his hand, but he did not care. She was right, he was every bit of the monster she thought he was.

27

There was silence over the deck of the ship as Remington kept his fist against the hull. He could feel his emotions rising though he tried to choke it down. Faintly he could hear the whispers of his crew around him, discussing what just happened. All he could focus on were Maeve's words repeating in his head. "You are a monster, why don't you just kill yourself." Nothing she accused him of was wrong, but how could she ever understand that he does not have that option. That his punishment was life.

His downward spiral was broken by a hand on his shoulder, it was Nicky. "Who was that Captain? Why did we let them go?" she asked him. He could see the confusion and concern in her face. It was about time they knew. He turned around to face the crew, his hands moving up to the seal skin on his shoulders trying to find some comfort.

"That woman, Maeve, was the owner of this selkie skin. We took," he corrected himself, "I took who she was from her, and as punishment we were cursed. She... she meant a lot to me for our short time together, and I betrayed her. Neither her nor her friends deserve the mayhem that we bring to these waters." His voice began to rise with confidence, "But her visit opened my eyes to the truth. For too long we have blindly accepted our fate, unable to find relief from the

River King, but there is something we can do. Someone out there put out the call for these skins, someone out there was the catalyst for our misfortune. I say we find this person, and we deliver a message from the Feylands. To show them what tricks the creatures of legends bestow upon those who betray them. What say you?"

There was silence as Remington told his story, then rose into a rousing cheer as he sent out his call to arms. T'kocht gave him an approving nod before ordering the crew about to get the ship moving again. Remington walked to the helm, though he wanted to be alone, to hide, he had a job to do and a crew to take care of. He saw Nicky follow him, though he did not acknowledge her. He hoped uselessly that she would let him be, but he knew he would not be that lucky.

"Why did you not tell me earlier?" she demanded, her voice angry at him. Not because she was actually mad at him, she was worried for her friend.

"I didn't think anyone needed to know. It's my problem, not the crew's. They had enough to worry about. I am fine really" Remington responded, not daring to make eye contact with her.

"Are you though?" she retorted. "Captain, Remington, I remember the days, weeks, months, after the death of Atrigul. The look of emptiness in your eyes, pain was the only thing filling the void in them. That same look is growing in your eyes now. It's okay to not be okay. Have you talked to anyone about this?"

"T'kocht knew." Remington whispered. If he raised his voice at all, he knew it would crack. She was right about the void, it always followed him, always beckoning him toward a salvation he could never achieve. He was tired of running from it, he had to turn and face the darkness head on, do something useful with his miserable life. He glanced toward Nicky, the look in his eyes conveying all the determination he wanted. Nicky seemed to get the message.

"I wish you had come to me earlier, I was there before, I know you. You are my friend and I could have helped, but I am glad you at least had T'kocht. He's a good man and no one should be alone going through something like that. I am going to help now though. We will find the bastard that put out the call and we will make sure he wishes that he never had money in the first place."

Her fiery spirit always put a smile on his face. She was right, he probably should have talked to her. She has always provided him with much needed wisdom, and he respected her advice. However, his mental walls still stood strong, and even now was still reluctant to talk about himself. Only T'kocht had the keys and even then, some of those doors were permanently locked. Remington was too terrified to attempt to open them.

That night Remington feared the retaliation that the River King would send for defying his chaos, but none came. Remington decided that the pain of seeing Maeve again was worse than anything the River King had thrown at him, and the River King knew that. Remington did not sleep that night, staying by the helm until the sun rose over the horizon welcoming a new day.

As the day crew filled the deck, preparations were made to make for shore. Remington wanted to talk to Elianne more than ever. The plan was to dock just outside of view of the city of Rivenport and then he and T'kocht could enter the city under the cover of night. The weather seemed to be with them as a thick fog rolled in. Remington couldn't help but wonder if this was the work of the River King helping him for some reason. Didn't matter, all that mattered was that they arrived unseen.

By the time the moon was high in the sky, Remington and T'kocht had made their way into the city center, hooded and cloaked. They were both skilled in the art of hiding, and Remington used his gifts from the River King to become one with the shadows. Eventually, they saw the building they were looking for: a large house just on the edge of the nicer part of town. Remington and

T'kocht had purchased this house for Elianne when they asked her to move off the island of Halitona. They knew it would be safer for her in the Saxe Empire if anything were to happen to them.

Remington saw a small light on in the house. He knew Elianne would be awake. Even after moving, she continued to help out the women that worked in the local brothels, watching their kids who would never know their fathers. It was a noble cause, and Remington and T'kocht always sent her money to support her, to make sure she stayed safe and happy.

Remington felt a hand grab his and give a tight squeeze. He turned to look at T'kocht who was looking at him with concern. Remington only gave a nod of affirmation before releasing his hand and knocking on the door. The seconds felt like eternity, it had been over 2 years since they had last returned home. He heard the door open and saw her staring at them. She looked tired as if she had just woken up. They were still hidden within the shadows, the night obscuring their faces. "Who goes there" she mumbled, still waking up apparently.

"Hi Ma," T'kocht whispered, his voice barely audible. Immediately, Elianne woke up and rushed toward them bringing the both of them into her arms in embrace. Both of them grunted at the unexpected strength of the hug.

"My boys," she said, her voice a little teary, "you're home! Come in where it is safe, I don't want you to be spotted." She ushered them in, locking the door behind her. As Remington entered, he could see the many bunk beds lining the living room, some of them occupied by small children. He made a mental note to send more money, even though they brought along a large amount of gold with them. They moved quietly past the children into Elianne's room, the only place she could be alone in this house.

As soon as the door closed behind them, Remington rushed in

to hug her. "Are you alright? Are you okay? Did they threaten you?" He started asking frantically, his own troubles melting away. He needed to know she was okay before asking further questions.

"I'm fine. Nobody threatened me, in fact they were quite nice to me. But she did threaten you. It has been so long since I have seen you both, and you look so tired and scared. What happened?"

Her voice was ever calm and soothing as she looked back and forth between T'kocht and Remington, taking in the changes though she dare not mention it. As she made eye contact with Remington, asking what happened, his strength crumbled and he burst into tears. All of the emotions that he had held in were released. T'kocht remained silent but embraced Elianne as if he was trying to absorb all the support she could give.

She held onto them both for a few minutes, giving them time to collect themselves, reassuring them that everything would be okay. Eventually Remington was ready to speak. "You said that Maeve stopped in, to speak with you. Well, she found me. Seeing her again, it just reminded me of the monster I have become. You should have heard her Elianne, the anger in her words, how much she hated me. And I deserved every minute of it. Every word she spoke, her begging for me to reverse my mistake, for me to end everyone's suffering by removing myself from this world stabbed into my heart until I felt I was about to die. And there was nothing I could do. Nothing."

"All I did was told her to leave, I wanted her to hate me. I don't deserve her forgiveness, but I desperately crave it. How could I tell her that there was nothing I could do. That I tried to kill myself multiple times, only to be rejected by the River King."

At this T'kocht looked up in surprise, this information was news to him. Remington gave him an apologetic look and continued, "I know she wants revenge on someone, and I couldn't even tell her who hired us. It was anonymous. Elianne, what do I do?" His voice now was small, as if he was once again that 16-year-old boy she met all those years ago. He felt lost.

Elianne squeezed the both of them, remaining silent. "Remington, you have been through more than anyone your age deserves to go through. You once told me that you have to be a harbinger of chaos, to kill wantonly on the seas. That doesn't have to be the case."

Remington looked at her confused. "I have to. How else do I protect my crew, T'kocht, from the pain that the River King holds over us. I have to..." Remington fell silent again.

Elianne looked at him, tears filling her eyes. "All you have to do is bring chaos. Why don't you focus that chaos, find out who hired you, and make their life a living hell? Forge your own path, right the wrongs done to you. Maybe if she sees you trying to do some good, searching for penance, then you might be able to forgive yourself."

They both looked at her in shock. Remington had never heard her speak a violent word toward anyone, and yet here she was telling him to seek vengeance. Her eyes were stone cold, nothing else mattered right now except the three of them, and that is all that would ever matter. "Sleep on it," she said finally, "You have been out at sea so long, enjoy a night and leave tomorrow. Please?"

Remington realized how tired he was and headed to an empty room. T'kocht stayed behind to talk to Elianne, he knew he had his own issues to talk about though Remington would never ask. Keep your deepest secrets hidden he thought to himself, and he let one of his biggest slip tonight. He would deal with that, or ignore it, later.

When Remington opened his eyes, the sun was blazing through the window, the sounds of kids in the street echoing in the alley. Sitting up he saw T'kocht sprawled across the bed on the other side of the room dead to the world. Remington wondered how much later he stayed up, T'kocht was known to stay up until the wee hours of the morning talking to his mother when he had a lot on his mind. Remington looked out the window at the streets he grew up on. He could not go out and wander them, to feel the warm cobble stone under his feet. Anyone walking out there would recognize him immediately and those who didn't, would scream in terror.

Remington sat back down on the bed, crossing his legs. "Alright, I thought you would talk with me last night," he said out loud, "I've done some thinking, well listening, and we need a talk. I want to discuss our agreement."

No response.

"Come on! I know you are there, chose your poison and face me." Remington almost shouted before remembering T'kocht was right there. He looked toward the other bed to make sure he did not wake T'kocht. Still sound asleep. When he turned back, he found the bed soaked in blood and Areliel sitting in front of him, mirroring his crossed legs and blood draining from the slash in her stomach.

"Hello darling," she said smiling at him. "This is a pleasant surprise. I never would have thought you would be begging to speak to me. How delightful."

Remington shifted uncomfortably, he hated being at his mercy. "Enough with the chit chat," Remington stated flatly. "I approach with a proposition. A change in our, situation."

"Why don't you just state the truth my love," Areliel said. "I own you. Your soul is in my possession and therefore, I can punish you in any way I find amusing. I know this body had many ways of doing that." Her hand cold as ice brushed his face. Remington did all he could to not flinch.

"I understand that," he responded. "I know your orders, but I would like to make a change of course in them. Give them pointed direction."

Areliel looked at him curiously, "What are you suggesting?"

"You wanted me to cause chaos, to do your bidding as punishment for my indiscretion," Remington started. "All I am asking is you allow me to direct my chaos towards the person and people of my choosing."

"Where is the fun in that? Chaos is much more fun when people aren't expecting it. Plus, why should I let you do anything that you want, that could potentially make you happy."

"Do you actually believe I could ever be happy?" Remington retorted. "As to why, think about how much more destruction I could cause if I actually put effort into my mission. And it would not just be for me. I know you hate the pirates that have poached in your lands for all these years. Think of the satisfaction you will feel knowing that one of the cruelest, most influential patrons of them is gone, forever. I can make that happen, but I need to know that you will not torture my crew as we work toward this goal. Our usual business will be on halt."

Areliel stared at him for a long while, attempting to judge him. Eventually she spoke, "Interesting you did not include yourself in that ask. Very well, I accept. But know I will be watching, so I hope you don't take too long. And be sure to cause plenty of chaos in the meantime, I know you will find a way to fit it in. Remember, you are and always will be a monster, nothing will ever change that." As she finished her statement, she leaned in and kissed him. Remington shuddered at the unexpected coldness of her lips. As he moved to return the affection, his hands moved through nothing and when he opened his eyes, she was no longer there. He was alone.

Remington grabbed a nearby blanket and burying himself as deeply as possible attempted to go to sleep, the face of Areliel burning behind his eyelids. His mission for his own revenge started now, his life finally having a purpose, and he knew exactly who he needed to talk to.

28

Remington woke up some time later to smell of fresh bread baking below. He moved towards the door before remembering to grab a hood in case there were any children downstairs. As he descended, he could hear T'kocht laughing with Elianne, they seemed to be in good spirits.

When he rounded the corner Remington was met with the sight of warm breads and freshly brewed tea, neatly set up at a small table where Elianne and T'kocht were seated. Remington chuckled to himself, the tantalizing scents teasing him with the prospect of enjoyment, but knowing it will taste like salt. Not wanting to worry Elianne, he sat down and grabbed some bread, the food was incredibly salty, as expected, but he forced himself to choke it down.

Elianne smiled at him before turning to T'Kocht, "Do you really have to leave today? I am sure you and your shipmates would enjoy some shore leave, there is plenty to do in the city"

T'kocht looked at her sadly, "It's too dangerous here Ma. You know we are wanted by the Empire; we have messed with one too many of their ships. Plus, have you seen us? I don't think any of us would be welcome in this city." T'kocht motioned to his face and the tentacles growing on it.

Elianne gave a sigh of resignation, "Oh all right then, but stay safe, will you? I don't know what I would do if either of you got hurt. And tell Remington to send me more messages, I don't hear from you nearly often enough."

She shot a teasing look at Remington who started to laugh. "Alright, I will send more messages," he said, "But we do have to go I'm afraid. There is plenty to be done and we need to make it back to the Fortune before it gets too late. You stay safe as well, and remember to use the stone if anyone causes you trouble, okay? We will be here as soon as we can."

Elianne nodded and the three of them quickly said their goodbyes. By midnight, T'kocht and Remington had returned to the Fey's Fortune. They did not talk the whole walk back, just enjoying the silence of each other's company. Under the cover of darkness they left their secretive harbor and headed out onto the sea.

"Where to, Captain?" Nicky shouted the next morning, the crew in full force in preparation for the next stop.

"Make for Tortuga," Remington stated firmly, "the Fey's Fortune is going to be deciding its own fate from now on."

Nicky looked up at him confused, but she was not going to argue. Quickly his crew hauled the sails, and the course was set to return to Tortuga.

It would be 3 weeks before they arrived in Tortuga, giving Remington plenty of time to think. Remington needed to talk to Vanhorn, for it was Vanhorn who put out the call in the first place for an anonymous buyer. He would know who the buyer is, but Remington knew it was going to take a lot to force that information out of him. This would also create a new enemy between him and the Master, who was very influential in the criminal underworld. It will be worth it.

Halfway through the journey, Remington was standing at attention at the helm of the ship. It had been quiet, no sightings of any ships since leaving Rivenport. He was thankful. Remington was fighting to keep his eyes open, it had been 43 hours since he last slept, but the fear of his dreams kept him going. He watched as a figure climbed the stairs toward him. It was dark out, the light of the stars only gave an outline of anything on the deck but Remington knew it was T'kocht. They had not spoken of anything besides business since leaving Rivenport, though T'kocht always watched him barely letting him out of his sights. Remington did not want to talk, but as he looked around trying to find an out, he realized he was cornered. They would have to talk eventually, he thought.

"Why?" T'kocht asked when he finally arrived, his eyes reflecting the dim moonlight. It was not the question Remington was expecting.

"Why what?" he responded, not wanting to steer the conversation in any direction.

"Remi, we haven't talked in 11 days. Why do you feel like you have to hide from me? Why did you not tell me sooner? Why did you try? Please, just talk to me." T'kocht was pleading by the end, his voice trembling in worry.

Remington sighed, he knew he would have to talk at some point, but still he did not want to. "I didn't tell you sooner because I knew you would react like this." Remington grumbled, refusing to make eye contact.

"Act how exactly?" T'kocht shot back, his voice becoming defensive. "Like someone who cares for his best friend? I care about you Remi, more than you know. We all do. If you are going about trying to leave this world, I'd like to know why so that I can help you. Let me help."

"You want to know why. Do you want to know the hell storm I protect this crew from? How every time I close my eyes, I am visited by the River King disguised as either Maeve or Areliel? How they torment me with the guilt of my past so that I never want to sleep and when I do I awake in terror and pain. Every minute I look out and I am reminded of the pain that I have caused my whole crew because of my damn arrogance. I am broken, T'kocht, and there is no hope of repair. You asked me why I tried to end it, it's because I am a coward who couldn't take the pain. However, I have learned that he won't let me. So, you see? Nothing to worry about."

Remington struggled to catch his breath, everything that he had been holding in for three years beginning to rush to the surface. He felt as though walls were closing in around him and his head began to swim. Slowly he sunk to the floor.

T'kocht knelt down next to him. Even in the darkness, Remington could see the tears flowing down T'kocht's face. "Remi, I-I had no idea. I can't even begin to imagine what you are going through, but I can tell you one thing. You cannot blame yourself for what happened to us. We all made our choice and we all faced the consequences, none of which are nearly as bad as what you face. Ask anyone on board and they are proud to serve on this ship under your leadership. We care about you, I care about you. You are the bravest man I know, don't you ever call yourself a coward."

Remington didn't move. He could hear the honesty in T'kocht's voice, but everything in him told him not to believe a word. What did he ever do to earn their admiration, all he has ever caused anyone is pain.

T'kocht leaned in for a hug, squeezing Remington tightly. "You might not believe me right now, I can see you are tired, but know that you do bring joy to those around you. When you need to, please just talk to me, and I will listen and support, because that's what friends do. I promise you it will make you feel better. Share the weight."

Again, Remington did not move. He felt weak and he was angry at himself. There was no need to share what he went through; it would only bring the suffering onto others. T'kocht had already seen so much of what Remington had gone through, he didn't need to see more.

"I don't know what lies the River King has whispered to you," T'kocht said as he left. "But I wish you would trust me like in the old days. What happened to that Remington, I miss him. I wish he would come out from behind that mask."

Remington broke down as soon as T'kocht was out of ear shot. The depth of T'kocht's words finally sinking in. T'kocht had always been there for him, no matter what, so why was he hiding from him now. The River King, Remington thought. His words whispered in the night, that he wasn't good enough, that he was a coward and a villain, that if people knew the truth, they wouldn't respect him. It had to be kept secret, but secrets only pushed those closest to him away. It was time to fight back, to pull his friends in closer and build himself back up with their strength.

Remington fell asleep on the deck of the ship, only to be awoken by the blaze of the morning sun a few hours later. It was an uninterrupted sleep, one of the first he has had in a while. A new day was dawning, and Remington was now as intent as ever on his mission to find the man responsible, to get his revenge.

Remington's mood vastly improved over the rest of the journey. He spent more time sitting down and talking with the crew and sharing the contents of his dreams with T'kocht. They discussed plans for Tortuga and potential issues arising from double crossing the Master. One unlucky boat did happen to cross their path, which they were obliged to dispose of in their usual fashion. No survivors this time.

Eventually the familiar island of Tortuga appeared on the horizon. Remington wanted to make a show of his arrival. He wanted the person he was hunting to know he was looking for him. For the first time since returning from the Feylands, the Fey's Fortune docked in Tortuga in the middle of the day, where everyone could see.

Remington took a deep breath and held his head high as he deboarded his ship. He could see everyone watching him, gasps of shock echoing through the crowd at the sight of the Drowned Captain. Many averted their gaze for a rumor said that one look from him was enough to doom someone to death. Their lives did not matter to him, he was on a mission.

The crowd parted for him, giving him clear walkway as he made his way toward the Busted Bottle, the only place on the island that he knew he would find Vanhorn. Apparently, news of his arrival reached the bar before he did, for when he entered, all eyes were already watching the front door, hoping to get a glimpse of the infamous devil of the seas.

Glancing about the room, Remington spotted the familiar dark skin of Vanhorn sitting alone at a booth with a large mug of ale in front of him. Wasting no time, Remington walked across the dining hall and sat down across from him not saying a word.

"Ah Remington," Vanhorn commented, a brief puff of smoke exiting from the pipe that rested in his mouth. "Rumor has it that you were not allow to step on land, though we can all see that is false. So, what brings you back to me, I can't imagine that you are looking for a job."

"I don't need a job, for your past job gave me and my crew a whole new outlook on life." Remington responded, the sarcasm in his voice coming off aggressively.

"I only offer up jobs," Vanhorn responded calmly, "It's up to the captain if they want to take it. I hold no responsibility for what happens on a job."

"Great, if you hold no responsibility for what happens, then I am sure you would have no issue giving me the name of your customer." Remington replied, leaning in closer to Vanhorn, water dripping off his forehead.

"Remington, Remington," Vanhorn laughed, "You know I can't

do that. Customer confidentiality is what keeps businesses like mine going. I cannot just give out a name because a pretty face batted their eyes at me. Sorry to disappoint, but if that is all you are looking for, you won't get anything. You are welcome to stay for a drink or a smoke if you would like." Vanhorn leaned back in his chair exhaling another puff of smoke.

Remington sighed, "Don't make me make this hard for you Vanhorn. I just need a name, they won't even need to know where I got it from. I can walk away with the information, look as sad as you want me to, pretending you denied the Drowned Captain. Think of the reputation you would gain."

"Sorry Remington, but secrets always come out, they cannot be locked away forever. If my boss learned I was divulging customer names, I would be in more trouble than you are right now."

Remington's eyes flared with anger at the comment, but he regained his composure. "You are right, secrets do always come out. But I am sure that your secret son would never be uncovered. Not with you keeping him so close to home on the island. That is one you will take to the grave will you not?"

Vanhorn's eyes widened with terror, sweat beginning to bead on his forehead. "H-how did you..."

Remington only laughed, "Does it matter? I am sure the Master will not be happy with you if he ever finds out. Isn't one of his rules 'No personal connections'? I am sure the Master would reward me greatly for taking care of this little mishap of yours. How old is he? My first mate estimates the boy to be no more than 7. So unfortunate that his life must be so short. However, I could be convinced to keep a secret." Remington stopped laughing and stared at Vanhorn, daring him to make a move.

"Really, Remington?" Vanhorn said nervously, "You would threaten a child to get what you want? He is only seven, leave him out of this. It is between you and me."

"You have heard everything that I have done over the past 3 years. You should know better than to underestimate how low I would stoop to get what I want. Just give me a name, and I will tell my crew to let the boy go, and we can forget this ever happened."

The two stared at each other, waiting for the other to show signs of a bluff, but none came. Vanhorn sighed and slid a note over to Remington. "Let him go. He is a good lad, he doesn't deserve death."

"Thank you," Remington replied, "your son will be just fine." Looking at the note, Remington saw it was a letter, requesting selkie skins at the price of 15,000 gold pieces each to be paid upon delivery. At the bottom of the request was a name, "*Dominus*".

29

"Who is Dominus?" Remington demanded. He ran through the list of names of people he knew, but none went by the name Dominus.

"I gave you a name, didn't I? My end of the deal is held. I don't know the true identity of Dominus, but he came with a letter of authenticity directly from the Master. There is nothing else I can offer you. Please leave."

Vanhorn looked frustrated and nervous, but he was truthful. Remington sighed. He was hoping to get a clear name and be done with the mission. It seems finding this Dominus would be more difficult than expected. He stood up and thanked Vanhorn for his business before heading back to the Fortune. It would be another week before they left to go to who knows where, and his crew needed a break.

During the week Remington had his crew asking around the island for any information on the true identity of Dominus. However, it was all in vain and the week passed with no new information gathered. Remington spent the week on his ship as usual, not wanting to make a reappearance on shore. He figured one sighting was enough to spread gossip.

Over and over he read the letter, looking for any sign or hint as to its original owner, but none appeared. He glanced over toward the floorboard where he kept his crystal ball. He knew Maeve did not want to speak to him, but her words repeated in his mind, "At least give me that." A name. That was all she wanted and he couldn't give it to her.

Before he realized what he was doing, the ball was in his hands, and he was thinking her name. His vision swirled until before him he could see her. She seemed to be somewhere very cold, the icy snow was blowing into her face causing thick snowflakes to stick to her eyelashes. Remington could not help but think how beautifully the ice contrasted with the fiery determination in her eyes.

"You must really hate me if you traveled all the way to the icy south. That's one way to guarantee you will not see me." Remington flinched at the same time she did. Why did he just say that? He shook his head, trying to hide that broken version of himself deep down. He waited for a response from her, but none came, she kept walking.

"Sorry. Look I know I am the last person you want to talk to, but you should know I have a name for you. The person who hired me was named Dominus. That is all I know. I will leave you alone now." Remington waited, hoping she would respond, hoping she would say anything to him. The silence was worse than the criticizing. After a few minutes, he gave up and exited from the vision returning to his ship.

Though she did not acknowledge him, seeing her rekindled the flame of revenge in his heart. Remington and the crew worked into overdrive. Each ship they encountered they interrogated, looking for any information on the name Dominus.

Many would make up information hoping for mercy, but between the lies, there was truth. Remington was able to gather that the name has been heard in the underworld connections in the city of Belward. Belward was the capital of the Saxe Empire, home to some of the richest people in the hemisphere. The rich were protected there, for the inner circle of Belward was enchanted 30 years ago to float 500ft above the rest of the city. It was a sight to behold, and on the other side of the country from Rivenport.

The Fey's Fortune turned southwest and began the long journey to the oceans off Belward. The journey was surprisingly uneventful. The River King continued to visit Remington in his dreams, but they were less frequent than usual. Remington was suspicious of how quiet it all was but was thankful for the sleep he was finally able to get.

The crew fed off of the increased positive energy from their captain. Their devotion to the creation of chaos increased, no ship standing a chance against their might. However, try as they might, there seemed to be no information about the person known as Dominus. With each passing massacre, Remington became more frustrated with this phantom. He began to wonder if Dominus ever existed if this was all a ruse from Vanhorn to trick him into leaving.

After a month of terrorizing the seas of Belward, the trail picked back up. Remington and his crew had just boarded a small Saxe Empire naval vessel and quickly took control. As per usual now days, the invasion did not start with death. Instead, Remington paced back in forth in front of the enemy crew.

"Now we can make this easy. All you have to do is tell me what I want to know, and you can go home, knowing mercy was bestowed upon you. My patience is short though. Someone better start talking, or someone's sword might slip, and we don't want that to happen. So, tell me, who is Dominus."

There was silence across the crew. There always was. Remington motioned to his crew and in a second, two bodies dropped to the deck. "You might not want to talk," Remington continued, "because he might be rich, powerful, maybe even threatening. But I am here in front of you now and I can guarantee your death now. Which one of you is a betting man?"

Remington turned around, waiting once again for the silence, but this time someone spoke up. "If I tell you what I know do you promise to take me with you?"

Remington pivoted in his tracks to face the unexpected speaker. It was a young woman, about the same age as Remington, shakily standing. "Well, that is an interesting thought, no one has asked to join my crew before. Let's hear what the information is first, then I might decide."

"If you are after the rich and powerful in Belward, there is some-one who can help you," she said, her voice trembling. "I can tell you where to find her, set up a meeting, but you have to take me with you."

Remington moved over to her, watching her curiously. "What is the name of your contact, and why are you so desperate to come with me?"

The woman straightened herself, Remington appreciated the attempt at composure when looking death in the face. "Because sharing this information will mark me as a traitor to the Empire, so mouth shut or mouth open I am a dead woman. You promised mercy, and my mercy would be taking me off this ship. I am a member of a group known as the Bloodroots. Our leader, Justice, is very knowledgeable about the rich and powerful of the Saxe Empire and is willing to burn them to the ground."

Remington broke into a smile. He had heard faint rumors of this organization though he never paid them much attention. This was just the lead he was looking for, and this woman was telling the truth. "I commend you for your bravery and thank you for your information. Lucky for you, I believe you. What is your name?"

"Tabitha, sir," she responded quietly. Her burst of bravery seemed to have faded.

"Well Tabitha, please go get whatever you may need to contact this Justice. For everyone else, don't worry we will make it swift. Leave one alive to spread the tale of this treachery. We need some assurance dear Tabitha is not going to betray us now don't we."

With swift strokes, Remington and his crew dispatched the remaining crewmen on board save one. They were allowed to board a life boat and leave the burning hull behind. Remington escorted Tabitha onto the Fey's Fortune, his clothes covered in the blood of her former crewmates.

"So tell me, where are we off to?" he asked her, wiping some of the blood off his cheek. He could see her shaking, doubt on if she made the right choice creeping up inside her. "Don't worry," Remington reassured her to the best of his ability, "You are safe under my protection. As long as I say so, no one will touch a hair on your head."

"Right," she started hesitantly. "I, uh, need to, uh, contact Justice, set up a meeting location. I am not sure where she is right now."

"Very well, make your call and let my first mate know as soon as you have a location." Remington turned and walked toward his quarters; the crew would keep an eye on her. She did not seem very dangerous.

Before he reached the door a voice appeared in his head. It was that half elf boy that traveled with Maeve. "Maeve wants to talk to you." A short and to the point message that caused Remington to stop breathing. She wants to talk. What about and why now?

"Understood," Remington responded, now racing to reach his crystal ball. He was out of breath by the time he pulled it out of its hiding spot. Taking a few moments to collect himself, he thought Maeve's name and felt himself being pulled into the vision.

The darkness faded to Maeve standing on a beach, Remington could not tell where. Her eyes were ablaze with anger, though he could also see confusion as she paced back and forth, unaware she was being watched. This was not going to be a pleasant conversation.

"Hello Maeve, you wanted to talk?" he asked hesitantly.

"Who is Anlini?" she asked without hesitation, spinning around not sure where to address him.

Remington would have laughed at her confusion if he was not so taken aback by the name. Anlini was the second selkie that he tricked, that he stole from. A naïve girl, who had been alone on her island for too long. She was too trusting of him, and it made his job easier.

"Just a business transaction," he responded. He did feel guilty, but it was just business at the time.

Maeve took a second to process this comment. He could see she was not satisfied. "Was I just a business transaction?" she asked. Her voice was softer than usual, it reminded him of her before all of this.

"No, you were not."

"Was I the first or the last?"

The first or last of his victims he thought to himself. He could finally answer her questions. He wanted to be honest.

"The last." He did not want to elaborate but wondered how much she already knew.

"Did any of it mean anything to you? Why would you do such a thing. To me, to Anlini? The poor girl is stuck on this island because of you. Do you feel proud of yourself?" Her voice once again rising with a heated passion.

"I have no pride in what I did, it was unacceptable. But every minute we had together meant something to me. I almost stayed that night, I wanted to stay." Remington paused. Why was he telling her all this? She would never forgive him, and he did not want to play mind games with her, but he wanted to tell her the truth, to be honest. Why was it so hard?

Maeve seemed to get more and more confused by his words. "Then why didn't you stay? You didn't have to go."

Remington inhaled sharply. He could have stayed. He could have left his crew in good hands and stayed with her forever. He knew that was never an option. "Because I didn't deserve it." The truth was out, and he could not deny it.

Maeve paced back and forth, contemplating what to say. Occasionally she looked like she was ready to say something before deciding against it. Remington decided to break the silence.

"I am trying to atone. I found a new focus for new revenge and it's because of you. Maybe you did talk some sense into me that day on the ship, and I plan on making something of my life."

Maeve stopped her pacing and looked down at the sand. She didn't know where else to look. "Why are you telling me this?" she asked.

"I don't know," Remington responded. He wondered himself why he was telling her all this, but it felt good. Remington allowed himself a rare smile.

"Goodbye Remington," Maeve stated unexpectedly. He was not ready for her to go, but he wanted to respect her wishes. Remington forced his way out of the vision, returning to his room on the Fortune.

30

Remington took a second to compose himself. He was not sure what to make of the conversation. The hatred in her eyes seemed to have dimmed, he wondered if she still cared. Remington shook his head, there was no way she would ever forgive him. He needed to get out of the fantasy.

Making his way back onto the deck, he found Nicky talking with Tabitha. Nicky seemed to be doing a good job at calming her down. Remington walked up to them, putting on his best fake smile. "So, where are we off to then?"

Tabitha jumped at the sound of his voice and quickly spun to face him. "Oh, hello, right. Justice says they are somewhere between Toperpoint and Murkstrum, but she is willing to meet you. She warns she will come protected though."

"I wouldn't expect anything less," Remington responded. Toperpoint and Murkstrum were north of where they currently were, not too far away. Depending on which city they were closer to, they could be there in a week, maybe less. "I hope she expects the same courtesy from us, I would hate to learn I was being led into a trap." His last words he made sure to emphasize as a threat. He didn't know much about this Justice and did not trust her to not be an ambassador to the Pirate King.

Tabitha audibly swallowed, "Yes of course." She then backed away from them, to find somewhere out of the sight of the dreaded captain.

"Give her a break," Nicky reprimanded him. "She just committed treason against the Empire, which to a pirate might not seem like a big deal, but to a soldier, it is everything. Speak against the empire and you find yourself living the rest of your short life in the slave camps of Fredlos." Nicky turned and also strode off, quite angry.

Remington tried to figure out what made Nicky so angry. She was always private about her time before joining as a crewmember of the Sickening Rose. Remington considered it had to be something about her past but was not going to push it.

The crew moved swiftly around the deck preparing to make their way north, and out of these dangerous waters. Remington spent his time carefully, planning as to how he wanted to address this meeting. He spent some time interrogating Tabitha, but she proved useless in getting any background information on Justice. Seems Justice was just about as much of a ghost as he was.

As they neared their destination, Tabitha was better able to coordinate a specific meeting location. It would be another week before Justice's group would make it to the location, and a few days for the Fey's Fortune, but it was the safest place to dock between the two cities.

Communication had been quiet from the River King. He had not visited Remington for over a week now, though Remington was not complaining. For the first time in a long time, he was finally feeling rested, and his guard was slowly dropping. Uselessly, he hoped that maybe the River King was done toying with him, that the nightmares were over.

Unfortunately, it was only a small calm in the storm. For as night fell, Remington felt the darkness of sleep give way to a very warm tropical island. Immediately he recognized it as the island where he killed Brend and realized this must be the River King playing games again. He turned around to find the River King, "So what is it that you want to talk about this..." His sentence trailed off, as standing before him was both Areliel and Maeve. The River King had never appeared as two people before, always only one. The sight of them side by side caused Remington to freeze.

Composing himself the best he could, Remington started, "Oh you learned a new trick huh, appearing as two people now. Just finding new ways to mess with me. What do you want."

Areliel looked offended, "What makes you think I want something? Can I not just stop in for a chat? It has been a while since I have seen you, and I missed you so dearly."

Remington watched as she approached him, leaning in close and circling him like a vulture. He couldn't find the words to say, her proximity to him, the smell of roses, the words "I miss you" all flooding his senses such that he could not process anything.

"You would never say such cruel words to me," she continued. "Plus my new friend here has some questions for you."

Remington now looked over toward Maeve, who did not seem to be making any movements, maybe the River King could only control one at a time. "We had a deal, and I am still holding out my end of the bargain so why are you here," Remington once again demanded.

"What deal?" he heard Maeve ask.

"You know our new arrangement, I am done here," Remington responded, getting annoyed.

"Now, now, my dear Remington," Areliel reprimanded, "answer her question. You don't want to disappoint me do you? But I did always have so much fun with you when you did. Would you like to feel that again?" Remington felt her push up against him even closer, the coldness of her breath on his ear sending chills down his arms as he did his best to not move.

"I will find the man responsible for this curse. I am so close, I just need a bit more time, please. I have a contact I am meeting with to help put the final pieces together."

Maeve stepped forward a bit, "Who is your contact?"

Remington did not want to answer but one glance from Areliel said he shouldn't try to fight it. Reluctantly, Remington stated, "There is a group of people that are against the Empire. Their leader is a woman known as Justice. I have word she can help me, so I am meeting with her in a few days. Happy?" Remington was tired of playing these games.

"Oh my," Areliel exclaimed, "Another woman coming to help you out of your miserable life. Are you going to kill this one too, or only betray her leaving a wake of scorn and vengeance. You really think she will help you? You are a monster Remington, nothing more. You can look and look but you will never find what you are looking for. This curse will always follow you."

"And to think too," Maeve chimed in, "that all of your crew is trapped on the boat, because of you. Think how much better their lives would be if you weren't there. Why do they stay?"

Remington growled, "Because unlike some people here, people actually like me. They stay because they want to."

"Are you sure about that?" Maeve retorted. "Where else would they go? How does it feel knowing you trapped all of them with you, knowing the pain you put T'kocht through every day."

Remington looked at her confused. He thought he saw a conflicted look on her face, as though she questioned what she said. The River King had never mentioned T'kocht before, he was always a source of happiness not pain. Though he was a source of support, Remington had not talked to T'kocht about some of the more recent activities, especially the conversation with Maeve. He was not ready to talk. Remington scrunched his nose at these thoughts.

"Sailing some rough waters there I see," Areliel stated. "Is he finally seeing the horrific thing that you are? The evil that lies just under the surface." Her hand slowly lifted his chin before brushing it back toward her.

Remington turned to Areliel and snapped, "No, he is just finally finding out the monster you have made me. What did you think I would be able to hide our little visits from him? Hide the fact that I have tried time and time again to end my existence and this contract only for you to prevent me? He actually cares about me, but now won't keep his eyes off in case I attempt to do anything stupid again."

Maeve once again spoke up, "If he cares for you so much, why do you torture him every day?"

Remington was becoming more confused and noticed even Areliel's curiosity was increasing. "I don't understand what you are referring to," he said.

"Yes, do enlighten us," encouraged Areliel. Remington shot a glance at her. What game was the River King playing at.

"Do you really think he wants to be on a ship day in and day out stuck with someone who will never care the same way. You are incapable of showing anyone that level of devotion, of love. Why don't you just let him go, and maybe he can move on from the poison that you are."

Remington looked at Maeve, though she seemed conflicted about what she was saying, her words were honest through the fire of hatred. What did she mean by that? Suddenly, as if time slowed down, many puzzle pieces began to find their place. The care that T'kocht always shared with him, was it something more? He remembered back on the Fey's Fortune when they had that fight over greed. "Because I care about you, because I love you," were the words that flew of T'kocht's mouth. Remington always assumed that the flush rushing to T'kocht's face was always of anger, and they were speaking as brothers. He never thought...

"No," he said out loud, "no,no,no." Remington did not care that the River King was still there. He had to run somewhere. How could he be so stupid, he thought to himself. After 16 years together he never once noticed, never once saw the signs. Each day torturing his best friend with his own obliviousness. T'kocht was in love with him, and he did not know what to do.

31

Remington woke up drenched in sweat. It was still dark outside, he guessed early hours of the morning. Not wanting to attempt to sleep Remington walked out onto the deck of his ship. He mind kept wandering back to T'kocht. They were friends, that was it. Remington knew in his heart that was a lie, T'kocht wanted more.

He wondered how long T'kocht had felt this way. Had it been this way from the beginning? Ever since day one in his life as a pirate, T'kocht had been there, but so was Areliel. In the silence of the night Remington's mind began to spiral. He stayed on the Sickening Rose because he did not want his friend to get in trouble. Every time he talked to T'kocht about the pain and torture he went through at the hands of his captain, T'kocht told him to hold on and helped him through. Why would he do that?

Remington started to connect dots in his mind. T'kocht was not his friend. Once again another person was manipulating him from behind the curtain. He was working with Areliel to break down Remington, to strip him of everything he was. T'kocht created this façade of friendship, to lower Remington's walls. It must have been his plan all along for Areliel to attack T'kocht. The perfect opportunity to remove her from the equation so that he may be the sole source of manipulation. The master puppeteer finally rising to take his place.

Remington was angry. How could he have not seen this all along. "No more," he said to himself. Remington had learned his lesson. No more will he trust anyone, for no one can be trusted. People were only tools to be used, as he was. Remington noticed the sun rising over the cliffs that his boat sat beneath. Only a few more days until his meeting with Justice, until he could be a few steps closer to his goal. Now more than ever he wanted his revenge. That maybe he could be freed of this curse and go where no one would ever find him again.

Remington's thoughts were interrupted by the sound of T'kocht's voice breaking through, "Remi are you alright? Did the River King speak to you again?"

Remington spun towards T'kocht and stared at him. However, he did not see the familiar dark black eyes. Instead, the icy green eyes of Areliel stared back for just a second. Remington took a step back. "It's none of your business. And you will refer to me as Captain when we are on this boat. Prepare the crew to head to shore, we need to be on time to our meeting."

He saw the look of confusion and hurt on T'kocht's face. Remington felt guilt begin to build and shoved it back down. T'kocht knew what he was doing, Remington had just finally figured out his game. "What happened Remi? You can talk to me. Whatever he told you are lies. Please, talk to me." T'kocht pleaded. Remington was not about to give in.

"I said, you will refer to me as Captain. Now get!" Remington almost shouted, the rest of the crew looking up in surprise at his outburst. Remington looked at them all but did not say anything, this was not their fight.

It was a long 3 day hike to the agreed upon location. It was only a small group going on the journey, just Remington, T'kocht,

Tabetha, and two crew members. Remington had invited Nicky, but she refused to set foot on Empire soil, so she stayed back to defend the ship. Throughout the travel, T'kocht continued to prod Remington, attempting to figure out what had happened, but Remington remained silent. He had nothing to say to the traitor. Eventually, T'kocht gave up and Remington relished in the silence.

On the third day of travel, the group entered into a small clearing in the marshy terrain they had been traveling through. This was their agreed upon meeting location. Remington was on high alert, keeping a tight grip on Tabetha incase this turned out to be an ambush. He heard a twig snap off to his right.

Quickly spinning about, he saw a group of three individuals enter the clearing. Two of them seemed to be a set of brother and sister elves, clad in greens and browns each carrying a wooden staff. In the center walked a woman in her late 20s. Her lavender-colored skin, pupilless green eyes, and horns growing from the side of her head in the fashion of a ram immediately gave away her demonic heritage. Her pointed tail flicked behind her as she took in the scene as well. Remington wondered where in her family history their curse began. The metal of her all-black armor clanked as she stepped forward, one hand on the hilt of her blade in caution.

"Hello," she started, "You must be the Drowned Captain. I have heard much about you." Her voice was commanding with authority but yet lacking the arrogance carried by those in power. Remington was intrigued.

"And you must be Justice. Unfortunately, I have not heard much about you. However, I do have something you might want." Remington reached back for Tabitha bringing her by his side.

"There is no need to play games, Captain. Especially when there is a person stuck in the middle. Why don't you let the poor girl go and we can talk like civilized people, unlike the person you are hunting." Justice was very persuasive and her pupilless eyes unnerved Remington, reminding him of the eyes of the River King.

Slowly, he took his hand off of Tabitha's arm letting her walk away. He needed Justice's help and as angry as he was with T'kocht, he did not want to pick a fight today.

"So, you know who I am looking for?" he asked curiously.

"You are looking for a man named Dominus, so I have heard. There are those with connections to the underground that have heard the name and fear the power behind it though few know the face. Luckily for you, I know the face and want him dead as much as you do."

The fire in her emerald eyes gave away the hatred she held towards this man. "I know why I want him dead, but who is he to you?" Remington asked. He knew the Bloodroots were typically anti-Saxe Empire, but just minor mosquitos in the swamp. Staging protests against technology and such, not necessarily violent until more recently.

"Have you heard the name Elizabelle Cresthorn before?" she asked.

Remington shook his head. He recognized the name Cresthorn. They were a very powerful family in the Saxe Empire, one of the Lords of Lebdi. But he had not heard the name Elizabelle in relation to it. "The Cresthorns are a powerful family, though I don't know an Elizabelle under the family."

Justice let out a small chuckle. "You wouldn't. For Alexander Cresthorn made sure to erase any and all knowledge of her existence. For why would a man who is so powerful admit to being cursed. The first born of each generation destined to outwardly display the demons that live within. So, he hid her from the world, from the rest of the family, and when she became too much trouble poisoned her and dumped her in a meadow in the middle of nowhere to die."

Remington nodded understandingly. Dominus is the famed Alexander Cresthorn, head of the Cresthorn family and leader of the Lords of Lebdi. This complicated things and was going to make it much more difficult to get to him.

"Well, it is a pleasure to meet you Elizabelle. It seems I have some competition for the pleasure of his death. Thank you for the information, is there anything I can do to help you since you have been so helpful to me?" Remington was surprised at how open she was about all the information.

"Elizabelle is dead, please call me Justice. And let's consider this a prepayment for future help for the Bloodroots. I might call upon you later for ocean-based backup. And if you reach my father before I do, make sure he knows that I sent you."

"With pleasure," Remington responded. He did not like being in debt to this woman, but he had the answers he needed. There were more questions formed, but at last he had a name, a real name. Alexander Cresthorn.

The two groups slowly backed away from each other, their trust still not solidified. As soon as they were out of sight and ear shot, T'kocht approached Remington. "That went well. We have a name now, maybe we will finally find some peace. What is the plan?"

Remington turned to T'kocht. Once again, the monster trying to break down his walls, to know his inner thoughts so he can manipulate them. "Don't talk to me of peace. The only peace I will have is when people stop caring about my every move. That includes you." Remington harshly whispered at T'kocht before picking up the pace and putting some distance between them. He just wanted to be alone but that would never happen.

It was a long and awkward hike back to the boat, but eventually they returned. Remington updated the crew on all that they had learned about Alexander Cresthorn before retiring to his cabin. He needed time to himself.

Remington's moment of peace only lasted an hour when a familiar voice rang in his ear. He looked to his left to see the River King in the form of Maeve sitting beside him. "Oh Remington," she said in a sing-song voice.

"Can I not get a moments peace. What do you want?" he asked angrily.

"You are never alone with me here," she responded. "But Maeve does need your help."

Remington's attention snapped to the creature next to him. Was she in trouble?

"I thought that might intrigue you. Apparently, her and a few friends are stuck in the Feylands and need a lift."

"I am a ship captain, not a ferryman. Plus, I don't know if you forgot but you banned me from the Feylands." Remington stated flatly.

"I am sure I can temporarily lift it for just this once. She so desperately needs your help. You wouldn't let her freeze to death in the icy tundra would you? Don't you want to see her again?"

"Of course I do," Remington responded. "Why are you doing something nice for me for once?" Remington was genuinely confused.

"Do not mistake this for something nice," she responded. "I fully expect this reunion to be very painful and disastrous, the last I saw her she is still very angry at you."

The River King was right, Maeve did hate him and all that he has done. But Remington was determined to be better, to prove that he was worthy of her forgiveness. Maybe this was his chance. "Alright, give me some time to find a lay line and we will make the jump." It has been a long time since Remington made a jump and he was not looking forward to it.

"See you soon," Maeve said before giving him a wink and fading away. Letting out a deep sigh, Remington stood up and walked outside into the setting sun, to let his crew know they were returning to the retched land of the fey.

32

The crew of the Fey's Fortune was flooded with mixed emotions at returning to the Feylands. Some were excited at seeing the colorful sky and breathing in the intoxicating scents. Others were nervous considering how well the last trip went. And almost all of them were wondering what could be so important that it would cause the River King to lift their ban, even if temporarily.

Remington told most of the crew only that they were going for a day to pick up some wayward travelers. However, he did tell Nicky, and reluctantly T'kocht, who they were actually picking up. He wanted the crew to be on their best behavior, and he knew the jump would be rough on him. Remington would have to put a little faith in his first mate to get the process going all over again. They had never performed two jumps so closely together; Remington was worried about the toll it would take on his body but was not going to admit his fears.

Remington began the ritual for the jump, T'kocht assisted with drawing the arcane circles to speed up the process. They did not say a word to each other as they worked, though occasionally Remington could see T'kocht staring at him out of the corner of his eye. Remington wanted to tell him off, to tell him that he figured out his plan. That he refused to be anyone's puppet and was forging his own path. But Remington knew this would cause discord amongst his crew, and he had put them through enough pain he couldn't add more to it. So he remained silent.

The ritual took them 9 hours to finish, working together on the setup. Remington began the arcane chant, the words to call upon the weave and the lay lines that rest below them to bring them where they needed to go. He felt the energy flow through his veins, burning as it moved through his feet and up into his hands. He could see the lay lines clear as day, as if they were spiderwebs tracing the sky. Carefully he traced his hands through the webbing, willing the ship to follow to where Maeve was awaiting him. He strained against the resistance the ship was providing, forcing it across the boundaries of the worlds. The all too familiar white light began filling his eyes and he let himself relax, letting the energy build and burn inside him.

As his eyesight cleared, Remington immediately felt the cold around him. He saw that the Fortune had landed in an alpine lake of sorts, the frozen mountains towering above them and ice forming in the lake around them. He felt his legs buckling underneath of him, but he stubbornly willed them to stand strong.

As Remington focused on remaining conscious, he heard the splash of the rowboat hitting the lake. Nicky must be on her way to pick up Maeve. *Maeve*, she was really here. His thoughts were broken by a hand supporting his arm and his weight.

"Remi, are you okay? I can greet them. You need your rest," T'kocht suggested.

Remington ripped his arm away from T'kocht. Even that little effort made him stumble. He would not show weakness and he would be the one to welcome them aboard. He was not going to let T'kocht take that from him too.

"No, I'm fine," Remington shouted. The world around him was slowly starting to spin, but he tried to block it out.

A few minutes later, the rowboat had returned to the ship and was being hauled aboard. Remington felt his breath leave his lungs as he watched Maeve step out of the boat. Her clothes were tattered as if she had been in a fight, though she seemed healthy. Remington's leg buckled once again but he caught himself.

He felt the beginnings of arcane healing flow through his body. Looking around, he found it to be coming from the young half elf boy that traveled with her.

"I don't need your help," Remington said, using his own gifts to stop the spell from taking hold.

"Welcome aboard The Fey's Fortune. We will be taking you back to the Prime Realm tomorrow. Until then make yourself at home. If you need anything you can just ask my first mate T'kocht, and he will..."

Remington was unable to finish his sentence as darkness took him and he slipped into unconsciousness. He woke up not long after that, with Maeve's hands on his chest, arcane healing soaking into his body, and his head protected from the deck of the ship by T'kocht. Remington scrambled away from both of them. How could he be so weak in front of them?

Remington quickly stood up, and almost fell over again from the blood rushing out of his head. He could not be near them, not now. "If you will excuse me, I need some rest," and Remington slowly moved to his cabin, trying his best to ignore the black splotches filling his eyesight. Closing the door behind him, Remington did not even make it to his hammock before collapsing onto the floor in a deep sleep that not even the River King could intrude upon.

Remington was not sure what time it was when he finally woke up. The everlasting light from the Feylands snuck in through the cracks in the cabin, it could be any time of day. As he exited out onto the deck, he saw the night crew in full force, it must be sometime in the middle of the "night". He also noticed a large opaque dome sitting on the deck of the ship. It must belong to the travelers he thought. Not wanting to wake them, he strode to the other side of the ship and began work on the arcane circles. He was still exhausted from the jump but did not want to return to sleep. There was still work to be done.

As he sat down and started drawing with his chalk, he heard footsteps behind him. Looking over his shoulder, he saw Maeve sitting cross-legged next to him, not saying anything. He looked at her in acknowledgement before turning back to his work. He did not know what to say.

"I want to apologize," Maeve said quietly.

Remington turned to look at her in shock. "You're joking right? You have nothing to apologize for. I'm the one who should be apologizing. I was terrible to you, and now I can't even do anything to fix it."

"But what I did hurt you," she continued. "I gave the River King more ammunition to use against you. And I can see that you are suffering because of that. I never should have said the things I said to him, but I was angry at you."

So that's how the River King knew about T'kocht. Remington thought back to that dream. Was Maeve really there too? Was it her that opened his eyes to the truth? How could she see this and he couldn't? He let out a pitiful laugh, "Was I the last idiot to figure it out. No, I actually thank you for telling me. Now I can see him for the villainous manipulator he is. My eyes are open, and I cannot trust anyone."

His eyes met hers at that last sentence, his heart fought against him, but it applied to her as well. He knew she had every right to be angry with him, he could not let his guard down, though it was difficult to fight against.

"Not everyone is out to get you Remington," she reassured him. "Your crew loves you like family. T'kocht would not do anything to hurt you. I talked to him and he is worried about you, genuinely. You put so much effort into protecting them all, and they appreciate you. You can't be so hard on yourself."

Her voice was soothing and calming. It lacked the fiery flame of teasing, but yet had the conviction of a mountain standing strong. He found it comforting and yet destructive as it tore down the walls he desperately tried to keep up. She would understand, he could talk to her.

"How can I go on?" he asked. Honesty, finally, with himself. "How can I go on knowing every single day I am torturing my best friend. Knowing every day, he stands teased by something he could never have. Something I could never give him. I'm tired Maeve, I'm so tired."

He could see the pity and sadness in her eyes. He had denied himself the truth for too long. He was never mad at T'kocht, it was always himself. It would always be himself.

"T'kocht values your friendship too much. He knows just being here as a friend is more than he could ask for. You should talk to him, he is so worried." Maeve's voice was soft, no pressure, just calming advice.

"Maybe," Remington responded. He could feel sleep overtaking him. The short hours he had gotten was not enough. He slowly lowered his head onto Maeve's shoulder, a place it had rested many times before during their time together. They fit together perfectly, as if Sepp forged them together himself. He waited for her to move away in disgust, for the kindness to melt away in the heat of anger. Maeve did not move away. She put her arm around him and remained quiet as he slipped into sleep.

Remington once again awoke abruptly to the sound of the morning crew taking their shift. He looked over to see Maeve sleeping next to him, his head still on her shoulder. Quickly he scrambled up, pretending like nothing happened and grabbed a piece of chalk to keep working. He tried and failed to notice the look on T'kocht's face as he walked out. The pain and defeat in it chilled Remington to the bone.

Remington worked the rest of the day switching off with T'kocht on drawing the necessary arcane circles. The crew kept themselves entertained with the newcomers. Nicky at one point, destroyed two of them in a playful dual, though the elderly dwarf gentleman got a hit against her. Not many get the honor of saying that. Others were conversing here and there, but Remington did not feel like talking.

He moved his way to the bow of his ship to stare off into the falling snow. He wished he could be like the snow, falling and floating with no destination, unaware of the turbulence of the air surrounding it. Just water, frozen in time.

His attention was snapped back into reality by a soft bell ringing in his mind. Someone had opened his personal chest. Someone was in his cabin. He turned toward the deck of the ship and noticed Maeve was missing. Remington considered confronting her, how could she just invade his personal secrets like that. That chest held objects that not even T'kocht knew he still had, all things that shaped Remington and reminded Remington of his past. But then again, did he not do the same to her when he walked away with her skin? What would she think of him now?

Remington turned his back to the cabin, pretending as though nothing was amiss. He was not ready to talk to her about that, not yet. He avoided her the rest of the day as they finished up the ritual circles, they were ready for the jump back. Remington began his arcane chanting, finding the weave to manipulate. Already he could feel his hands shaking with exhaustion, but Remington pushed through it. He looked toward T'kocht, his deep friendship pushing through any fear he might have, looking for strength. He worried he was not rested enough.

The snow started to pick up into a full blizzard before Remington lost memory of what happened next. He has a vague recollection of feeling the warmth of the sun on his face, Maeve by his side. He could remember the feeling of his legs unable to move, the shear pain of just existing, and being lifted off the ground before once again darkness overtook him.

The darkness, the exhaustion, was accompanied by nightmares worse than Remington had ever experienced. His dreams were a psychedelic trip reliving the death Areliel over and over but this time as she lay dying her face would melt away to be that of Maeve's. Remington's blade constantly slashing and bleeding her dry. The cycle was broken when he heard Maeve call his name and turning to face her, he felt a blade slip into his heart.

Remington woke up screaming, before realizing it was just another nightmare courteous of the River King. He stayed in his hammock, though not quite sure how he got there. Either way, he did not want to go to sleep. His heart rate already elevated, Remington jumped when he heard a knock on his door. Slowly getting up, he moved across to the door, his head throbbing in pain. Carefully opening the door, he found it to be night outside and Maeve and the goliath woman were at the door.

"Maeve?" he asked, surprised to see her at his door. "Is everything alright? Do you need something?"

"We, uh, heard a scream," she explained. "We wanted to make sure you were alright."

Remington flinched. He did not like that she heard his screams, why must he be so weak? "I'm alright, just a visit from an old friend. Nothing to worry yourself about." Remington was mumbling his words, though he tried to fight it, sleep kept pulling him back into the darkness.

"Alright," she said, looking as though she didn't quite believe him. "Let me know if you need anything."

She started to walk away. Remington wanted to ask her to stay, to lay by his side and keep the nightmares away. But he just slowly closed the door behind her. He did not want to bring her into his everlasting nightmare.

33

Remington was woken up many hours later by T'kocht entering his cabin. He shoved his face into the blanket, for not only was he still thoroughly exhausted from back-to-back jumps, he was still not ready to talk to T'kocht, not yet.

"I'm sorry to wake you, Captain, you still need your rest. But there is a ship on the horizon. I can lead the charge, you should stay here, but I thought you should know." T'kocht said, moving closer and rearranging some of the blankets.

Remington pushed himself up, grumbling about the ship. He began to shuffle over to put on his shoes.

"Lay back down, Remi," T'kocht demanded. "You are not strong enough yet, you are going to get yourself killed if you go out there. Let me take care of it."

"No," Remington asserted. "I will lead our crew as I always have. I will not sit back while they slaughter innocents in protection of themselves. And if I get myself killed, then maybe I will finally have some rest."

T'kocht moved to argue against him but decided not to pick a losing fight. Instead, he helped Remington gather his things before heading out. They were greeted by Nicky who gave them a quick rundown of the ship in question. It was flying a Saxe flag and, on the outside, appeared to be a simple fishing vessel. However, on closer inspection it seemed to be heavily guarded by foot soldiers.

Remington turned toward Maeve and her traveling companions. "You don't need to partake in this," he insisted. "This is my war not yours. Go below deck, and I can get you once it's over." Maeve and her friends did not move. Remington looked at them curiously, why would they help murder people who did nothing to them? It was their choice; he was not going to waste what little energy he had.

It did not take long for The Fey's Fortune to catch up to the other ship. The crew quickly boarded the ship and battle commenced. Remington went straight for the captain, though he was not at full strength. The captain demonstrated fighting stances and styles taught to all members of the Saxe army, he has seen Nicky fight with a similar style.

Remington was able to get a few good hits in before the captain drew is massive great sword and swiping it at Remington, sent him flying across the deck. He could feel the hot sticky blood flowing from his chest and he struggled to stand up. One more blow like that and he would be dead.

Smoke was starting to flood the deck of the ship, obscuring his view of most of the battle on the ship. Nicky had taken his place by the side of the captain, nimbly dodging his attacks and getting well placed strikes in of her own. He could see the look of recognition and fear as the captain realized who the woman he was fighting was. Most Saxe Empire soldiers had this same look when facing down Nicky. Remington used this opportunity to sneak behind him and deal the final blow, the final breath of the captain mixed with blood as Remington's sword found its home in his chest. With the captain dead, the rest of the fight would be a sinch.

Remington saw the last of the other crew quickly going down, blood soaking into the deck. Remington approached one of the remaining crew members with steady steps. He could feel the air around him grow colder and could see the fear deepen in the man's face.

Remington grabbed him, pulling him uncomfortably close, "I need you to deliver a message. Tell Alexander Cresthorn that I am coming for him, and he will regret ever crossing my path. Now run, I hope you can swim."

The poor soldier took off running, diving off the side of the ship into the dark waters. The smoke began to clear away, though no fire was to be seen. He quickly looked around and saw Maeve, she seemed fine, barely a scratch on her. Relieved, he began to shuffle back onto his ship, "Search the ship for whatever they were guarding. It must be valuable whatever it is."

Remington, moving slowly, barely made it to the plank to cross over when he heard Rinva shout, "Uh, Captain, I think we found what they were guarding."

Remington turned around and felt his heart sink in his chest as he saw grasped tightly in Rinva's hand was a young girl, no more than 8 years old. He could faintly hear the sounds of Maeve's companions talking to the girl, learning who she was, but he did not need to hear. Anyone who had grown up in the Saxe Empire would recognize her family emblem and her history. This was Lady Clairabelle Cresthorn, only known daughter of Alexander Cresthorn.

"You know the rules," the voice of Areliel echoing over his left shoulder. "You already let your one survivor go. We can't let any more get away, can we? But, oh look, our little Maeve is here watching your every move. What would she think, to see you drain the life of a child with no remorse. She thinks you are a monster now prove it. Don't make me punish you."

Remington did not want to respond, the River King did not deserve that satisfaction. However, Remington knew he was right, the girl would have to die. He began to take a step forward when he saw Maeve watching him. He saw a look of recognition in her face, she knew what he was about to do. She turned and ran to the half elven boy, who Remington finally learned was named Kel. Remington sighed and continued moving forward.

"Hold it my dear," Areliel returned. "Your friends just gave me a better idea. Don't you think you will feel so much more satisfaction if you were to bring her home? Think about the happiness of reuniting a little girl with her father. Think about the horror of the court as you slice her throat in front of them. Your revenge will be as sweet as ever."

Remington let out a sigh of relief, at least she was safe for now. The River King just gave him the time he needed to get out of this situation.

"Rinva, let her go get what she needs," he ordered, "we will be taking this little one home."

He waited for her to return carrying a small porcelain doll, and escorted her across the plank onto the Fey's Fortune. Curiously, he leaned down to her and whispered, "Welcome aboard my ship, my lady. Tell me, how is your sister Elizabelle doing?"

Clairabelle responded with a commanding fire, "I don't have a sister!"

Remington chuckled softly. He did not expect such a powerful voice to come from such a small body. "My apologies, I must be misinformed."

As The Fey's Fortune departed from the burning wreckage of its victim, Remington turned towards Maeve. He needed an answer. "Why? Why did you help. These were innocent people, there was no need for you to get your hands tainted as mine have been."

"We needed to protect you, you idiot!" Maeve exclaimed. "Look at you, you are barely standing upright, I was not going to let you just go out there and get killed."

Remington froze. Did she really mean that? Why would, after everything that had happened, she still want to help him? He watched her carefully as she walked away, a faint spark of hope growing in his heart. He wanted to go talk to her more, but she was right. He could feel his legs beginning to buckle underneath himself. Remington had not yet fully recovered from the back-to-back jumps. He returned to his cabin, for the first time looking forward to the future.

Remington woke up midday the next day. There was only a few days left until Maeve reached her destination and they would be parted once again. He exited onto the deck and saw her huddled with her friends. He needed to talk to her alone. Using his arcane gifts from the River King, he sent her a message, one only she could hear: "Can we talk?"

She quietly slipped away from her group, none of them noticing and followed him below deck. He turned around to face her, the candles flickering in the darkness illuminating her eyes with the fire in her soul. He needed to know the truth, "Did you find what you were looking for?" He could see the look of shock on her face as she realized he knew she was digging around in his room.

"I'm not sure. I was looking for something, any reason to not trust you. In that point, I guess I didn't find anything," she responded sheepishly.

Remington knew what was in the chest she was looking in, knew the ghosts of his past and reminders of the poison of his life. "Did what you found change your opinion of me? Did it reveal to you the truth?"

She thought for a moment. "No, it did not change anything. Though I am not sure of the truth you are referring to."

Remington looked up at her in surprise at both answers. "The truth you always knew. That I am a broken man, remade into a monster. Even now I have to wait knowing that I am taking this girl to her death."

"What do you mean?" Maeve asked.

So she did not know how the River King changed the deal. "I am ordered to return this girl to her father, and kill her in front of him," Remington stated stoically. He flinched at the expression of horror on her face, but it began to melt away.

"I can see you don't want to do this," Maeve whispered. "You keep telling yourself you are a monster, that you are broken. But a monster would not hesitate like you are. You are not irredeemable. We can find a way out of this, together."

Remington opened his mouth to protest but was cut off as Maeve quickly leaned in and kissed him. For the first time in almost 3.5 years, he felt warmth flow through his body. He breathed in the salt that coated her face, and felt the soft waves of her hair brush against his face. He could feel himself melting into her, bringing him back to those days on the island.

She slowly pulled herself away, her face was bright red. "My friends will be missing me," and with that she turned and raced up the deck. Remington took an hour to compose himself before going back up himself. For the first time in a very long time, Remington was truly happy.

34

Over the next two days, Remington spent time catching up on sleep and stealing glances at Maeve. He knew she was in a rush to complete whatever mission she was on, but he wanted to savor every second he had with her. However, this light that had re-entered his life was shadowed by the young girl still on the ship. He knew he would have to follow through with the River King's plan, and though he hated the idea of putting a young girl's life to an end, it was his best chance at getting close to Lord Cresthorn.

On the last day, as the ship was approaching land, Remington was standing on the port side of the deck, watching as their destination grew over the horizon. Soon Maeve would be gone, and he would have to make his way to Belward once more to enact his revenge. He wondered if he could follow through with it.

He felt a hand gently brush his shoulder. Maeve was standing besides him, resting her arms on the railing. She looked towards him, "What are you going to do?" she asked.

He knew she was talking about the girl. "I am going to do what I have to, my crew will always come first. Though I take no pleasure in it."

He could see disappointment flood her face and guilt weighed on his heart. "You know," he continued, "I could turn a blind eye. Let you just walk her off my ship and my obligation with her."

Remington regretted the words as soon as he said them, the River King would never allow that. The cold wind that suddenly passed confirmed his suspicion. However, Remington was surprised when he heard Nicky speak up behind him. He did not know she was there.

"Captain, you can't just let them leave with her," she stated quite aggressively. "This is the best shot we are ever going to get at the Cresthorns. We can't just throw this gift away like this."

Remington turned towards her furious. He was aware Nicky had a strong grievance against the Saxe Empire and they were somehow involved with her injuries, but he did not realize how deeply her hatred ran. She never talked about it.

"A gift!?" he shouted back. "Nicky, she is an 8-year-old child. We have done some terrible shit in the past, I know we have, I started it. Have we turned into such monsters that we are willing to kill a child? No more. I don't want us to lose the last shreds of humanity we once had. At some point we have to say no."

Remington did not know where this defiance came from, but he began to fear the very words he spoke. He looked towards Maeve for encouragement, and she responded with a smile.

Nicky gave him a bit of a shove, "Are you serious? Do you not remember our predicament? What do you think will happen to us if we don't do as we are told. Or have you been lying to us about all this bullshit? She doesn't know what we have been through, don't let yourself think this sudden burst of humanity is going to change anything about the past."

Remington could tell that she too regretted the words as they left her mouth, but she was too angry to admit she was wrong. It did not change the fact that her words were unacceptable. But she was also right, there would be consequences and there would be no changing the past. "That's enough," he commanded, "go get ready for harboring. I will talk with you later."

Maeve grabbed his hand in support, "Are you okay?"

"No," he whispered. "Nicky is right, we can't just turn an eye, no matter how much I want to. I'm tired of having to make these decisions. I'm so tired Maeve."

Wanting to be alone, Remington moved to the top deck. He could see the shore not 500ft away. As he was walking, he saw Kel by the girl. Remington could see him grabbing the girl's hand and beginning an arcane spell. Remington could see the portal forming next to the girl, they were trying to escape. Remington felt the powers of the River King stir inside him and he focused on the portal.

He watched the portal fizzle out, the boy Kel looking at him with concern. Remington began to walk towards him, and once again Kel attempted to take the girl, and once again Remington negated it. Remington could feel the power in him draining, he would only be able to do this once more. Remington was closing in, and a third time, the boy tried, and for a third and final time, Remington put an end to it.

"You will stop this nonsense if you want to continue to live," Remington threatened grabbing the boy's hand. Kel nodded, fear growing in his eyes.

Remington could not believe they would try something so openly defiant against him. He knew he did not have the strength to stop them if they tried again. He hoped his threats were enough, he did not want to hurt them, but would fight to keep the girl no matter what.

As he stormed off back to the helm of the ship, he heard footsteps following him. Maeve joined him at the helm.

"I'm sorry about Kel," Maeve started, "he is such an idiot sometimes. Doesn't think before doing things."

Remington shook his head, "This is not something you or your friends can help me with. I have to help my crew, even if it means letting go the last of my humanity. I wish I could say I have a choice, but I don't. I'm sorry you had to get involved with this, but I hope you can forgive me. You see the best in me, the chance to change. For once, I don't feel the pressure, you would never make me do anything I don't want to. You have never tried to manipulate me. I trust you, Maeve, though I accept you may never fully trust me back."

As he finished his sentence, Remington was silenced as Maeve leaned in for a kiss. He felt his legs grow weak and he melted into her, feeling her strength build his soul from the corpse it was. Everything in that second was perfect, then his reality shattered.

"Captain!" Nicky cried out. Quickly pulling himself away Remington looked up to see the goliath woman flying through the air toward shore, with the girl with her.

Remington stumbled back, "T'kocht stop them," he shouted. It did not take long before he could hear the loud explosions of T'kocht's gun echoing across the boat. Remington did not care, his eyes were focused on Maeve. He felt every bone in his body, every scar that formed over his heart rip open. There was no good left in the world around him. He trusted her, to help him, to support him, and all she did was lie.

"I'm sorry Remington," Maeve said, "but it's for your own good. I am doing this for you." She turned and jumped over the side of the boat, making a swim for shore.

Her words slammed into him like a ton of bricks. Echoes of those words from his past, constantly spoken by Areliel as she beat him down, turning him into nothing. The whole time, promising him it was for his own good, that she was helping him.

"That is what she told me too," Remington said as Maeve dipped below the railing of the ship.

He looked around, her other companions were already off the ship, almost at the shoreline. He saw T'kocht shoot down the woman and child into the sea, but their friends were already there to help. Time seemed to slow around Remington, there was nothing he could do, they would be long gone by the time he made it to shore, he didn't want to make it to shore. The group disappeared over the grassy knoll, Remington not moving or saying a word. Nothing mattered anymore, there was no one left in his life.

He could hear the talk of the crew around him asking if they were to follow, but the voices sounded distant and distorted. They were all drowned out by a strong laughter ringing in his ears, the River King's laughter, his true voice coming through on this rare occasion. Remington could only shake his head; he was not going to follow them. He couldn't.

35

⬥

"You failed me," the River King stated, his laughter finally dying down. "You let the girl get away, your one chance at your revenge. Not to mention you have ignored my orders to take her back home. Let the punishment begin."

Remington barely heard the River King, his eyesight focused on the shoreline, where Maeve ran off, betraying him. His thoughts were quickly brought back to his ship as a scream of pain echoed across the deck, quickly followed by a loud thunk. Looking to see the source of the sound, he saw T'kocht on the deck of the ship, writhing in pain, the wood around him collapsed and splintered from where he impacted from the crow's nest.

"No!" Remington shouted running towards T'kocht. The crew quickly made room for him to get by as Remington slid to the ground, resting at T'kocht's side. T'kocht was still screaming, holding his hands to his head as if he was trying to prevent it from exploding.

"T'kocht, speak to me, what happened?" Remington desperately asked. He attempted to hold down T'kocht to keep him from further injury, but it was in vain. T'kocht was always much stronger than Remington.

"Make it stop Remi!" T'kocht pleaded, tears now streaming

down his face. "The voices, the pain, make it stop. Please, I can't, I'm sorry." T'kocht repeated over and over, begging for it to stop and apologizing.

Remington looked helplessly at his friend screaming in agony, before turning his face to the sky. "What do you want from me, I will give you whatever you want, just stop hurting my crew. Let me carry their pain."

"It's amazing the regret and guilt so many of you mortals carry with you with such a short life," the voice of Maeve echoed in his mind. "You bottle it up, make sure nobody else sees it, make sure nobody else knows the true monster that lies beneath. You want to help your crew? Release the smoke from that bottle. Tell him the truth you never wanted to face. Tell him."

Remington looked down at T'kocht and saw blood starting to flow down his face as T'kocht clawed at his own head, desperate to make the pain stop. Remington shook his head, this was not a conversation he was ready to have, not in front of his crew, but he could not bear to see T'kocht in pain. He wondered how much pain he would leave T'kocht in by telling him.

Remington bent down and grabbed T'kocht by the head forcing him to be still. "T'kocht, look at me. Look at me."

T'kocht opened his eyes, and looked at Remington. He could see the fear and panic set deep within his black eyes, reflecting Remington's own face back at him. Remington could see the guilt in his own eyes, but he had to push through.

"I know T'kocht. I tried to pretend like I didn't, tried to continue to remain blind to the truth, but I cannot deny that my eyes are now open. You have loved me since I first stepped onto this ship." Remington paused, and he could see T'kocht's eyes widen, attempting to look anywhere but at Remington.

"I know that you love me," Remington continued tears starting to flow himself, "but I cannot give you the same love back. You are my brother, a friend that I cannot bear to be without. But I am broken, T'kocht. A husk of a human that has always destroyed both people in any relationship I enter. I couldn't do that to you, you deserve better. I am sorry for the pain that I have caused you. I'm so sorry."

Remington released T'kocht, burying his face into his hands. He could hear the crew whispering around him, some attempting to pretend that they heard nothing, others debating if they should attempt to comfort him. The screams from T'kocht had stopped and was replaced by a deafening silence. Remington did not want to look up.

"Everyone move, give them some space," Nicky began ordering, "don't any of you have a sense of privacy, move it."

The entire crew began to shuffle around the deck, some of the more curious attempted to stay nearby to eavesdrop but were quickly moved by Nicky. Eventually, Remington and T'kocht were alone on the ship, both remaining silent in between their tears.

T'kocht was the first to speak, "How long have you known?"

"Not long, I figured it out just before we met Justice. I was angry and confused, and I took it out on you. I lied to myself, told myself that you were just using me as a pawn, anything to hide the fact that everyday I was leaving you in pain, blind to the struggle that you faced. That if I could push you away then the pain would end." Remington stared at his lap, he could not bring himself to look at T'kocht.

"I never wanted you to know," T'kocht stated. "I always knew what the answer would be, always knew that while Atrigul stood, I had no chance. Her hold over you was always stronger than anything I had seen before. I'll admit that on the day she died, and you saved my life, I thought that maybe there was a chance. You chose me over her, but it was false hope. Even the Pirate King knew."

"The Pirate King?" Remington asked, surprise entering his voice.

"That first day I met him, he told me, 'he will never be yours'. I refused to believe him, but reality eventually took hold. Atrigul left her mark on you too deeply, and I accepted that you would never be capable of loving anyone again. I was okay with that, as long as you were in my life, I was happy. I always hoped you would be able to find happiness, and always hoped it would be with me. Then Maeve appeared."

Remington felt the weight on his shoulders grow heavier and heavier, finally understanding the full force of the struggle his friend had gone through. All he could do was listen.

"That first day you appeared on the ship after meeting her, I could see a new light in your eye, one I had not seen in a long time. Someone had caught your eye, but you were blinded by the poison still flowing in your heart. I tried to warn you, but I was angry. Angry that some nobody was able to capture your heart so quickly where I had failed. I spent that month in resentment, questioning why I tortured myself every day, keeping the one thing I wanted just out of reach. I almost left, thinking if I did, I would untie the ropes that bound me to you that you would never see."

Remington began shaking. How could he have let this go on so long? Let his friend struggle so desperately with no one to support him?

"Then you returned, and I saw the anguish within you. Saw the destruction caused by your own self sabotage. It made me realize something. He was right, you would never be mine, but that does not mean I could not be yours. You needed a friend, a brother, to help guide you out of the darkness. But the entire time you were always my light leading us out. My life would be nothing without you, I would not give up our brotherhood for anything. And I knew I needed to make sure you never knew the truth, as I knew how much it would pain you. Lousy job I did at that huh."

Remington finally looked up at T'kocht, taking in everything that was being said. "I'm so sorry, T'kocht, I'm so sorry. Please forgive me." Remington leaned over bringing in T'kocht into a tight hug.

T'kocht hesitated for a second before returning the hug. "You have nothing to apologize for, but can you promise me one thing?"

"Anything," Remington responded.

"No more secrets between us okay? All it does is hurt each other. If we are to survive, we have to trust each other. No more lies."

Remington froze, T'kocht was right, if they were to survive, there needed to be no more secrets. How could Remington tell T'kocht that he did not plan to survive. "I promise," Remington lied. He felt as though a massive stone appeared in the pit of his stomach, but he had made up his mind. Even after all he learned, he could not see a future for himself. He was going to get his revenge, and die trying.

36

Over the next week, various others of the crew members fell to the same fate as T'kocht. A sudden onset of pain and screaming as their minds were filled with every action they ever felt guilty about. Remington did his best to comfort his crew, occasionally convincing the River King to pass the pain along to him. This only worked for those who had less guilt in their mind.

The length of time the pain lasted varied person to person. It seemed the more guilt one had, the longer the pain lasted, and the stronger the pain. Many of the crew shared in the pain, watching their friends scream in agony, with no way of helping them until it passed. The worst session was experienced by Nicky, who was writhing and screaming in agony for over 3 hours. Her weapons had to be ripped from her hands to prevent her from removing her remaining ear. She hid away from the crew for two days after that, not wanting to talk to anyone.

Eventually, the episodes seized. Remington wondered if the River King got bored or if the punishment was completed. It did not matter, his crew were finally given the opportunity to recover. He could see the horror and pity creeping into their eyes with full realization of what he was protecting them from setting in. Remington knew he had to end this soon.

The Fey's Fortune was on its way back towards Belward, towards Lord Alexander Cresthorn. T'kocht had been able to convince Remington that going after Lord Cresthorn alone would spell the death of the entire crew, that they needed help. Remington sent a message to Justice, asking for one more meeting, to help each other out in their journey for revenge. She agreed. They were to meet on the coast south of Topperpoint, where this potential partnership might form.

It took 3 weeks to reach Topperpoint from Maeve leaving the ship. Remington tried his best to keep her out of his mind, but the River King would not allow it. Every attempt to get rest was filled with betrayal, hatred, and pain. He could feel himself growing weaker as the increased lack of sleep started to take its toll on his body.

Remington and his crew were preparing to leave the ship, and make for the shore to meet with Justice and her group the Blood-roots. "I hope you are okay," Remington heard Maeve's voice enter his mind. He wondered if it was really her or the River King. There was no chill between his shoulder blades, it was her. He felt his blood begin to boil.

"You know I was only doing what I thought was right for you. I hope he didn't punish you."

Remington let out a scoff. The games, the dishonesty sickened him to the bones. Her mind tricks would no longer work, he would not let himself fall victim to another Areliel. He responded, "Know that all their pain is because of you. You did this." In the back of his mind he winced, he began regretting his words, wondering if her concern was genuine. He quickly walled in that thought, he could not afford to think that way.

"Are you alright Remi?" asked T'kocht, startling Remington out of his thoughts.

Remington nodded, "Just some lies finding their way into my mind. Don't worry about it. Let's go find Justice."

The crew walked for 2 days inland, only a small subsection of the crew remaining on board to keep it safe. Even Nicky was convinced to come ashore, though she was very reluctant. It did not take them long to find the Bloodroot's campsite, there must have been at least 100 people at the camp.

As Remington approached, he spotted Justice walking toward him, at her side a pyllbanor man. The man stood tall, Remington estimated him to be about 7'9". His fiery red hair contrasted with the light grey fuzz that covered his skin and cow like ears and nose, common to the forest dwellers. The pyllbanor wore a fully grown beard, which was highly unusual for folk of his kind. As they got closer, Remington was surprised to recognize the pyllbanor. The man was with Maeve when he picked her up in the Feylands, though Remington could not remember seeing him after the jump.

"Hello Remington," Justice proclaimed, "I am surprised to hear from you so soon. This is my partner, Elaren, the true leader of the Bloodroots. I don't believe you were properly introduced when you rescued him. Thank you for bringing him home."

Elaren studied Remington though he did not say anything. Remington could tell that Elaren was uncomfortable with his presence, though he seemed conflicted by his thoughts.

"We have a lot to discuss, Mr. Darkwalker," Elaren finally spoke. "Please get yourselves settled and come into camp for dinner. We have plenty of time to discuss politics later. You are safe while you are under my protection, so rest, you must be tired from your journey."

"Myself and my crew have no need for sustenance. If it is all the same to you, I would prefer to start discussions as soon as possible," Remington replied. He did not want to waste any time, he was ready to be free.

"It is not all the same to me Mr. Darkwalker," Elaren calmly said. "You may not need food, but I do. And I will not have discussions with a man who looks like he is barely on his feet with exhaustion. Justice is to leave shortly for a mission of her own, and maybe we can have a discussion on why you look like you have not slept in 3 days after she is gone. Please, stand around and wait if it makes you more comfortable, otherwise try to relax."

Remington let out a small growl under his breath. His personal life and health were none of Elaren's concern. Remington knew however, that he needed this man's help and begrudgingly dropped his bag onto the ground. "Make camp, I think we might be here a while," Remington ordered to his crew. "When you are done, you can go mingle with those of the Bloodroots if you choose. Nicky, T'kocht, I want to talk with you."

Remington, Nicky, and T'kocht moved away from the others for a little bit of privacy. "This Elaren character doesn't trust me," Remington began. "We are going to have to tread carefully if we are to get anything out of him, he is much more level-headed than Justice. I was not ready for his hesitancy."

"He is not wrong, Remi," T'kocht stated. "I know you do not like sleeping but it's been a long time since you have had any time to relax. This delay might be good for all of us. It might be the rest we finally need."

Remington shot a glare at T'kocht. He knew he was right, but had accepted that there was nothing he could do about it. He turned to Nicky, "I know you never talk about the empire, but I also know you very closely follow their news. What do you know about these people."

"Well, I know Elaren scares me a lot more than Justice does," Nicky began. "Justice acts on pure emotion, makes her violent, quick to decide, but predictable. Elaren tends to think things through much more, and always seems to be 10 steps ahead of the authorities.

He disappeared about 8 months ago and wasn't seen again until he hopped aboard the ship. No one knew where he was or what he was doing. Both of them have very large bounties on their heads by the Lords of Lebdi. Anything we try to convince him to do needs to be logical. He will not put his people in danger unless needed. He is a lot like you really."

Remington nodded, taking in everything she said. He was going to have to be patient, no matter how much he detested the idea. "Alright. I want both of you at all discussions with him. Stop me if I get hasty. Let's return to the group, I don't want to worry Elaren more than I already have."

The crew had already set up camp and began intermingling with the strangers when the three of them returned. The Bloodroots seemed welcoming to the cursed crew, not paying mind to their disfigurements. Remington found himself a seat away from the crowd, contenting himself to people watch and keep an eye on Elaren and Justice. They were talking amongst themselves along with a young man in his mid-twenties. Elaren seemed concerned and was talking very sternly to Justice, who seemed to be doing her best to ignore him, though she was not doing a good job at it. The man seemed aloof, unable to keep still, though he occasionally chimed into the conversation.

Eventually the three people walked over to a rather large tree nearby. The man placed his hand on the tree and traced his fingers down its trunk. Remington found his feet walking curiously toward them as he watched what appeared to be a portal open in the center of the tree. At this point he was close enough to hear their conversation.

"Remember, you are not your father. Return to me quickly please," Elaren was saying, looking deep into her eyes, his hands cradling her face.

"I know. I will be back soon," Justice replied. Elaren bent down, kissing her forehead before she walked through the portal.

"Shall we continue our conversation," Remington asked as the portal was closing.

"Yes, if that is what you wish," Elaren replied shortly. Elaren turned to the man, "That is all for now Milos, stay close though, she will need a ride back when she is done."

"Why does she get to have all the fun?" asked Milos. "I'm kidding, I'm kidding. I will be in the trees if you need me." And in a flash, Milos transformed into an eagle before taking to the sky.

"That's a neat trick," Remington stated. "I can see that being quite useful."

"Milos does what he wants," Elaren explained, "he is too old to take orders from anyone. Luckily our beliefs seem to align closely, so he occasionally helps out when it suits him. Enough about him, we have much to talk about, before I agree to work with you. We can meet in my tent, come." Elaren quickly walked away without checking to see if Remington would follow.

As Remington followed, he motioned T'kocht and Nicky to follow him. Rejoining each other, they followed Elaren into the tent. Elaren watched him curiously, "Your friends are welcome to join if you wish, though I might recommend you think otherwise. My business is with you."

Remington bit back his tongue, "Any decisions made here affect the whole crew. They will stay."

"Very well," continued Elaren, sitting down and grabbing a cup of tea. "I told you before that I will not discuss business with a man barely walking, so tell me, what did you do to anger such a powerful being. The River King is not a creature you want to anger."

Remington flinched, but quickly regained himself, "I took the skins from multiple selkies against their will through well placed deception. The River King caught us and granted us our lives at the cost of this curse. I avoid sleep to avoid discussions with him. I can assure you that I am well enough to hold an intelligent conversation."

"There is no use lying to me, Mr. Darkwalker," Elaren stated after a long sip of tea, "I can hear the slight slur in your words and I can see the shaking of your limbs as you fight back the darkness of sleep. I would recommend you refrain from lying to me from now on. I think you are smart enough to know that I am less willing than Justice to put my trust into you and your crew, especially when you travel with the Oblak Executioner." His eyes glanced towards Nicky with harsh accusation set within them.

"So, in order for you to convince me to help, you must first learn patience, and learn that I take decisions like this very seriously. I am not going to throw my men into a suicide mission on the whims of an angry man." Elaren returned his attention to Remington, unphased by Remington's admission of guilt.

Remington glanced toward Nicky, but she showed no emotion in her face. T'kocht gave him an encouraging nod. "Very well," Remington stated, "we will go at your pace. I appreciate a leader who looks after his people. However, any rest you make me take will be pointless. While he haunts me, I find no relief in the unconscious."

Elaren finished off his tea, letting out a deep sigh. "Mr. Darkwalker, you are under my protection now, and that includes being a part of the sanctuary that is this camp. I am sure you saw the arcane circle as you entered into camp. While you remain within this circle, nothing can find you. Your patron cannot see your activities here, and your mind is safe to find rest. So please, sleep, and tomorrow you can convince me that you are not using me as a vessel of your own death."

Elaren stood up and exited the tent into the campsite, saying nothing more to Remington. Remington, looked toward T'kocht and Nicky, "Do you think that's true?"

"We will find out tonight won't we," replied T'kocht.

37

Before Remington retired for the night, he pulled Nicky off to the side. Elaren seemed to have knowledge of her, and it was not favorable. He had heard the name Oblak Executioner a long time ago as a child. He tried to remember where, he thought maybe from some soldiers back in Rivenport but he did not pay much attention then. Remington needed to know now, if this deal with Elaren was going to play to completion.

"Nicky," he started, "who are you?"

"That's a stupid question," Nicky responded sarcastically.

"I mean it," Remington emphasized, "Elaren referred to you as the Oblak Executioner, and he said it as though it left a foul taste in his mouth. I have seen how some Saxe Empire soldiers look at you during raids. I haven't asked you about your past as I respected your privacy, but I know you hold some grudge against the Cresthorn family that is above just this curse. If we are to secure this alliance, I need to know what happened, so we can convince him to trust us."

Nicky rubbed her nose; he could tell she was very agitated. "The past is the past, I've moved on from that. It doesn't matter anyways, everyone thinks the Executioner is dead. Whatever side motivations I have won't affect the crew, I swear."

She was clearly avoiding answering his question, which annoyed

Remington. "Well clearly Elaren knows you are not dead now," Remington retorted, "please, just tell me. Maybe I can now return the favor of helping you when you so often helped me."

Nicky was now pacing at this point and began chewing on her fingernails. "What do you know about the high society of Belward?" she asked.

"Not much to be honest, never cared about it," Remington responded.

"The Oblak Palace is a magnificent mansion located in the Cloudtop District that floats above the rest of Belward, looking down on the rest of the population. It is the workplace to high-ranking military personnel and some of the Lords. It was also the home of the Cresthorn family. When the Executioner was a young girl, she lived on the lower streets of Belward after being abandoned by her parents. As any kid would do, she often got into tussles with the local law enforcement, often kicking their asses before running away. Well apparently, her reputation became known to some higher ups.

She was snatched off the streets in the middle of the night and taken to some training facility who knows where. There, along with a few others, she was trained to become a world class killer and assassin. To take orders without question, but also to not need orders. They learned military strategy, politics, and to think only of bettering the empire.

Well little Nikola grew up and quickly became a favorite of General Diluhd. She became one of the youngest Lieutenant Generals in Saxe Empire history and was often praised as a hero for the acts she did in the public eye. Behind the curtain, however, was a different story. She was the Lord's personal assassin. If someone needed to be gone, there would be no sign of them left in the morning.

This was all fine and dandy, until one day the late Lord Cresthorn and the General approached her with a mission of utmost secrecy.

Said she needed to go south into Fredlos, to deal with a threat to the empire. Told her that she needed to teach those who would defy them a pricey lesson. So, she did what any good soldier would do and she did as she was told. She arrived in the city of Storstad under the cover of night, and by the time she was gone in the morning, over 40 children hung dead from their parents' front door, their blood painting the Lebdi symbol into the wood."

Nicky had stopped pacing, her eyes focused on nothing as the memories returned to her. Remington was struggling to process all that he was hearing, he could not imagine the Nicky he knew now doing such acts. He was also concerned that she was talking as if this was a whole different person, that the Executioner and herself were not the same. He wondered if she truly believed they were different people. Her refusal of any position of authority began to make sense. He moved to place a hand on her shoulder to give his support but she aggressively shoved it off.

"It was a long walk back to Belward," continued Nicky, her lips curled in a scowl. "And during that long, lonely walk, she had time to think about what she just did. Not quite sure when it happened, but eventually she snapped. This horrific act was not her fault, no, it was the empire's fault, and anyone who chose to follow them willingly were to blame.

So, she returned to Belward with a little surprise. Instead of reporting the success of her mission, she stormed into Oblak palace and began killing anyone she could find that was part of the military. Worked her way up the floors leaving a blood trail behind her. Eventually she beheaded the general, and presented the head to the late Lord Cresthorn. She would have taken his head too, but he cast some bullshit magic at her that knocked her unconscious. Thus, she earned the name. It doesn't matter, since she died in the winters of Fredlos anyways. The Oblak Executioner doesn't exist anymore. Happy now?"

Nicky stared at Remington, daring him to judge her, but he only looked at her with understanding. "How many?" he asked cautiously.

"67 privates, 19 officers, 2 generals, and 5 minor lords," she replied as if she were just repeating a fact in history.

Remington wrapped his arms around her in an embrace, not knowing what to say, for nothing there was nothing he could say. "Thank you, and I'm sorry."

"Yah, whatever," Nicky stated ripping herself away from the hug. "I will finish what she started and complete my judgement. The good lord should have made sure I died, big mistake. I promise though, I will be on my best behavior just for you." Nicky made an x over her heart and held up a salute.

"I understand, at least now I better understand what Elaren may be thinking, but that is something we will have to deal with in the morning. Go get some rest."

Remington patted her on the shoulder before retiring to his tent, making sure that it was well within the circle that Elaren had pointed out. As he laid down and slipped into unconsciousness, he prepared himself for the onslaught of nightmares that awaited him behind closed eyes. The nightmares never came.

Remington awoke to the sun blazing into his tent, the chatter of people quite loud around him. He was not sure how long he had been asleep for, but for the first time in 5 weeks, he awoke feeling refreshed from long uninterrupted sleep. The smell of food drifted into his tent, reminding him that the curse still remained though the ache in his bones was lifted.

Poking his head outside the tent, the sun was high in the sky, well past noon. He cursed at himself for wasting so much of the day but decided Elaren probably would not have talked if he woke up any earlier. Stretching his muscles, he headed out into the camp to find his crew and to find Elaren, which did not take long, as Elaren towered a full foot taller than even the tallest man there.

"Ah much better," Elaren exclaimed seeing Remington approach. "I hope you enjoyed some brief respite from your patron. Now that you are rested up, I think it is time we begin talking. I need to who I am to be working with if I chose to do so. Please follow me."

Remington quickly looked for T"kocht and Nicky but did not see them anywhere. Not wanting to lose this rare opportunity to possibly move forward with Elaren, Remington followed him into the tent, out of sight from the world.

38

"So, Mr. Darkwalker, tell me, why did you come here seeking my help," Elaren asked. He sat behind a desk organizing various papers that were in slight disarray.

"Why can't he see me here," Remington asked, ignoring the question. He could barely remember what it felt like to be unwatched, but it felt good. "Can this be a permanent situation?"

Elaren shook his head, "I have been on the run a lot longer than you have Mr. Darkwalker. I have learned some tricks in the art of hiding and have been blessed with the support of Realta. This is not something that can easily be transferred. Like myself, you cannot hide forever. Now again, why did you come here?"

Remington watched him carefully, "I understand we share a common enemy. I want to see Cresthorn dead as much as you do. We can help each other, strike fast and strike soon. You will get the world that you want for the Bloodroots and I get my revenge. It is a win-win."

"What makes you think I want the Cresthorns dead?" Elaren asked without looking up from his paperwork. The question came as a shock to Remington.

"Is it not the goal of this organization to get rid of the Lords of Lebdi and the technology in this Empire?" Remington asked.

"It is," Elaren confirmed. "But dethroning Lords does not mean I wish death upon them. To achieve our mission, we must be smarter than that. I will not blindly run through the gates of Belward on a suicide mission. I will not aid you in your own death."

"It is not a suicide mission if we work together. We have strength in numbers," Remington retorted. "How long has your group been together and what progress have you made? Not much from what I see. I am willing to die for what I believe in, what about you."

Elaren let out a deep sigh and looked up at Remington. "Mr. Darkwalker, there is more to a cause than dying for what you believe in. If everyone did that nothing would ever get accomplished. Changing the world is a game of strategy, one that takes a long time to put the pieces into play. Rushing the game only creates carelessness and ultimately defeat. What you are suggesting..."

Elaren suddenly stopped talking, his expression quickly turning to concern. Remington even thought he detected a hint of anger in his eyes. Elaren quickly stood up and moved around the desk next to Remington. He grabbed Remington's hood and quickly forced it over his head, concealing his face. "You are coming with me. You need to see what you are proposing first hand."

Reaching into his pocket, Elaren pulled out a small candle that magically lit itself. Remington felt his body distort as the familiar sensation of teleporting took its toll. Remington landed slightly off balance onto a cold stony floor. Looking around the room, it was a blood bath. Remington quickly counted 7 dead bodies, and many figures soaked in blood. Seeing the body immediately next to him, he recognized the lavender skin of Justice.

Elaren was already kneeling next to her, "This is not how I wanted to present this to you." Reaching into his pocket, Elaren pulled out an intricate diamond ring and pressed it into her chest, muttering arcane words. Vines seemed to grow out of the diamond and into Justice before dissolving. Justice shot upright, gasping for air her body desperately desired.

"Do you see now," Elaren asked, his voice was level and unwavering. "Do you see now why I will not help you. You follow in the footsteps of these folk, of Justice, of the Executioner, on the path of revenge and all it leads to is death. Death of innocent people, who only wanted to help their friends. I will not participate in this suicide mission of yours as all it will lead to is more death. We are going to be here for a few days. You say you are willing to die for what you want, maybe in this time you will find something worth living for."

Remington scowled. He did not want to be lectured. If Elaren was not going to help then so be it, he would do this on his own. Taking now a closer look at his surroundings, he felt the air leave his lungs as he realized who these people were. Standing only 50ft away from him was Maeve. Anger once again flooded over his body and Remington stormed off towards the edge of the room, not wanting to be recognized, not wanting to talk.

Remington heard the faint murmurs of chatter as Elaren continued helping Maeve and her companions, but he did not listen. The sooner Elaren finished his business, the sooner Remington could return to his ship. Remington began pacing back and forth, unsure of what to do. The half elven girl, Gwen as they called her, approached him though he did not turn.

"Hi there, who are you?" she asked, though her tone indicated she already knew the answer. He did not respond. "What are you doing with Elaren?" she continued, this time attempting to maneuver her way so she could see his face. Again, he did not answer, and attempted to walk away.

"We know it is you Remington, stop being stupid and face us," a voice yelled out to him.

Remington stopped and slowly turning around took off his hood.

"I am not interested in talking to you after you stole my possession, now leave me alone," Remington grumbled.

"Well I don't want to talk to you either," Maeve shouted at him. "I was doing what was best for you, we agreed to let us take her. And she is not anyone's possession."

"I agreed to nothing. I can make my own god damned decisions!" Remington was shouting now, all his anger flooding out of him like the breaking of a dam. "I told you I was taking her with me. You have no right to make these decisions for me. No right to take what is rightfully mine!"

"What is rightfully yours?" Maeve accused, her voice now rising into a yell. "She is a child. You were in no state to make a good decision. You said to take her away."

"If I made a bad decision, then at least it would be mine to make. It was a child I barely knew or the suffering of my crew. There were no good choices there, but instead you made that choice for me. Condemning my crew to weeks of pain and suffering. You lied to me. Made me feel like you still cared and then you betrayed me." Remington was beginning to shake as his anger grew more and more.

"If that's what you believe then so be it," Maeve stated. "I did nothing wrong, though nothing I say will convince you otherwise. You know some people try to do the right thing for you. I'm done." Maeve quickly spun around, and Remington followed suit.

The silence in the room that followed was deafening as Remington paced back and forth once more. He wanted more than anything to get out of this hell hole of a building.

Gwen once again approached him. "We are going to explore the mansion a bit, want to come."

Remington paused. As much as he did not want to speak to anyone, it would at least get him away from Maeve, and Elaren did not look like he planned on leaving any time soon. "Anything to get me out of here quicker," Remington stated flatly. Turning around, he slowly followed Gwen out of the laboratory they were in.

39

Remington helped these folk search through this large dwarven mansion for a while. They seemed very focused on finding specific items, though Remington could not care less on what they were trying to do. He could tell they didn't like him, and they certainly did not trust him. This did not bother him, though he couldn't help but wonder why Gwen would have dragged him along if none of the others wanted him there.

As they were returning to the room they started in, after not finding much, Gwen fell in line with him. "Why do you think everyone is out to get you?" she asked. Remington looked at her curiously. He was taken aback by the bluntness in her questions, she had no fear in asking what everyone in the room was probably thinking. Yet, she had strange mannerisms that made her appear like she was not from this time.

"I think that because it is true," Remington responded. Though he did not like talking about his past, Remington felt a strange need to defend himself. "My whole life the world has been out to get me. Those around me manipulating me and making my choices for me, for the worse. I put up my guard to make sure that doesn't happen again."

"You know," Gwen said, "I actually know what you are talking about." Remington looked at her curiously. She continued, "For a long while I was under the lies and charms of a terrible person. She made me think I was doing good things, helping others, but in reality, we were performing horrific acts. Once the veil of the illusion was lifted, I realized what I had done and it was awful."

"Then you understand," Remington said. This girl knew what it was like, she understood. "I have worn and removed that veil too many times, I will not allow myself to put it back on."

She nodded, processing what Remington told her. "So, what was this suicide mission Elaren was talking about. He doesn't seem thrilled about it."

Remington let out a sigh, "I plan to storm Belward and dispose of Lord Cresthorn. I came to Elaren hoping to get his assistance, but he thinks I have no chance. I am going with or without his help."

Gwen seemed to hesitate for a second on this. "What if I told you there was a bigger threat than Lord Cresthorn?" she asked cautiously. "Have you heard of someone named Nemuah?"

Remington felt ice run up his back as Areliel's voice whispered in his ear, "Do not listen to this one. She is trying to distract you from your goals. Manipulate you. Isn't Cresthorn the reason you are in this situation. Is he not your prize?"

Remington looked curiously over his shoulder, though he knew he would find nothing there. The River King clearly did not want Remington to learn about this person, but why? "No, I have not," Remington responded to Gwen. "Please, tell me more."

Remington listened closely as Gwen went into lengthy detail about this Nemuah character. He learned Nemuah was once one of the Fey Court, known as the Night Queen, before the others cast her out and took away all of her strength. Over the many thousands of years Nemuah grew in strength in secret, leaving the others of the Court to think her gone for good. Gwen explained this was the woman she was charmed by before a friend of hers who was still captive rescued her. Supposedly Nemuah is planning some sort of revenge plot against the rest of the Court in an attempt to destroy the Feylands.

Remington struggled to catch every detail as the River King desperately attempted to keep him distracted. About half way through, Remington began to feel a searing pain begin to form between his shoulder blades that grew as Gwen continued her story. He did his best to ignore it, anything the River King did not want him to hear needed to be learned.

"I am not sure I see the threat," Remington said calmly. He could tell Nemuah scared Gwen, but he could not help but think that she could maybe help him. He did not want Gwen to know that. "Plus, she is in the Feylands from what you have told me. I cannot go there, I need to focus on what is in front of me."

"She has her fingers in so many groups, including Lord Cresthorn," Gwen emphasized. "He is just a symptom to a greater sickness. She will eventually come here to the Prime Realm and take out everyone here too. Take her out and he will fall with her!"

Remington smiled. Her passion and enthusiasm were charming, though misplaced. "I have to focus on what is obtainable, and right now that means Lord Cresthorn. I wish you luck though in your quest."

By this point, the group had returned back to the original room. Maeve was sitting by Elaren and Justice, who was sleeping on Elaren's lap. Remington did not want to talk with either of them and luckily, they felt the same way. He watched as the others gathered together for the night to sleep, putting up protective domes that Remington could not see into. Collapsing on the floor, Remington was finally alone. He did not want to sleep, but he could not handle the growing feeling of emptiness inside of him. Elaren had Justice, Maeve and her friends had each other, and Remington was alone, isolated and shunned.

Letting out a yell of frustration, Remington drew The Fortune Teller and headed toward the trap door. The least he could do was make himself useful and take care of the undead that he heard roaming about outside. As he was opening the hatch, he heard Elaren call to him, "Mr. Darkwalker."

Remington turned to face him, though he was impatient to get out of this building. "I know there is a lot going through your mind," Elaren continued. "She has always been my light when I found myself on the boarders of twilight. Maybe she can reignite something inside of you."

Elaren stepped forward and placed a metal medallion in Remington's hand. Remington turned it over and noticed pressed into it was the image of a sun surrounded by stars shooting out from it. The symbol of Realta, the goddess of flames and stars. Remington rolled his eyes, Elaren was just another cleric attempting to convince him the gods are helpful.

Elaren saw the distain in his eyes. "Roll your eyes all you want Mr. Darkwalker but take this with you none the less. Maybe it will convince me to help you eventually." Elaren closed Remington's fingers around the medallion before turning around to return to Justice.

Remington scoffed and trudged out onto the streets. Looking around, Remington found the city to be completely underground. The buildings were constructed of stone and metal. Each structure incorporating itself into the large cavern helping to support the ceiling. The architecture was dwarvish in nature. Remington figured they must be in the dwarven city of Khardarum, an ancient city built deep into the Asdiac Mountains.

Remington did not have a ton of time to admire the architecture when the first of the undead charged at him. It used to be a dwarven woman, but now a black necrotic poison seemed to infect her vanes. Her eyes glowed a bright purple which emphasized the burst blood vessels in the white of her eyes. There was no life behind those eyes, only an anger and a desire for violence.

Remington froze as he watched her fling herself toward him. He had seen that look before. He saw that look in his eyes every time he looked into the mirror. He wondered if that is all he was, a mindless undead aimlessly wandering at the whim of his patron. His thoughts were interrupted as the woman sank her teeth into his shoulder. Remington let out a yell as the pain spread down his arm. Quickly he brought up The Fortune Teller and decapitated the head, which stayed attached to his shoulder.

Remington ripped the head off his shoulder with a disgusted grumble. His focus back on the danger around him, Remington began fighting his way through the streets of Khardarum, knocking out one undead after another. Remington was not sure where he was going, nor did he care. It felt cathartic releasing his held in anger, occasionally screaming as loud as he could just to let go of the pressure.

As Remington turned a corner, looking for more of the undead, he felt a tug in his mind. Curiously, he turned his head and saw a small building to his right. The door to enter was open and a small brazier was burning in a central room. Every cell inside of him was screaming to enter, to stare into the flame. Remington did not resist as his feet started moving on their own through the doorway.

40

As Remington entered into the building, he quickly realized that this was a temple. He observed the murals painted into the walls of flames engulfing a forge, of a dwarven male with mechanical wings flying towards the sun, and stars seemingly glowing on their own speckled the room.

Remington let out another scoff, of course he wandered into a temple of Realta. He reached into his pocket and pulled out the medallion that Elaren had given him. "You sly bastard," Remington whispered to himself. Annoyed by this unexpected detour, Remington turned to exit the temple. As he turned his back on the brazier, the lights in the temple went out and the flames were extinguished.

"What the..." Remington's words of confusion were cut off as the perimeter of the room ignited in a massive wall of flame. Remington's eyes widened as the flames filled his vision. He could see the iron brand sitting in the fireplace, the smell of his own burning flesh began filling his nostrils reminding him of that night with Areliel.

Unable to think clearly, Remington ran. He hoped he could punch his way through the flames as quickly as possible and escape. He felt the heat blaze against his skin and as he ran closer, the heat became unbearable as his vision began to fade to black. Remington saw the blackness fade into memories. He saw himself, only 5 years old, at his parents' funeral, crying about concepts he could barely understand.

"Forgive," a female voice rang out. It was forceful but caring. The vision faded and Remington found himself back on the island with Brend. Brend was sinking beneath the mud as Remington struggled to reach out, attempting to change the past though he knew he could not.

"Forgive," the voice repeated.

"No!" Remington shouted, "Leave me alone!"

The vision shifted; Remington felt a warm sticky liquid spread across his chest. He looked down and saw the dying body of Areliel struggling on the ground. He rushed forward trying to help. "I'm sorry, I'm sorry," he kept saying. Everything around him felt so real, it began to overwhelm him.

"Forgive," the voice repeated.

"No," Remington shouted back, though weaker this time. He was not sure if the voice could hear him or not.

The vision once again shifted. He was on the beach, holding onto a selkie's skin, Maeve's skin. He could see her sleeping on the beach, unaware of the treachery around her. He could see her face looked much younger, free from the anger and strife that he caused. He struggled against history to move his feet and just return the skin, to turn back and leave her happy. But they would not move.

"Forgive," the voice continued to insist.

"Why should I?" Remington asked, "I don't deserve it." There was no response.

The vision faded, this time images popped up one after another of T'kocht. He could see T'kocht's goofy smile as he saw Remington that first day on the Sickening Rose. He heard a thud and as he spun around saw T'kocht sending his fist into the mantle at Elianne's old house when he first saw Remington's scar. He saw the hundreds of hidden glances and smiles that T'kocht snuck without Remington noticing. He felt the fear as T'kocht saw Rinva carrying Remington's limp body onto the ship. He saw the pain in T'kocht's eyes as they argued over Maeve.

"Enough, stop this," Remington pleaded. "Please."

"Forgive," was all the voice ever responded.

The vision switched, and Remington watched as every life he ended flashed before his eyes. There were hundreds of faces that flew past his field of view, each one mangled in fear and pain.

"Forgive," the voice repeated once more.

"I can't!" Remington yelled into the void, finally admitting the truth.

Remington found himself back in the temple, still surrounded by flames. His clothes were scorched, and he could feel the burns forming on his skin. He started retching at the smell of his own burnt flesh, the scar on his chest more painful than ever.

"Why do you resist?" the same feminine voice asked. The flames around him grew and shrank with the words, as if they were speaking to him.

Remington ignored the voice and attempted to run through the flames again. Once again, the visions flashed through his mind as he was thrown back by the flames. Each time the voice insisting forgiveness. Each time, Remington rejected it.

Remington groaned as he stood up from the ground. Half his jacket had burned away and he could feel the cool air on his back.

"Why do you insist on rejecting yourself?" the voice asked. Remington thought it sounded sad but brushed the thought aside.

"Why do you insist upon me finding forgiveness? What does it matter to you?" Remington responded. He was annoyed, but realized he was not going to get out of this through force.

"Everyone deserves forgiveness," she responded. "Forgiveness clears out the darkness and allows the light of hope to fill its space. You have been shrouded in the dark depths of guilt your whole life. Let the flames illuminate the truth and kindle life."

"How?" Remington asked, "How can I forgive? I am a monster. I have only hurt everyone around me. Innocent people who did not deserve the cruelty I dealt them. I don't deserve forgiveness, let me be lost to the darkness. You can't help me."

"You are right," the voice agreed to Remington's surprise. "I cannot help you, only you can help yourself. The guilt you carry is clouded by lies. Lies that were created by you to hide the truth, and to create the pain you think you needed. End the addiction and see past the guilt. Understand, then forgive."

Remington processed the words spoken. Was he truly addicted to the pain, to the anguish? Remington took a deep breath and walked towards the flames as calmly as he could. He could feel the chills over his skin from where it was burnt but did his best to fight the urge to run away. He had to face his past.

As Remington stepped into the flame, he braced himself for the onslaught of memories. He watched carefully as each one flashed before his eyes. He remembered the manipulation, the pain, the anger that led him towards each of his actions. He could still feel the guilt eating away at what remained of his soul.

"Forgive," the voice repeated.

The voice brought Remington out from the spiral into darkness he was falling into. He saw his friends around him, supporting him through every slip in his downward climb. Always reassuring him, telling him it's not his fault. That he shouldn't burden the guilt. Were they right, he wondered.

"I forgive you!" Remington shouted at himself. And he meant it. Remington felt a large weight lift off his shoulders as he flew forward, landing on his knees. As he looked around, he realized he was back on the streets of Khardarum. The flames were gone and the streets were quiet, as if nothing had happened. The smell of smoke rising from his ruined clothing confirmed for Remington that all that had really happened, though he was not sure what that was.

Remington raced back to the mansion, not even bothering to deal with the undead that he passed by. Forcing open the trap door, he immediately laid eyes on Elaren.

"What the fuck did you do to me?" Remington shouted at Elaren.

Elaren slowly turned towards him. At this point Remington saw Maeve in the room speaking to Elaren, along with her friends. "Ah, there you are," Elaren calmly spoke. "We were just talking about you. Did you find any answers?"

The soothing calmness of Elaren's voice was jarring to Remington. He could feel the calmness wash over the anger and confusion. "I did," Remington responded to his own surprise. He turned towards Maeve who was staring at his disheveled appearance, "Can we talk, in private?"

Maeve nodded her head and followed him down the trap door into the other room. Remington began to panic. Why did he ask her down here? What was he trying to accomplish? Before he could collect his thoughts, Maeve broke the silence, "What happened to you?"

Remington turned to face her. She looked concerned. "It's a long story," began Remington. "But first I need to apologize. For everything. I was in a dark place and I brought you into it. If I could go back and undo everything, I would. But I can't."

"I'm sorry too," Maeve said, stepping towards him.

Remington started laughing, "You have nothing to be sorry for. This is my fault, I recognize that. You should not be the one apologizing."

Maeve looked at him, then looked down at the floor. "What happened to you?" she asked again.

Remington reached into his pocket and pulled out the medallion.

"Elaren gave me this. I went out onto the streets to blow off some steam, ended up in a temple. I was forced to relive my guilts and learned to forgive myself for them."

Remington paused. He thought about what had happened. He might have forgiven himself for the past, but he realized he could not forgive himself for the future. As long as he was a slave to the River King, he would keep destroying the lives of those around him. He cared too much for Maeve to put her through that. He had to let her go, before he hurt her any more.

"I may have forgiven my past," Remington slowly continued, "but I can't continue to hurt you. You deserve so much better, a life that I cannot offer you. I hope one day your skin finds its way back to you, but while I am around it never will. So this is goodbye Maeve. I wish you well where you go."

Remington struggled to keep a stoic mask over his face. He did not want to say goodbye, but he had to if she was to move forward. He saw no escape from this curse, she did not deserve to be cursed as well.

Maeve began crying, though she struggled to keep herself together. Remington wanted to reach over and wipe the tears away, to tell her it was going to be alright. But he didn't. "No it is not," she said through her tears.

"I don't understand," Remington questioned. What did that mean? Why would she not just let him leave?

"This is not goodbye. You do not get to say that. Let me help you, we can find a way out of this. I have plans, ideas. Just let me help." Maeve was pleading. Remington could hear the desperation in her voice.

"I am not good for you Maeve," Remington shouted back, a little louder than he intended. If she knew the truth, she would run, she would give up on this idea that he could be saved. "I have killed so many people in horrific ways. Unarmed people who did not deserve to die. I have lied to my friends and I have lied to you. I killed my first mate within months of joining my first pirate ship. Later I killed my captain after betraying her trust. I am a monster, Maeve. Just walk away from me."

"What happened to forgiving yourself? Huh? Sounds like that went so well." The sarcasm in her voice reminded him of their time on the island and though she was insulting him, he felt his heart skip a beat. But the voice was right. He was addicted to the pain, and though he accepted and forgiven himself in the past, it does not change that his future would be filled with more guilt.

"A forgiveness of the past is not an acceptance of the future. I can't continue this way, I have to end this."

"Is that what this suicide mission that Elaren keeps referring to is?" she accused. "What is your plan for that anyways."

Remington let out a sigh. "I am going to storm Belward and go after Cresthorn, with or without Elaren's help. I don't intend to return." Remington did not intend to admit that part, but there was something about Maeve that made him want to tell her everything.

"So you expect to die?" Maeve asked. "What's your plan if you succeed? What if you actually make it out alive?"

Remington never considered that option. What if he made it out with his revenge and his life? He shook his head, that could not be an option and he would make sure of that. "That won't happen," he whispered. "I plan to make sure of that. I hope your skin will find its way back to you after." Remington turned and began climbing back into the main room. He worried if he stuck around, Maeve would convince him otherwise. He could hear her tears behind him as he left, though he dared not turn around.

4 1

Remington stormed off to a corner to sit alone. He just wanted them to be gone, so he could be alone. Unfortunately, this group was not one to let people sit in peace. It did not take long for Gwen to once again sit next to him.

"I noticed the mark on your back," she said. Remington had noticed the mark she was referring to shortly after his first encounter with the River King. It sat right between his shoulder blades and he could feel an icy chill emanate from it whenever the River King spoke to him. He had done some research on it, learning it to be the mark of being cursed or blessed by a Fey Lord. Knowing there was not much he could do about it, he ignored it. He did not answer her.

"I had a mark like that too, but my friends deactivated it. Maybe Elaren could do something similar for you?"

Remington continued to admire the unwavering optimism she held, but again it was misplaced. "This is a mark of ownership, not a blessing. Unfortunately I cannot get rid of it because of that."

Gwen pondered that for a bit. "Is he always listening?" she asked cautiously.

"When he is interested in what is happening around me," Remington responded. He felt the cold on his back.

"And suddenly I am interested," he heard Areliel say over his shoulder. "Are you singing my praises?"

"Shut up," Remington said out loud, forgetting that Gwen could not hear the River King.

Gwen scrunched her face as though she was upset by this response. She then resolved herself and turned to him. "Alright I am going to tell you something then flood you with other stuff so maybe he won't hear."

Remington looked at her curiously, not sure where she was going with this.

Gwen took a deep breath, "We think there is a way to kill the River King. Puppies! Rainbows! Ice cream! Gold!..." she continued shouting random words at him, hoping to distract him, but her words hit him like a brick wall. Was she telling the truth? Was it really possible?

"Wow that girl is even more ditsy than I thought she was," Areliel laughed into his ear. Remington thought he could hear a hint of nervousness in her voice. "I am a Fey Lord. You cannot kill me. Why get your hopes up? Is Lord Cresthorn not your enemy? I have given you so much, I think we have become quite the team. Don't forget, I can see and hear everything you think. You can't return to the Feylands. I will see you, and if you thought your life was miserable now, think how bad it would be if you tried to hurt me. You would fail. You always do."

Remington recognized the truth in her words. As long as the River King could see Remington, he had no chance. Though Gwen's words refused to leave his mind. Could he free himself from this hell?

Remington's attention was torn from his internal thoughts by a commotion in the center of the room. Looking up he could now see a new, but familiar face in the middle of the room. Her pure white hair was unmistakable as Lady Clairabelle Cresthorn, the child from the ship, stood in the room.

He could see all eyes turn toward him as the group attempted to quickly remove her from the room. She was yelling at Elaren about how her father was going to take them down. He stiffened up, "She is right there," Areliel stated. "You just need to walk over and grab her. Do it."

Remington wrinkled his nose but did not move. One way or another he was going to be free from this soon. He did not want to listen. He thought about the punishment that may come from this disobedience but at this point, he did not care anymore. It did not matter.

Areliel gave an annoyed grunt behind him. "Is this how we are going to play? Really? You think you can escape me so easily. I can make it so that your plan won't work. I am still having fun with you. Never before have I had a toy with so much to play with. I am not going to let that go so easily. I might overlook this small act of rebellion for now, but I always get what I want. Don't forget that."

Remington felt the coldness disappear from his back as the girl dipped under the trap door and out of his view. Maeve and her friends were gone, and he was finally left alone. Elaren and Justice were busy speaking to a young dwarven lad who seemed to have some form of leadership position of the city. They would be busy for a while dealing with the undead. It gave Remington the time he wanted to be alone.

Remington took the time to message T'kocht, letting him know where he was and ordering him to wait with the others for his return. The message was brief, Remington could still feel his emotions rumbling within him, ready to explode like a volcano. He could not handle talking out loud without fear of choking up. Instead, he sat down in front of a window and looked out onto the streets. He could see dwarves moving about the streets, cleaning up rubble and moving the countless bodies to a new resting point. Family members reuniting with each other, embracing, and crying knowing they are alive, knowing they are safe.

Remington began to think about Maeve, of their various reunions, of the kindle that grows then burns to ash at each meeting. The magnetic pull they feel between each other, the strings of fate pulling them ever closer. But the heat of a passion this raw, this intense, is one that neither of them can contain. At the end of the day, someone ends up hurt, betrayed.

Yet he could not help but picture her bright golden eyes flexed with the brightest of teals. The warmth that grows in his stomach like a nice whiskey every time her gayful laughter fills the air. The feeling that she can build anything new and beautiful from the ashes and rubble of his life.

All of that did not matter anymore. He sent her away for good, ripping off the bandage that kept her clinging to him. She wanted to help him, to be with him, even after everything they had been through, after everything he had done to her. But was this not the same way he felt with Areliel? All he ever did was make Maeve's life worse, tricking her into thinking that he was worth it, that she loved him. She was addicted to his poison even though it would kill her. The only way to save her, was to make sure she could never reach the poison again.

Remington was so lost in thought that he did not hear the approach of Elaren besides him, pulling up his own chair to join. "What do you think you are doing Mr. Darkwalker," Elaren asked. His voice was steady, though Remington could detect a hint of pity in his voice.

"What do you mean?" Remington asked emotionlessly. "I am not doing anything."

Elaren released a deep sigh, stroking his smooth ginger beard. "I thought the graces of Realta would help you. Would show you that there is hope for everyone, you just need to look for it. You have been sitting in a dark pit of despair for so long, and yet when that girl comes to you with a rope leading to the light you toss it aside. Even after you almost pull her down with you, she returns with the rope time and time again."

"Exactly," Remington responded. "I can't trap her here with me. She deserves to live in the sun. I have done enough to darken the world; I don't want to darken her light as well."

"What makes you think the dark would win?" Elaren countered. "Light, hope, all of that is stronger than you think. You just do not remember what the warmth of the sun feels like. Maeve shines with a light that is powerful enough for the both of you, but you just keep closing your eyes."

Remington thought on this for a second, staring at the floor, watching the water drip from his nose. He was not sure whether it was sea water, ever present on his body or tears he was trying to hold in. "How can I climb to the light, when the puppet master keeps my strings stuck to the floor. How do I make sure she does not get tangled into the strings too."

Elaren placed his hand under Remington's chin and slowly lifted it to look into his eyes. "You must truly be stupid to believe that Maeve is not strong enough to take care of herself. That girl is searching all the planes of the world to find an out for you. She has faced monsters you can't even imagine and passed through the frozen wasteland of the Ice Queen to bring me back home, a man she has never even met. Because her compassion, her strength, allows her to do what is right. And now she is contemplating facing down the trident of a demigod to save you. Are you going to let her do it alone?"

Before Remington could process this, Elaren stood up towering over him. "We will head back to camp tonight, think about it won't you," Elaren said before walking away, his words echoing in the empty halls of the mansion.

42

It was a very quiet trip back to the camp ground. Elaren's associate Milos had opened up a portal in a nearby tree that allowed them to effortlessly traverse continents in mere seconds. As Remington stepped through the tree, he could feel an invisible cloak surround him, blocking the view of his ever-present patron. Remington felt the weight that lifted off his shoulders return as T'kocht flung his arms around him in embrace.

"Are you alright, what happened," T'kocht asked, frantically searching his friend, staring at the burnt and tattered clothing he was still wearing.

"I'm fine, just some therapy," Remington responded, his focus on Elaren walking away hand in hand with Justice. "So are you going to help us," Remington called out to him.

Elaren stopped and turned around. "If you mean your attempt to lay siege to Lord Cresthorn, then no Mr. Darkwalker, I will not be assisting you with that. However, in the safety of my sanctuary I will say this. Young Maeve's quest is not completely in vain. The Summer Court is not untouchable, in fact they have been uprooted before. Have faith in her, that she will find a way to help you. To protect you from the eyes of one who has fallen. Just do not do anything brash until then. Good luck Mr. Darkwalker, I hope you can find your rope."

"What is he talking about Remi?" T'kocht asked, looking toward his friend. Nicky approached the two of them, interested in the conversation as well.

Remington glanced over at them, "Maeve thinks she can kill the River King, and Elaren agrees." He quickly turned around walking away from them. "Have everyone prepare to leave the camp. We might not have the help from the Bloodroots, but that doesn't mean we can't try. Lord Cresthorn must fall."

Remington could hear them calling for him, demanding further explanation, but he ignored them. Maeve was seeking out to destroy a creature more powerful than any of them could imagine. She was putting herself into mortal danger for him and it was going to get her killed. His plan to die at the hand of Lord Cresthorn must be completed before she dug her grave too deep. So that she had nothing she needed to fight for.

The crew of the Fey's Fortune quickly packed their gear, though many were loath to go, having enjoyed the short break from reality in the safety of the camp. Even Remington was hesitant to leave, feeling at rest knowing the River King could not see him there. But as Elaren pointed out, he could not hide forever. It was time to leave.

It would be days until they returned to the Fey's Fortune. Occasionally they would discuss their plans, how to enter the port of Belward, and the entire time Remington would contemplate the alternative. The opportunity to live, to remove his parasite and live peacefully. He wondered if what Elaren said was true, that the River King could be killed. But no matter how he answered that question the truth always remained. No mission could be a success while his enemy watched his every move. While he was slave to the River King, there would be no rebellion. But he could do something about Lord Cresthorn. To help Nicky find a conclusion, to help the Bloodroots rid the continent of a ruthless leader. It was a mission that was reachable, though it would be the end of the road for Remington. He was ready, it was time to rest.

The rest would be a long way off for Remington. With eight more days until the crew reached Belward and the River King holding true on his promise, Remington felt exhausted. But each time he thought about the impending mission, an itch in the back of his mind seeded doubt. His mind constantly drifted back to Maeve, about what Elaren said. He began to regret the words spoken, the pain that they both felt by Remington's goodbye. Never the less, he did say goodbye and he did not expect to see her again. There would be no remedying the situation, only eternal sleep.

One and a half more days. That was all that was left between him and Alexander Cresthorn. The crew were getting anxious, this mission was going to be difficult and dangerous. They had to be stealthy, and careful. One wrong move could mean the deaths of many crew members. Remington was pouring over maps of the city, looking for the best way to enter, and the best way to get to the Cloudtop district which floated 500 feet above the city.

"Where are you?" Maeve's voice entered his head. Immediately Remington knew this really was her, not the River King, the icy chill was not there. "I have a plan working, don't go through with your stupid mission. Just wait a little bit, please."

"Just outside Belward," Remington responded. His heart ached at the sound of her voice, but still he wanted to protect her. "I am doing this to save you. You need to stay safe."

The silence that followed was deafening as Remington stared at the wall in front of him. What was she doing, what plan did she have? He could only hope that she would stay safe, be happy. Even if it was without him.

Unable to sit still any longer Remington got up and began doing simple tasks around the ship, checking the weaponry, mending sails, anything to distract his mind over the next few hours.

"We got help," Maeve's voice once again entered his mind. "We will be aboard soon, so don't attack or anything."

Remington did not respond, his mind processing the words that echoed in his memory. How would she even get here, there were no ships to be seen within miles. A loud thunk followed by chatter sounded across the ship. Remington raced towards the noise, finding Maeve and her friends, standing aboard the Fey's Fortune, blinking from the blinding sun.

Remington slowly stepped forwards, trying to make himself believe this was real. "You actually came," Remington stated cautiously stopping a few feet away.

"Of course I came," Maeve retorted. "Why wouldn't I?"

"I thought I had sent you away for good the last time we saw each other. That I had let you go."

"I'm disappointed Remington," Maeve teased. "Have you really forgotten how stubborn I am?"

Remington chuckled, her stubbornness could move mountains if it wanted to.

"Put this on," Maeve commanded, holding out a green pendent that glowed with powerful arcane magic. "It will hide you from him, trust me."

Remington stared at her in shock. Slowly he reached out his hand, but felt resistance as though something was pulling it back.

"Oh no you don't," Areliel whispered in his ear, her hand holding onto his arm. "You are not hiding from me again."

Remington pulled against it, eventually finding a grip on the necklace. The closer it got to him, the stronger Areliel fought back until when it was mere inches from his face, he felt his hand become paralyzed, unable to move it. He could see Maeve watching him closely and it gave him strength. With a loud shout

Remington pulled with all of his might finally slipping the necklace over his head. Silence. He looked around but there was no sight of Areliel. There was no sense of something watching him, there was only peace.

Remington looked at Maeve and in the silence and the peace he felt the last of the walls he tried to build crumble into dust. Without thinking, he rushed to her, grabbing the back of her head and pulled her into a kiss. He could feel her surprise before she too relaxed into him, in the comfort of only their company. All of the pain he felt for so long trying to keep her away, crumbled with the wall. Hope for a normal, peaceful life returned as he saw the rope she lowered and began his climb to the light.

"I see the rope now," Remington said breathlessly. "I see you, and I will let you guide me. I always thought I needed to protect you, but you are the one saving me and now I will never let you go. How did you make this possible?"

Maeve seemed to become agitated by the question. Her eyes flittered in random directions, her hands unable to keep still, all signs of recent guilt. "I traded a man's life for this," she finally admitted. "You would be hidden, we now have an item that can extract your soul from the River King's possession. The Queen of Witches said he was dangerous, and he was trapped in my ring. He is from thousands of years ago, and apparently really powerful." Maeve continued rambling on, attempting to create any excuse to herself that what she did was right, worrying she might be lying to herself.

Remington was frozen the entire time she was talking. She had given up a man's life for him, for even just the shot of saving him from his hell. He never would have asked her to do such a thing. He had taken so many lives, it was another body to add to the blood on his hands. But this time it was not just on his hands, Maeve felt it too. He could see the conflict, the pain that the decision had caused. He would not let her sacrifice go to waste.

In the middle of her ramble, Remington closed in, embracing her with a hug. She stopped talking and held him close, their breaths comforting on each other's necks. "I will always follow you, no matter what. My devotion will never waiver again. I am yours." Remington whispered into her ear. For what felt like an eternity, they just held each other, neither one wanting to let the other go.

Eventually, Remington broke the silence, "So what's the plan?"

43

Maeve reached into her bag and pulled out a small book, no bigger than the palm of her hand. "This is another one of the gifts I was given," she explained. "It gives us the ability to take your soul back without having to kill the River King."

Remington looked at her with confusion, "What do you mean without having to kill him? He deserves it. Would it not be easier?"

Maeve looked uneasy, taking a deep sigh. "Unfortunately," she started carefully, "Another thing we learned is there are consequences to killing one of the Fey Lords. Their deaths leave a scar on the Feylands, and though we don't know yet what exactly these scars do, I don't think it is good. I want to protect my home, and if that means leaving the bastard alive, then so be it."

"How do we know he won't come after us, revenge for making him look the fool," asked Remington.

"We don't," Maeve responded looking deep into his eyes. "But if he does, we can face him together. My home means everything to me, if there is a way to protect it, I will."

Remington smiled, leaning down to kiss her forehead. "Then I will protect it as well. If I can be free of his hold on me, then that is all that matters."

Maeve beamed, her cheeks flushing a rosy pink under her golden skin. "Great! Now we need you to come with us, one because I want you there, and two you need to be near your soul when it is released. We do have two more spots in our planar travel spell, if you want to grab two of your crew members to come with you."

Remington let out a sigh of relief, he would not be needing to make the jump himself. Bringing the entire boat took a toll on his body, one that he could not handle going to face the River King. Giving Maeve one last hug, Remington went off to find T'kocht and Nicky. Their skills in combat were the best amongst the crew and he would not go into battle without them.

Remington didn't even finish asking T'kocht before he agreed to come along. He knew T'kocht would follow him anywhere, and he appreciated the support. Nicky, however, needed a bit more persuading. They were so close to the person she wanted her own revenge on. So close to the city she once called her own. The last of the people that had turned her into the monster she was. Eventually, Remington was able to convince her that it would be easier to end Lord Cresthorn without the River King interfering, and reluctantly she agreed. Then it was time to tell the crew.

Remington made his way up to the helm and waited while his crew gathered below. He gazed over his crew, his family, and the state that everyone was in. They would all soon be freed from the curse, from the ruthlessness so forced upon them.

"Attention everyone," Remington shouted out causing the deck to be enveloped in silence as the crew listened. "No longer are we cursed, for today we have been blessed. For too long have we suffered under the watchful gaze of the River King but no longer. We are invisible to his ever-watching eye and have been granted the chance to free ourselves from this curse once and for all."

A murmur broke out amongst the crew, discussing the possibilities. Remington held up his hand, "T'kocht, Nicky, and I will be accompanying our guest upon one final journey to the Feylands.

When they return, you will all be free. If you choose to leave this ship then you may, for you are no longer bound by curse. But for those that choose to stay, there will be no more pointless killings. No more unnecessary chaos. Your morality will be yours to set, no longer dictated by the threats of torment. We leave tomorrow morning."

As Remington walked down the steps, T'kocht stopped him. "What do you mean by they? You are coming back too, right?" he asked with concern.

Remington flinched slightly, he had hoped no one had caught that. There was too much grief, too much pain in the Prime Realm. When this nightmare ended, he just wanted to start a new life, one where no one knew his struggles, where he was not wanted by many powerful beings. One where he could be with Maeve, in the land she called her home. But he was not ready to say goodbye, not yet.

"I just misspoke, it's been a while since I slept," Remington lied. He could see T'kocht did not quite trust the answer but he did not question it. Not wanting to answer more questions, Remington rushed off.

He once again approached Maeve and her group of friends. "There are some empty hammocks down below, I apologize it is not the nicest place to stay, but it's better than the wood floor up here." He paused and looked at Maeve, "There is, uh, a bed in the captain's quarters if you would like to use it. I never do."

Maeve smiled and followed him while the rest of her friends followed Nicky below deck. As soon as she entered the room, she ran towards the bed cannonballing into the soft mattress. Remington could not help but laugh as she almost bounced off the bed, giggling, as a result. The laughter subsided as he looked at the scene. He often avoided looking into that corner of the room, one filled with so much deceit and pain. The sounds of feminine laughter reminding him of his many nights with Areliel, and he wanted to run. He reminded himself that Maeve was not Areliel. This was not laughter from the enjoyment of pain. This was pure glee and a love of life.

He watched as she buried herself into the blankets, watching him from the corner of her eye. He saw an expecting look, followed by what appeared to be disappointment as he climbed into the hammock he had strung up on the other side of the room. He thought about going over there, to join her, but the ghosts that haunted that area were too strong. Instead, he laid down in the hammock and listened to her breathing slow as she fell asleep. Listened as her comforting, rhythmic breath echoed through the room uninterrupted by the poison of his patron. He was not sure when, but eventually he slipped into a deep, dreamless sleep, giving him the strength to take on what was next to come.

When Remington awoke in the morning, he was alone in his room. Maeve must have woken up before him. Exiting the room, he saw the adventuring party preparing to leave. He was the last to arrive. However, taking a look around, Remington noticed there was someone missing. He did not see Gwen anywhere.

"Maeve, where is Gwen?" Remington asked, still looking to make sure he did not miss her. She was the one that put the possibility of this mission in his mind, he had hoped to have her optimism around to support. He noticed an immediate look of sadness pass over Maeve's face.

"She, she is not with us," Maeve carefully started. "We were investigating a powerful artifact and she was kidnapped out of a teleportation spell. We... we think she is back under the influence of the creature that manipulated her before."

Remington stood in horror. Gwen seemed so terrified when she talked about this Nemuah, so terrified of potentially falling back under the veil of manipulation. She was unable to escape the chains of her master. Remington worried if even if all of this succeeded, would he befall the same doom as her? Would the chains of servitude bring him back to the River King, as it constantly brought him back to Atrigul?

"When all this is over, I will help you get her back if I can," Remington responded quietly. He did not want to think of what she might be going through; he understood her pain and her struggle. "Let's get going."

The male gnome in the group, Zook, pulled out a piece of parchment with arcane symbols written all over it. Remington quickly recognized it as a very powerful spell scroll, one that will take them to the Feylands. With the assistance of Kel, Zook carefully navigated the casting of the spell, chanting the words that reminded Remington of his own planar travel ritual. However, much less energy was needed to transport 9 humanoids, versus an entire ship and crew. As Zook finished the spell, a blinding flash of light engulfed the party before they all descended into a freefall.

The party fell 15 feet before crashing into the water below. Immediately Remington saw that some of the party could not swim, or had armor too heavy to fight against gravity and were quickly sinking to the bottom. He dived down into the warm waters of the Feylands and released his arcane energy into the waters. He transferred his blessing, or perhaps curse, to those in the water, granting to them the ability breath the fluid as easily as they breathed air.

The panic in their eyes died down as they inhaled the oxygen their bodies desperately craved. Slowly, they made their way along the sea floor heading toward the cursed place where this all started. Remington could feel an emptiness inside him grow with each step toward the River King's tower. But with each step, he could also feel a pull. A force begging for two pieces separated for too long to be reunited. His soul was calling to him, it was so close.

After an hour of trudging through the sand beneath the crashing waves above, they finally reached the shore edge. Climbing the stone wall to land, the party was greeted by a ferocious storm, rain pelting down upon them, stinging their skin. Remington looked up, blinking away the rain as it ran into his eyes and once again saw the tower. It rose hundreds of feet into the air, looming over the land as though it was an ever-watchful eye.

They quickly made their way into the tree line, in search of even a little bit of shelter from the storm, an indication of the River King's growing anger. The rest of the party worked to begin strategizing. Nicky and the Sokyan warrior spent a lot of time discussing military strategy, where to best use the resources available to them, and theorizing what they might face in the tower. Remington thought he might have heard talks of potentially attempting to bargain instead of fight, but he struggled to pay attention.

His thoughts instead swirled around his own inner strength. He questioned if he would have the strength to stand up to the River King, to demand back what is rightfully his. Areliel had chiseled away at him all those years ago, turning his walls of strength into stone dust. Though he tried his best to rebuild those walls from what was left, it was still weak, prone to crumble with a single strike. Had the River King succeeded in breaking him again? Would he be able to stand up and once again begin rebuilding his life.

A twig snapped to his right, and he saw Maeve pacing. She was intently listening to the strategic planning, her eyes focused on the task at hand. He counted the rain drops as they fell on her head, her hair soaked through. The water glistened on her skin, as though it knew it belonged there. He tried to imagine what it would look like in the sun, dazzling and glittering as though her skin were made of diamonds. Just knowing she was there, that she went through so much to get to this point comforted him.

After an hour of planning, they were finally ready. Though they were not sure of what they would face, they bravely stepped toward the tower. The looming gates welcomed them, daring them to enter.

There was nothing guarding them, though Remington felt something watching them. The River King knew they were there.

As they walked through the long dark hallway that followed the doors, Remington could see it open up into a large cavern. Inside was an abandoned city built into the walls of the cavern. Coral growth spread throughout the crumbling doorways, slick mossy stairs wound their way up and through the city. But standing at the edge of the city, stood the towering form of the River King, his long cerulean hair crashing over his shoulders. His cold pupilless white eyes staring straight through Remington into the depths of his missing soul. He smiled.

"Oh, there you are," said the River King. "I thought you might come running back to me. Why did you hide, and why do you return to me?"

44

Remington stood frozen in fear. The monster that had haunted him these past three and a half years now stood directly in front of him. No barriers of the mind to protect him, no safety of being on a separate plane. He was right there in all of his fury.

The silence was broken by Kel. For once, Remington was happy that Kel could not keep his mouth shut. "Your majesty," Kel stated, dipping deep into an insincere bow. "We have come here to ask you to return this good man's soul. We mean no harm, we just want you to release him."

"And why, may I ask, should I do that?" the River King asked in response. The tone in his voice was teasing, as if anything they might have said would not change his mind. Remington could feel himself sinking further into himself.

"You brought about this punishment for what he did to me," Maeve spoke up, stepping forward. "At the time, I appreciated it. I was angry. But not anymore. He has redeemed himself, repented for what he did. Have you not punished him enough? This torture that you put him through, does it really match the crime? You did this for me, and now I ask that you stop for me. I love him, and I want this to stop. He is a good man, please."

The River King turned to face Maeve and began to step toward her. "How touching," he began, not even attempting to hide his sarcasm. "He has redeemed himself you say? Well, here is a secret. There is no such thing as redemption." At this point, the River King's voice had risen to a loud roar as though it was a crashing waterfall.

"Those that are wrong and cruel, will never be good. Those who betray will always betray. People do not change, and mortals do not deserve to. You say that this punishment is enough, that it should stop, but there is something you misunderstand." The River King continued, his anger growing with each word.

"This is not just a punishment for the petty theft of my subjects. This is a lesson and a warning. For too long, you mortals have dirtied my land with your filthy greed. Passing through thinking you can take whatever you want. This is a message to anyone who dares question my power, my rule, that forgiveness and mercy is a weakness of mortals. I will not relent, and the punishment will continue."

"You leave us no choice," Maeve countered. Her voice was slightly trembling but she was doing her best to remain strong. "We will take it by force. We are not leaving without it."

The River King let out a billowing laugh that echoed throughout the chamber. "Oh I would love to see you try. Unfortunately, squashing vermin such as yourselves is beneath me. I will let my tower deal with you. If you still find yourselves in my presence after, then you will wish you had turned around now. For I will make sure your deaths are as slow and painful as possible."

"Oh and Remington," the River King's voice switched into Areliel's voice. "We have been through so much together. You could never hurt me, could you. Not again." The River King smiled and melted away into the water, disappearing into the cracks in the cavern.

Remington's legs screamed at him to run, to give up on this ridiculous mission. Maeve looked back at him with a reassuring look, the knowledge in her eyes that they can accomplish this. With a deep breath he began to step forward into the cavern, T'kocht by his side giving his support.

As he took a closer look at the city around them, Remington noticed water leaking through cracks in the walls. About 70 feet above them, a large balloon was tethered to an equally massive stone block. He followed the party up to investigate, curious as to the oddity that stood out amongst the ancientness of the city. As they approached, he could see writing on the block, the same phrase written in a wide range of languages, "Break the Dam".

"What do you think that means?" asked Kel, looking all over the stone. "Maybe we cut the balloon?"

"I don't think so," Remington responded, placing his hand on the edge of the block. "I can feel a breeze behind the block. It might be a doorway. We need to find a way to move it, but it's too heavy to move."

"Maybe we can use the water," said the large goliath woman, Ruck. Everyone looked at her with interest. "Well things float in water, right?" she continued. "I think there is a bunch of water behind that wall over there. If we release it maybe the buoyancy with the balloon can help us lift it."

"We can all breath underwater, it's worth a shot," Nicky chimed in.

With that, they all moved down towards the wall, each chipping away at the rock. It only took a few large swings from Ruck before the wall gave way. A flood of water shot towards them, washing them all off their feet leaving them to tumble against the sharp corals of the city.

Remington was the first to regain control of himself, the long years at sea teaching him to be a strong swimmer. He could see that everyone seemed alright, though maybe a bit bruised. The cavern was slowly filling with water, the first of the ancient houses sinking beneath the surface. They looked as though that is where they belonged.

"Remi, I think there is something out there," shouted T'kocht, looking towards one of the houses. As Remington shifted is gaze to where T'kocht was looking, a large shadow began to move its way out of a doorway about 20 feet above them. As it got closer, Remington could see it was a greenish creature whose entire body resembled the head of a frog. Though it lacked legs, it exhibited a 15-foot-long wingspan that glided effortlessly through the water. Trailing behind it was an equally long tail, ending in a dangerously sharp barb.

Before Remington had time to fully process this creature, 4 more appeared, diving straight for the party. Remington quickly swam to the nearest one, swinging the Fortune Teller at it with a practiced sweep of the blade. The creature's thick slimy skin protected it from Remington's attack, his blade acting no more painful than a papercut.

Remington took a moment to look around for the rest of the party. Many were struggling with the environment, not having experience with fighting in the water. Their movement was slower, fighting against the viscosity of the water. Nicky at this point had joined him, doing her best to protect each other from the creature.

"REMI!" T'kocht shouted. Remington whipped his head around to the sound of T'kocht's voice to see Maeve trapped in the mouth of one of the creatures.

"No," whispered Remington with concern, his eyes widening as he watched her struggle. With one final swing he dug the Fortune Teller deep into the mouth of the creature next to him, causing it to go limp in the water. He swam as fast as he could towards the creature holding onto Maeve. He could see it was already badly wounded, Maeve had given it a good beating.

Before he could reach her, Remington watched in horror as the creature opened its mouth and swallowed her into its deep body. "MAEVE!" Remington screamed as he tried to swim even faster. His scimitar cleaved into the creatures hide, causing it to release an ear-piercing shriek. He turned attempting to use his momentum in the water to hit harder. However, the creature was fast. Its gaping maw clasped down onto his arm, pinning him to the creature.

Remington twisted to look at the creature and saw a blinding light emanating from the inside. His thoughts immediately turned to Maeve, and what must be happening to her inside. Using his arcane reserves, Remington focused on getting out of the creature's mouth, for that was the only way he could save Maeve. He felt the twist pull at his body that accompanied teleportation, and after disappearing, reappeared on the other side of the creature.

A crossbow bolt entered the side of the creature as Remington made his next swing, though he did not hit as cleanly as he wanted. The glowing light seemed to intensify, searing the creature with a radiant energy from within. He could smell the flesh cooking and looked at in horror as the life exited its body, the radiant heat cooking it to its death.

Remington froze believing he just watched Maeve cook with the creature before he saw the mouth twitch. Preparing his sword, trying to hold back his tears, he waited for the creature to attack. Instead, he saw a hand reach out of the mouth, and pulling herself out, was Maeve. A white radiant light was streaming out of the orifices on her face, boiling the water around her. Maeve turned towards him; her eyes completely consumed by the light. Remington moved back a little, fearful of the raw energy she was producing from within. It was a raw, primal anger and energy, eating away at her own life force as its own flames grew.

As her eyes met his and saw the growing fear, the light began to dim, eventually extinguishing. Remington could tell she was exhausted from the release of the energy, but he could also see the resolve to keep moving forward, to fight, return to her eyes. "Come on, we need to help the others," Maeve ordered him. Not wanting to think about it, Remington just nodded, they were not out of danger yet.

Before Remington could reach the rest of the creatures, the other members of the party had quickly dispatched them. Slowly the bodies were sinking to the bottom of the cavern. Remington looked up and saw the water level had finally risen above the balloon, the tension on the string pulling up on the stone.

"Quickly," he shouted, "We don't know how many more of them there may be."

They quickly swam towards the stone and using their combined strength, were finally able to feel it budge. The force of the water on the balloon lifted it just enough that with a massive heave, they shifted the stone. The stone now removed, revealed a long hallway which the water from the chamber immediately began to flood into.

Remington felt himself flashing back to that first visit with the River King, to being at the mercy of the water's current. Though he knew he could breathe, Remington still felt panic set in as he fought against the power of the river. He felt the left side of his body crash hard against dry land as the water spread out around him, coalescing into a calm river. Maeve was coughing next to him, her limbs shaking from the experience.

"I, I think we need to rest," mumbled Kel, blood gushing from his side where one of the barbs had pierced his body. The rest of the group was in not much better condition, though Nicky seemed to be unharmed, and T'kocht only a few scratches here and there. With a grateful sigh, they all sunk down, hoping they would be safe for a while in this room, to nurse their wounds.

The calmness did not last long though. After only 10 minutes, a thick fog began to roll into the room, surrounding the resting party. It moved unnaturally, as though it had a purpose, a mission.

"It's not poisonous," Zook spoke up. "It's just water, regular fog, though something is controlling it. I can sense a lot of arcane power flowing through it."

Remington carefully watched the fog, not trusting anything in the heart of this creature's lair. He was right to mistrust it. The fog began to condense forming into 2 featureless humanoid shapes roughly the size of two dwarves. He could hear the fog begin to project a conversation, the dwarves seemed to be arguing over the massacre of a small town. Remington looked around and saw the dwarven Sokayan warrior in the group twisting his face. Remington recognized the look in the man's eyes, the look of shame, of guilt from a mistake of the past. This must be one of the man's memories. The River King was playing games with them, and now that they were in his territory, no one was safe from the terror that he brought.

The scenes in the fog began to shift, digging deep into the memories of each member of the group and bringing into the light the guilts of their past. Remington recognized Nicky's, the faceless shape tying off a rope revealing a small child hanging in front of a doorway. Some scenes showed people getting hurt, or people not protecting those they care about. Remington saw his own guilt, the moment he chose to walk away from Maeve on that beach leaving her there alone.

The scene shifted, a figure walked towards a doorway, its crossbow loaded and hidden behind its back. Remington looked around, curious to see who this guilt belonged to. He was surprised to see the deep-set look of anger enter into T'kocht's eyes. Remington had only seen this look once or twice before, and it scared him. The figure rested their hand on the door handle, preparing to turn it.

It hesitated, and frustratedly shook its head. The hand pulled away and walked away from the door. Remington looked back to T'kocht, who had looked away at this point, making every effort to not look at anyone and to hide his face.

Remington started to move to go talk to him when the next scene caught his attention. He heard Maeve's voice ring out, though slightly garbled, "It's for your own good. I am doing this for you." He turned to look just in time to see the figure fling itself over a blurry railing.

Remington looked over at Maeve, and just as with all the others, the guilt began to overwhelm her. He wanted to do something, to say something, but he knew it was best to leave her in the silence. He remembered the agony of guilt he felt the first few weeks of torture with the River King. After all these years, his feelings had dulled to only a tight knot. But to these folk, this was their first time facing the full force of the River King and they would need time to process it themselves.

45

◈

Eventually, the fog retreated after replaying everyone's guilts a few times over. Wanting to move on and get out of this area in case the fog returned, the group began packing. Remington glanced at his crew. Nicky appeared to be fuming, though he knew better than to talk to her at this moment. T'kocht, however, was pointedly avoiding contact with everyone and eventually Remington's curiosity overcame him.

"What did he show you?" Remington asked, carefully putting his hand on T'kocht's shoulder.

T'kocht shrugged his hand off, focusing on making sure his gun was completely dry. "It was nothing," he grumbled, not saying anything else.

Remington looked at him with concern, "It clearly wasn't nothing. What did you do? I could tell this was before I was captain, it must have been a while ago. Talk to me, it will help."

T'kocht scrunched up his nose, clearly starting to get frustrated. "It's not what I did, it's what I didn't do that I regret. But it is in the past, I was a coward."

Remington paused, what was T'kocht talking about? "What didn't you do?" he asked carefully, slowly seeing T'kocht open up.

T'kocht let out a deep sigh, still not looking toward Remington.

"It was about two weeks after that very first stop we had in Halitona," he began. "I was angry at what she did to you, what she was still doing. I wanted to protect you, to keep you safe. I could see you were trying to fight it, the pain that is, but I could not stand to watch it. So, I planned. One night, I grabbed my crossbow, and made my way onto the deck. I made it all the way to her door, ready to kill her in her sleep, even if it meant my death. But I couldn't. I couldn't do it. So instead, you suffered for 9 more years because I was a coward."

Before Remington had time to respond, T'kocht walked away. T'kocht had attempted to kill Areliel all those years ago and never said a word about it. If he had followed through, if he had succeeded, Brend would have ripped T'kocht's arms off his body and fed him to the sea. It would have been his death sentence. Though Remington suffered under Areliel, he would not have wanted to lose all those years with his best friend. But Remington could not help but wonder what his life might have been like without her.

Lost in his thoughts, Remington mindlessly followed the rest of the group to a large river where a ferryman was waiting. The ferryman was speaking to them, presenting a riddle for them to cross the river safely, but Remington did not listen to what was said. His attention was focused on the man's face. Though the man was talking with pep, and smiling at the group, Remington felt something was wrong.

While the others discussed the riddle, Remington continued to stare at the man, who only patiently waited, occasionally answering questions. It was only when the first 3 members of the party began to board the boat when Remington realized what bothered him about the man. The man was in the same situation as Remington, his soul was missing, at the mercy of the River King. He could see the anguish behind the man's eyes, moving like a puppet unable to control his own destiny. There was nothing Remington could do to help him, besides move deeper into the tower and teach the River King a lesson.

The last members of the group finally deboarded from the boat on the other side of the river, regrouping in preparation for the next trick ahead. They made their way through a long winding hallway, occasionally stopping to allow Zook to look for traps, though he never found any. About halfway through, the tunnel walls began to change. The wet moss filled stone walls gradually faded into clay and dirt. Remington could see a bright light ahead where the tunnel probably opened up into a cavern.

As they got closer, Remington could hear the howl of wind as it flowed through the tunnel. It screamed as if a thousand voices were calling out in agony. The clay, the sound of the wind. Remington knew he had been here before, he remembered.

Remington did not have time to stop before the movement of the group herded him into the chamber and as his eyes adjusted to the light his fears were confirmed. They had returned to that cursed cavern, to the home of the Fountain of Youth, to a place he yearned to forget.

"Captain?" Nicky asked, confusion and shock in her voice. Remington, thinking she was talking to him, looked in the direction she was looking and froze. There, in the center of the cavern, sitting on the dried-up fountain, was Captain Areliel Atrigul. Her strawberry blonde hair was newly washed, soft and silky tied up in her typical ponytail under her large hat which covered her eyes. Her legs were stretched out and crossed, her stiletto boots hugging her calves up to her knees. He heard a slight crunch as she took a bite out of an apple before she set it down.

"Ah there you are," her silky voice spreading throughout the chamber. "It's so good to see you all, especially you my dear

Remington." She stood up, tilting her hat so that her predatory smile could be seen by all.

Remington scowled, "I will not drink your poison anymore. You are dead. I watched your life leave your body." Remington looked up to nothing in particular. "Is this all you got?" he yelled to the River King. "Is this not getting old?"

"I know you watched me die, you killed me remember?" Areliel continued. "That was a mistake wasn't it. Look what a mess your life has become. You have misled my crew into disaster after disaster without me. But don't worry, his majesty has brought me back to clean this all up. By my side, we can finish my plans and together we will become legendary."

Areliel was slowly walking towards him, each step, each word drawing her closer and closer. Remington instinctively reached behind him, searching for Maeve's hand, searching for support as he felt the draw of her poison pulling him toward Areliel. Maeve grasped onto his hand and squeezed.

Areliel looked at Maeve curiously, "I have heard much about you." Areliel smiled, walking past Remington, pulling up behind Maeve leaning close into her ear. "So, you think you have found something better than me in this bitch. After she lied to you, hurt you, and now is using you on this pointless mission of hers. She has corrupted your crew around you, and cannot be trusted. How long did she think she could get away with this?"

A fire began to grow in Maeve's eyes. She turned around to face Areliel, glaring slightly upwards to match her eyes. "We are here to support Remington, to save him from further cruelty. Step aside, bitch."

Areliel started laughing, "You are going about this all wrong. You don't need to fight, to hurt others. Just come with me Remington. Turn around and walk out by my side, and I will protect you as I always have. You still owe me a debt. After killing me even though I have saved your life countless times, don't I deserve a little thanks in return?"

Remington attempted to speak, but the smell of roses filling his lungs made him feel sick and all he could do was focus on keeping his stomach down. He could see Areliel was losing her limited patience and his body began bracing itself for the oncoming punishment for disobedience. Instead, Kel spoke up, his sword pointed at Areliel's back.

"Okay, okay that's enough," Kel stated calmly. "Either help us out and come with us or step aside and let us pass. We will force our way through if needed."

Areliel stepped back a bit, clicking her tongue. "Unfortunately, I can't let you do that. His majesty needs to be protected. If it is a fight you are looking for, it's a fight you will get. But it is not very fair, one versus nine. You have served me faithfully for so long, why don't you help me again."

Areliel looked toward Nicky, her eyes flashing with a brilliant green light. Nicky's body froze up before relaxing again. Slowly, Nicky turned to face the party, a deadly look in her eyes and drew her rapier, preparing to fight. With lightning fast speed Nicky lunged toward the Sokayan warrior engaging him in combat.

Remington felt his adrenaline pumping through his body as the heat of battle grew around him. Remington turned towards Areliel, "Don't make me do this again. Please." He swung the Fortune Teller towards her, lightly cutting her arms in a failed attempt to disarm her. She looked down at the blood that was flowing down and dripping off her hands.

"You hurt me. Once again, my poor Remington has been corrupted to break his promises." Areliel took a few steps back, separating herself from the group. Inhaling a deep breath she released a dreadful wail, filled with hurt and anguish that resonated throughout the chamber causing some of the stalactites to come crashing to the ground. Remington clutched his ears as all the pain and anguish filled his head burning him from the inside. He could hear the thump of bodies around him as multiple members of his group fell unconscious, unable to withstand the pure and raw emotion.

The rest of the battlefield blurred around Remington, his only area of focus was around Areliel, she was all that mattered. He searched desperately for the madness that had taken her before, looking for anything that would explain her actions. But there was nothing. Her eyes were focused, and her smile made it seem as though she was even enjoying it. Remington looked over his shoulder to see Maeve with her double-sided scimitar pulled and ready to attack the nearest enemy. He needed to protect her.

Remington raced forward to meet her in combat. He once again slashed at her with his blade, unconsciously aiming at non-vital areas. "I do not need you," he said. "You never cared for me, I see that now. The only creature of deceit in this room is you. I will free myself of you once and for all." Remington's voice shook as he said it. No matter how much he wanted to believe what he said, he could feel the addiction pulling, tugging at his mind.

"You do not even believe that yourself," Areliel responded. "Do you remember what happens when you lie to me?" Her blade swung around digging deep into Remington's shoulder. He could feel is shoulder weakening as a dark smoke surrounded her sword, draining the life out of his body, filling it with a necrotic poison.

"But you always cared more about others than yourself," Areliel continued, twisting the sword in his shoulder. "Why don't I get rid of that pesky little distraction, so you can always be mine." A chime rang out from Areliel. Remington could hear Maeve scream as the ringing reached her. Spinning around he could see she was holding her ears, black ichor dripping from underneath her hands. He could see the energy draining from her body, though she still stood strong.

"You hold no control over me anymore," Remington repeated. "She is not a distraction. She is my strength. I will not allow you to pull me down again." Remington charged with his sword, clipping her side as blood began to stain her coat.

Areliel touched her side, examining the blood on her fingers. "I will always hold control over you Remington. Deep within, you know that I loved you, that I cared for you. Our feelings were real. You crave that love and with each passing moment you feel the pull. The want to return to what we had, to the absolute trust that we shared. The respect that others viewed us with. Or have you forgotten. Let me remind you of what happens when I am disrespected."

Remington once again heard the bell chime out, this time the cry of T'kocht filled the room. Remington flinched and began to turn to check on his friend. Before he could though, Areliel took advantage of his distraction, digging her blade through his back and between his ribs. Once again he could feel the necrotic energy flooding his body, a deep sense of dread entering his mind. He could feel the heat of his own blood running down his back soaking his jacket.

Remington felt his vision start to blur, the injuries he had incurred started to become too much. He turned back to face Areliel, the fury he felt slowing melting away, her poison finding its way in, quenching his flames. He wanted her to hold him, to forgive him. A battle cry echoed through the chamber, a cry of hope amongst the screams of pain. Remington's wounds began to close just a little, just enough to keep his will to fight in burning embers.

His breathing was growing heavier. He could feel his blood flowing with each breath, the pain in his lungs like a knife. Each sharp jolting of pain bringing him closer and closer to the memories of his past, to when the pain was a part of him. To when he believed he was happy.

Remington felt heat emanating from the depths of his coat, but it was not a painful heat, it brought comfort. He rested his hand on the heat and felt the medallion that Elaren had given him. The symbol of Realta, a symbol of hope.

"You know in your heart where your devotion lies," a familiar calming feminine voice echoed in his mind. "Don't fall back into the blinding dark. Find your light, find your flames. Let your devotion be the key you need to break your chains of the past."

Remington took a shaky step forward. Every part of his body screamed at him to stop, to melt into Areliel as he had been trained to do in the past. He did not want to be that person anymore. He had seen this scene repeated over and over again in memory and now he was reliving it. This was his chance to be free.

"I have not forgotten," Remington stated between heavy breathes. "I have not forgotten the pain you inflicted upon me." He swung his sword cutting deep into her side. "I have not forgotten how worthless and how useless I was." Another slice, hard across her chest, each hit transferring all of his anger from his body into hers like a poison. He paused, her blood dripping from his blade, mixing with his own pooling onto the ground. "And I have not forgotten that I loved you. But that Remington is gone, and you will only remain a memory to him." With one final swing, the Fortune Teller sank deep into her chest, slicing through her black heart.

Remington watched as blood pooled in her mouth, preventing her from speaking as she collapsed to the ground, once again dead from his blade. He felt his blade slip from his hand, clanging onto the cavern floor. Remington fell to his knees, his pants soaking in the blood around him. Without thinking, he scooped up Areliel's dead body once again and held it close while the battle around him continued, though he paid no mind.

46

Remington felt a hand rest upon his shoulder, snapping him out of the emptiness of his mind. He looked up and saw Maeve looking at him, a sadness in her eyes. "Are you okay?" she whispered, kneeling down to be next to him.

Remington choked down his emotions, trying to keep it together. "I have relived this moment over and over again in memory. And now he made me kill her again. Why must he play games like this. Why." Remington stared at the dead body in his hands, unsure what to do.

"I'm sorry," Maeve said. "I am so sorry he is doing this to you. But that is why we are here. We are going to end this. I'm here to help you. Come on." Maeve grabbed his arm lifting him up off the floor.

Remington slowly got up, the shock wearing off as his exhaustion set in. He looked around to see the rest of the group also looking fairly hurt, slowly working on healing their wounds.

"We should burn the body," Zook stated flatly as he looked over Areliel. "Just in case."

Remington moved to protest, but he knew Zook was right. They could not risk her coming back and ruining the mission. Not when they were so close to their goals. Instead, he nodded his head and moved as far away from the flames as he could, holding his breath from the smell of searing flesh. Luckily the heat of the flame was strong enough, that her body was ashes in less than a minute. Too fast for Remington to change his mind.

"I will be the first to say it," Kel spoke loudly. "I think we should rest again." His eyebrows raised at the group, looking for opinions.

"No," Remington responded. Though his body ached and his wounds needed tending, he did not want to stop. He feared what would happen if they did. "After what happened the last time we rested in the cursed place, I don't want to think about what he might send next. We cannot grant him the time to plan. Keep moving."

Remington did not even wait for a response before heading towards the doorway, ready for the nightmare to be over.

The group wound their way through the following hallway. The twists and turns threatening a danger with every footfall. The air around them began to cool, and Remington felt chills flow through his body. But ever present was the slight heat from the metal in his pocket.

The people in front of him stopped abruptly and as Remington looked up he saw the floor drop out from in front of them. This new cavern seemed to go on forever with no floor or no ceiling to be seen. Floating in the center of this chamber was a torrent of water, flowing like a river, spiraling to and fro spanning the length of the chamber.

"Gods hold the power to manipulate the elements, something mortals will never be strong enough to do. When can man walk on water?" Maeve read aloud, staring at the words written into the cavern wall.

"What do you think that means?" Kel asked, looking at a strangely labeled compass rose on the ground. Remington recognized the symbol where south west should be. It was the same symbol marked on his back, the symbol of the River King's ownership. Remington noticed that the group was staring at him, waiting for a response.

"I don't suppose any of you know how to make ice?" Remington eventually responded. Anyone can walk on water once it is frozen. There were a lot of looks of recognition of the obvious answer followed by looks of disappointment as they realized they did not possess that arcane ability. Did they really come all this way to get stopped by this? They had come too far, there had to be another way.

"The Ice Queen!" Kel shouted. Remington tilted his head in confusion as Kel ran around the compass rose, eventual stopping at the symbol to the west. "Who makes ice better than the queen herself?" Kel rhetorically asked. With a swift motion he stomped his foot down hard on the symbol. The floor beneath him shifted downwards and the chill that Remington felt increased tenfold.

The suspended river began to form a layer of frost over it. A wind picked up as a white out blizzard filled the entire chamber. Remington wasn't sure if he could see even 10 feet in front of him. But within the minute, the river was frozen solid allowing a path to walk across.

Zook was the first to attempt the crossing. The wind was buffeting at his small body but he held firm against its force. Zook disappeared into the blizzard and a minute later Remington saw a bolt of fire streak downwards. The party waited in anticipation, hoping to see how deep the cavern was. Eventually the bolt disappeared. They all looked at each other, amazed at the depth this cavern posed, when the same bolt of fire streaked past them once again, falling from the ceiling. Remington realized it was in a loop. After repeating this fall 3 times, the fire eventually died out.

Taking a deep breath, Remington stepped out onto the ice. He had to get across it. He felt the wind forcefully pushing him towards the side of the walkway, his feet struggling to find traction on the slick ice. He took another step, and felt his foot land on a particularly smooth area of the ice. Unable to catch himself, Remington slipped, crashing hard onto the ice, sliding uncontrollably off over the edge.

The snow was too thick for the others to see him go over. Remington saw the icy path retreat further and further away as he fell into the abyss below. Before he had time to attempt to get back up, Remington felt himself slam into what felt like a wall. The pain echoed up his arm spreading across his body. He looked down to see what he had hit only to see himself above the icy path falling back down towards it.

Remington reached out, attempting to grab the path, to pull himself out of this infinite loop. His hand brushed the edge of the path, but he was falling too fast. He felt his wrist bend too far back and he let out a welp of pain as once again he was falling away from the path, back down towards the abyss. Remington knew the invisible shelf, the starting point of the loop, was coming up. Rotating in the air, Remington positioned himself in preparation. He felt his feet hit something solid and using the force of his fall pushed himself in the direction of the path. He heard a crack in his knee as it hit but he ignored the pain.

The push was just enough to change his trajectory and Remington came crashing down onto the ice. He pulled out his spare dagger and stabbed it into the ice preventing him from sliding off once more. He thought he heard others crash down behind him but the snow was still too thick to see anything. Crawling along the ice shelf this time, Remington made his way forward on his hands and knees towards where he hoped the exit was.

Eventually, his hands numb from the cold, Remington rejoined the rest of the group who were staring at the exit door.

"He has an alarm set up," Zook explained. "We could easily dispel the magic but it would take a lot of arcane energy to do so."

"He already knows we are here and we are coming right?" asked Remington. "Do we really need to get rid of it?"

"Yeah, but we can have the element of surprise on our hands!" Kel said with a little too much enthusiasm. "Its fine, I got this." Kel moved his way to the small silver thread that marked the boundary of the alarm. Whispering some arcane words, Kel worked to dispel the magic, causing the thread to drop to the ground, no longer able to alert its creator.

With a knowing nod, the group crept forward, moving slowly and quietly so as not to be seen. The shadows around them seemed to cling tightly to the group, hiding them from the visions of others and dampening the clinking sounds of their armor. Remington did not question this, thankful for the assistance in hiding their presence.

Before long, the tunnels they snuck down stopped and opened up into a magnificent cavern. The floors resembled a lake, variety of oceanic life swimming underneath, though in attempting to dip his hand into the water, Remington found it to be as solid as a tiled floor. On top of the water in the center of the room sat a magnificent throne created from living corals in every color of the rainbow, glistening with the water that peppered the nooks and crannies.

Remington held his breath at the magnificence before noticing the occupant of the chair. His legs stretched over the arm rest, fingers twiddling in his hands, sat the River King, unaware and looking very bored.

47

They all paused, holding their breaths hoping the River King would not see them. So far, their presence remained hidden. Remington looked toward Maeve. He was so close to ending all of this, to finally be able to return her skin to her, and to finally escape the nightmare of his life. She smiled at him and silently pointed at him, T'kocht, Kel, and Zook. She then pointed towards the River King and mimicked the firing of a cross bow. She wanted them to attack, using the element of surprise to help them.

The 4 chosen nodded in agreement for they were the only ones with any ability to hit their targets from long range. Positioning themselves for the best angle, they took their aim. Remington could see his hand shaking, attempting to align his arcane blast with the River King's chest.

One finger, two fingers, three. At the signal they released their attacks, most of them hitting their mark. As the smoke cleared from the throne, Remington saw the River King standing up, hardly a scratch on him and a sickening grin growing across his face.

"You dare use my own power against me Remington!" the River King bellowed out, his deep voice shaking the cavern around him in anger. "You have no chance of defeating me."

Remington let out a battle cry and with Nicky by his side ran as fast as they could, straight for the River King swords drawn together. He swung his blade, slashing toward the River King, but it passed through him, as if Remington was cutting through water. The River King let out another laugh, "Do not forget boy, that your powers come from me. Now face the full force of my wrath."

Taking a step back the River King extended his hand. Electrical energy began building up along his shoulder wrapping its way down his arm like a vine before releasing into the cavern. Remington turned to see one of the bolts of lightning heading straight for Maeve before time stopped.

Remington watched as an echo of the lightning bolt continued on, striking Maeve in the center of her chest, electrifying her whole body, the smell of searing flesh faint in his nostrils. The echo began to fade, and Remington knew he did not have much time. "Duck, Maeve!" Remington yelled as loud as possible.

Maeve did not question his order and dropped to the ground just in time for the lightning to skim over her head, barely missing her. Remington's sigh of relief quickly turned into a gasp of pain as in his distraction the River King had slammed his sword into Remington's abdomen, sending electricity pulsing through every nerve. The River King's strike was precise, piercing Remington's lung.

Remington could feel the room around him begin to go dark, blood pouring from his chest. He fought against the call of unconsciousness, his one lung struggling to keep up with the rest of his body. He saw Nicky from the corner of his eye releasing every move she had in her arsenal onto the River King. Occasionally a gun shot or arrow would pass his head, finding its mark in the River King, though he did not seem to mind any of the hits.

Remington pushed himself off the floor, using his full body weight to push his blade deep into the River King. As he attempted to pull the blade out, Remington realized the blade was stuck, and his hand locked onto the handle unable to move. He felt a coldness seep into his body as his life force flowed from deep within him, through his sword and into the River King.

"How pathetic," the River King stated absorbing Remington's last bit of energy before Remington fell into the darkness. His entire body felt cold and empty, frozen in time and space. His thoughts dwelled on Maeve, knowing she was still out there, fighting for him and his freedom, while he lay here dying, slowly approaching the halls of Mirtis.

As Remington began to feel himself accept his imminent death, the darkness was interrupted by a small flame. Remington looked towards it, his eyes struggling to stay open and he felt comfort.

"I am here with you," the familiar, calming voice rang out.

Remington smiled weakly, relishing in the warmth the small flame provided, though it flickered, constantly threatening to go out. "I tried," he whispered. "I hope they can forgive me."

The flame began to grow, its strength and its heat increasing until it erupted from over flowing energy filling the darkness with millions of stars. The flame itself reforming, holding itself in the shape of a human, though no features could be seen. It walked towards Remington, each step leaving behind a trail of new stars and galaxies.

"You are the pebble that begins an avalanche Remington," the voice continued, this time coming directly from the flame. "The hope and devotion that you and your friends hold within you are strong enough to change the world. Fates are in motion and they will travel through the darkest and coldest of nights. They will need every bit of hope they can hold on to if they are to right the imbalance that is coming. Your part in this story may be ending, but your story is not over. She will need something to fight for, to remember when the darkness blocks my light."

The voice was interrupted by another, though this one was faint. Remington thought he could hear Maeve calling his name.

"She is calling for you," the voice confirmed. "Go to her, and be the light that burns brighter than the sun itself. You will be whole again."

Remington began crawling his way toward Maeve, each inch regaining his strength until he was on his feet in a full sprint. Remington felt himself crash through the darkness awakening on the floor of the River King's chamber, with Maeve next to him. Her hands, glowing a brilliant white, were resting over his punctured lung which was slowly mending. He could feel the air rushing into it, his cells desperate for the oxygen needed to function.

Seeing that Remington was conscious again, Maeve stood up, barely dodging the River King's sword and bounded out of his reach, keeping just out of the sword's range.

The River King looked down upon Remington, "See how she does not even stand with you. How cowardly." The River King reached out his hand sending a blast of water towards Maeve. It hit her dead in the temple of her head, and Remington watched as she went unconscious, the water taking her with it across the room. The River King laughed and bent down picking up Remington by his neck. Remington tried to look around for his friends, but could not see anything besides the vengeful face of the Fey Lord.

"Release him," the Sokayan warrior shouted, slowly drawing a massive sword that was almost the same length as the dwarf himself. As the water glistened off the blade of the sword, Remington thought he could see genuine fear in the eyes of the River King. Remington crashed to the ground as his throat was released, Nicky now holding onto the River King's back in a bear hug.

The warrior rushed forward, cleaving his sword into the River King. To the shock of everyone, a golden liquid, almost like blood, began to flow from where the blade impacted. Remington realized what was happening: the sword was made from cold iron.

Remington had heard legends about cold iron, a technique for making swords that was lost long ago. There were many rumors about various techniques for keeping yourself safe from fey creatures like iron and keeping salt in one's pockets, though many of them were just cons to make money. Tales said in the golden age of arcana, cold iron was in abundance and was feared by the fey creatures for its particularly cold bite against them. Many humanoids from the Prime Realm used this to manipulate the fey and gain power. The Fey Lords decided to put an end to the threat and destroyed all of the cold iron, and those who made it. Apparently, they did not destroy all of it, and it was a deadly mistake.

The warrior swung again, hitting the River King square in the chest causing him to fall to his knees. True panic had now entered his eyes.

"I will give him his soul back," the River King shouted, almost pleading. "Please, don't kill me."

Remington looked on in shock, never imaging the River King to beg for mercy, to be afraid of anything. The warrior looked at Remington looking for a decision. As much as he wanted the River King dead and was basking in this change of character, he shook his head. He needed to show mercy, for Maeve, because she asked.

The warrior swung his blade, stopping just short of the River King's neck before pulling back and sheathing the sword. The River Kings released the breath that he was holding. Remington heard the sound of a blade cutting through flesh and looked down to see a blade clean through the River King's heart, the blow opening the dam of life to flow out. As the corpse fell to the ground, Remington saw Kel standing behind the Fey Lord, his hand still tightly gripped to the blade, now dripping with the River King's life force.

Time seemed to stand still as everyone processed what happened. No one wanted to move or say anything, for what could one say in a moment such as this. The confusion was broken by a glowing thread of silk exiting from the River King's mouth, shining like a star. Slowly, more and more of these strange lights flowed out of his mouth, rocketing into the world as if they were looking for something.

Remington watched as one of them headed straight for him, as if being pulled by a magnet. The thread forced his way into his mouth, and he knew this was his missing piece of his soul. He felt the thread reabsorb into his body, the emptiness that he had felt for so long being filled with hope for the future. The coldness that he had felt within him quickly changed to an intense burning heat as he felt a large amount of energy being released from his body, filling the room around him with a blindingly bright red light pouring out of his eyes and mouth.

"Be my champion," the voice whispered. "Save her."

Remington felt the heat subside and without thinking ran straight for Maeve. She was still breathing, though it was weak and he could see her fading fast. He focused the energy that was fading onto her and watched as her wounds began to heal up, her eyes opening.

"What happened," she asked bolting upright ready to get back into the fight.

He placed his hands on her shoulders, attempting to calm her down. "It's over," Remington said. "But, the River King is dead. Kel killed him." Remington was not sure what else to say. He promised her he would not kill him, and he failed.

48

Maeve stormed over to the group, who were now in a heated argument, attempting to figure out what to do next. Nicky and T'kocht had backed away from the chaos, not wanting to have any part in these strangers' personal business.

As Remington walked over to them, he thought he felt something dangling from the right side of his face. Reaching over, he peeled it off, revealing the starfish that for so long made its home on his right ear. Remington looked up to see the others were experiencing similar transformations, the tentacles sloshing off of T'kocht's chin. Nicky was peeling the fins off of her forearms like a bandage. The curse had been broken, and they were freed.

Remington wrapped his arms around them, squeezing them tight in case they disappeared. They were all hurt, bleeding, but for the first time in three and a half years, they were their own. There was no master to answer to anymore

Remington stepped back admiring his friends who had followed him through so much. How would he be able to say goodbye. He turned to find Maeve standing behind him watching him. He smiled.

"I believe this belongs to you." He said, taking her selkie skin off of his shoulders and passing it over to her. Her face glowed with joy. They were both complete now.

"What are you going to do now?" she asked, her hands carefully tracing the smooth skin.

Remington took in a deep breath. He was not ready for this moment, but it had to come at some point. "I am going to stay here, in the Feylands," he said carefully. T'kocht's jaw dropped, and he moved to protest before Remington stopped him.

"I can't go back," Remington explained. "There is too much pain, too many horrific memories that I don't want to face anymore. Yes, there are happy moments, and I am thankful for every single one of them. But it is not enough to block out the bad. The Fortune is yours T'kocht. Tell the crew I perished, and be a better captain than I could ever be. Stop the unnecessary violence, and be the leader you were meant to be. Stay out of the wrath of the Pirate King, it's not worth it. Apologize to Elianne for me." Remington held T'kocht in a tight embrace, he could feel the tears running down T'kocht's cheeks, though T'kocht said nothing.

Remington turned to Nicky, "Thank you for everything. I know you won't listen to me, but don't try to go after Cresthorn. Don't become the monster you believe he made you into. You are better than that." Nicky scoffed. He could tell she was mad at him, but she knew he was doing what was best for him.

Finally, Remington turned to Maeve. "I know you have a lot you need to do, and a home that needs to be saved. Gwen needs someone to find her, to save her like you saved me." Remington reached into his bag, pulling out the crystal ball. "I used this to dwell on my past. Maybe you can use it to help fight against the future." He handed the ball to Maeve who held it carefully. "But when you are done, and when you are ready, will you come find me? I will be waiting where we first met. I will see you soon Maeve."

Maeve set her stuff aside and held Remington close, not wanting to let go. "I will see you soon, I promise," she whispered. Remington could feel his own tears running down his cheeks. Taking a step back, he looked at her one more time, taking in every detail that he could before vanishing out of the cavern, using his new found powers to return to that island where it all began. Where it will all begin anew.

49

Epilogue

"You ready for the start of tourist season, Rem?" The elvish bartender asked, sliding a drink across the table. Remington looked up and smiled at him, gladly accepting the drink.

It had been over a year since Remington had made his way back to the island town of Vauxquet, to start his life over again. He used what funds he had to purchase a small fishing vessel and during the tourist season, when members of the Prime Realm made their way from the city of Cairnathoul, he converted it into a site seeing boat, *The Green Eagle*. This would be his third tourist season, and Remington thought his business had started to make a good name for itself. He expected this season to be his best season yet.

"Absolutely," Remington responded. "What about you Gaelin? Think you got enough raykish fruit for the season? I could make a trip up the mountains to get you some more if you need it?"

Remington had become good friends with Gaelin, the owner of the bar Remington usually hung out at. The bar where he first met Maeve. Gaelin was a talented barkeep, mixing up concoctions that would put even the strongest of constitutions to the test by the end of the night. One of his specialties was a very strong cocktail made from the raykish fruit that could only be found in the high mountains of the island. Most people would not risk going that high due to some dangerous inhabitants that guarded the trees, but they were never any threat to Remington. So, he would occasionally help his friend out and harvest the fruit in exchange for free drinks.

"I still got plenty from the last trip you made," Gaelin replied. "I still don't know how you carried them all down, but I know better than to ask."

That is what Remington liked about Gaelin. He never asked questions about Remington's past, never questioned how Remington got things done. Gaelin enjoyed the company and the business deal. Remington took a large sip from his drink, though the day was still young.

"Ahoy captain," Gaelin yelled out in his most exaggerated sailor voice he could muster. "There be a ship on the horizon. Looks like the first group has finally arrived."

Remington chuckled, turning his head to see the large mast approaching the harbor. The first of the visitors to arrive for the season. He considered going down to the docks to watch their faces of wonder and confusion as the various locals attempted to scam or make a deal with those who did not know better. Remington was enjoying his drink too much though, and the company of Gaelin. He would get his boat set up tomorrow, once the first day chaos had died down a bit.

The sounds and chatter of people making their way through the city filled the typical quiet that enveloped the island. Remington could hear the families talking about what they wanted to do first, what creatures they were hoping to see, and what dangers they may face in this strange new land. The streets filled up quickly and a few of the newcomers took a seat near Remington, causing Gaelin to shift his focus. Remington just shrugged his shoulders and went back to focusing on his drink. It was going to be a busy 3 months.

Remington felt someone sit next to him, though he did not pay them any mind.

"I thought I had seen all the beautiful wonders of the Feylands but clearly I missed one."

Remington stopped mid drink and turned slowly towards the voice, towards the person sitting next to him, towards Maeve. Her hair had been chopped to just above her shoulders, the waves of gold and teal extenuated by the release of the weight. She had a new scar running along her left cheek but her eyes were as bright as ever and her grin spanned from ear to ear.

Remington without missing a beat responded, "Is that really what you are going with? Why don't you try that again?" He broke out into a massive smile and sprung towards her, wrapping her into his arms. He felt her melt into his arms as he picked her up spinning her around. He took in a deep breath, soaking in her familiar scent of salt, oceanic water.

Remington had wondered for a while whether she would actually come, if she would survive her tasks ahead. But here she was, home at last and safe. He could not stop smiling as he stepped back and just looked at her, basking in her presence.

"You made it," Remington finally said. There was nothing else he could say.

"I made it," she confirmed. "We won. Our home is safe, the journey is over."

"Our home," Remington repeated. "I promise to never leave your side. My devotion will always be to you. Together, we will overcome anything."

"Together," Maeve stated, once again falling into his arms. "Forever and always."

www.ingramcontent.com/pod-product-compliance
Lightning Source LLC
Chambersburg PA
CBHW071236300726
48975CB00002B/446